≥ Also by Charlene D'Avanzo ≤
Mara Tusconi Mysteries:
Cold Blood, Hot Sea and *Demon Spirit, Devil Sea*

PRAISE FOR *Cold Blood, Hot Sea*
(Foreword INDIES 2016 Finalist)

Sleuths will have to figure out who done it, but the real crime is the backdrop here: the endless heating of a fragile planet.

—BILL MCKIBBEN, author of *Eaarth*

A great read that gives us more to think about than just the plot twists.

—GARY LAWLESS, co-owner of Gulf of Maine Books

Paddlers will love this book's hero—an oceanographer who uses her kayak to thwart climate change deniers.

—LEE BUMSTED, Maine Sea Kayak Guide, author of *Hot Showers! Maine Coast Lodging for Sea Kayakers and Sailors.*

PRAISE FOR *Demon Spirit, Devil Sea*
(2018 IPPY Silver Medal Winner)

Another great read ... D'Avanzo writes compelling novels that take you to wonderful ocean-side places where terrible things happen.

—GEORGE SMITH, outdoors writer for the *Bangor Daily News*

A fine entry in D'Avanzo's oceanography-themed series, which fills an unusual niche in the mystery genre.

—Kirkus Review

Demon Spirit, Devil Sea *is a mysterious, fast-paced novel that immerses the reader smack dab in the wild.*

—MARY WOODBURY, curator at Eco-fiction.com

Charlene D'Avanzo

SECRETS HAUNT
THE LOBSTERS' SEA

Charlene D'Avanzo
A MARA TUSCONI MYSTERY

Secrets Haunt the Lobsters' Sea

©2018 Charlene D'Avanzo

ISBN: 978-1-63381-136-2

front cover design by
Rick Whipple, Sky Island Studio

designed and produced by
Maine Authors Publishing
12 High Street, Thomaston, Maine
www.maineauthorspublishing.com

Printed in the United States of America

This series is dedicated to scientists struggling to better understand the exceptionally complex phenomena associated with climate change.

AUTHOR'S NOTE

THIS NOVEL INCLUDES NUMEROUS REFERENCES TO CLIMATE change research and to scientists who study lobsters in the Gulf of Maine. I attempt to represent the science as accurately as possible in a fictional story. I note, however, that remotely operated vehicles, not manned subs, have been used for deep-sea coral research in the Gulf of Maine. Similarities between Matinicus Island and the fictional island Macomek are coincidental. Scientists who recognize their research discussed by characters in the story will find appropriate journal references on my website, where I also list several books about Maine lobsters and lobstering I found especially useful.

SECRETS HAUNT
THE LOBSTERS' SEA

What is past is prologue.

— Shakespeare (*The Tempest*)

1

NATURE FAVORS LOOPS, TWISTS, AND TURNS. ALL corners and straight lines, Gordy's mussel aquaculture raft looked like a soggy oversized matchbox riding the swells off Spruce Harbor.

From my office window at the Maine Oceanographic Institute, I eyed the thing through binoculars. Bobbing up and down, my cousin's raft called to me. Damn. Back-to-back fall research cruises had left me with zero free time. Folders labeled "Data for analysis," "Grant proposals to write," and "Research papers to review" called for attention from my computer's screen.

I dropped the binocs and rubbed my eyes. Despite the piled-up work, I absolutely should have checked out Gordy's pet project. The office phone interrupted my guilt riff. I reached over the desk and picked it up.

The man himself was at the other end. "Mara," Gordy said, "I need ta talk with you."

"Now?"

"Since I'm standin' ten feet away, ayuh."

The door was ajar, and Gordy strode in before the phone had settled into its cradle. He wore his usual warm-weather attire—tan canvas shorts fringed at the hemline, brown, ankle-high leather boots with white socks, white T-shirt.

"Good to see you, Cousin," I said. "Weren't we getting together for beers at the Lee Side tomorrow afternoon? Did I get the day wrong?"

"Nope. I said tomorrah all right." He pretended to study the framed photo of his lobster boat *Bulldog* on my bookcase.

"So what's up? Are you okay?"

It came out in a tumble. "I'm wonderin' when you're gonna look at my mussel raft. I think it's goin' real good, but you might see somethin' that needs work."

"Actually, I was just checking out the raft with my binocs," I said. "It's really amazing what you've done. I'll paddle out there in a bit to see it up close. Okay?"

Gordy answered with a grin and added, "By Godfrey, that's terrific. See ya tomorrah."

I stared at the door my cousin had left ajar. An independent lobsterman with Irish stubbornness thrown in, Gordy Maloy rarely asked for anything. Getting the right permits, never mind learning how to grow mussels, *was* a big deal. Still, his urgency that I check out the raft seemed over the top.

Gordy and *Bulldog* had saved my life when a madman tried to dump me into icy Maine waters the previous spring. Needless to say, I owed him. On top of that, he was my closest—really my only—blood relative. Over corned-beef dinners, drinking green beer on Saint Pat's day, filling in as sternman on his lobster boat, I'd done everything I could think of to express my affection and gratitude. Could he really think I wouldn't check out his mussel raft when I had a moment?

For the second time in minutes, a visitor interrupted my musings.

My grad student Alise stuck her head through the half-open door and said, "Mara, can I come in?" Reminded as always that the future was in capable hands, I took in Alise's message of the day. The bold green lettering of her "Earth Is the Only Mother We Have" T-shirt nicely complemented the colored snake tattoos running down her arm.

Smart and sassy, once she got her PhD, Alise was going to shake up the male-dominated realm of oceanography. I couldn't wait to watch.

She handed me a stapled document. Since the woman didn't print anything that could be electronically sent, I knew something was amiss.

"Thought it'd be easier for you to critique my proposal if I printed it out," she said. The anxiety evident in Alise's eyes was painful to see.

"I know you're worried," I said. "There's nothing worse than having a grant proposal you really need get turned down."

She shrugged. "I know it comes with the territory, but if Sea Grant doesn't fund me this time, I'm in big trouble."

I wanted to assure her that she would get her funding and her doctoral research wasn't in jeopardy. But we both knew that scientists decreeing who got money and who didn't sometimes made inexplicable decisions.

"When can you get it back to me?" she asked.

The promise to Gordy poked my conscience. "I have to do something that will take about an hour. Then I'll come right back and read your proposal."

She nodded, but the shrug was there was as well.

I stared at the door after Alise closed it. During the last Sea Grant go-round, I had been fifty miles off the coast of British Columbia investigating an international law of the sea violation. Events during the trip—including the inexplicable death of a young Haida man who had prevented me and my sea kayak from drifting into the frigid Pacific—had consumed me. I hadn't given Alise's proposal the attention it deserved and felt the sting of its rejection almost as much as she did.

"First Gordy, then Alise." I said aloud. "I *really* owe them both."

The computer's chime announced a new email message. Annoyed at my usual inability to ignore this electronic summons, I leaned in to check it out. Harvina—called Harvey—Allison, my best friend, sister oceanographer, and Watson to my occasional Sherlock, had sent a missive entitled "#!!!Grr." There was no note above the signature that identified her as a chemical oceanographer at MOI.

I powered off my computer, refused to look at the to-do list on my whiteboard, locked the office door, and glanced at the nameplate—"Dr. Mara Tusconi." I had been hired right from my post-doc three years earlier and still couldn't believe my good fortune. Jobs for oceanographers, especially females, were scarce. That I could do my own research and work with terrific students like Alise on my home state's coast was a gift from the science gods.

I was halfway down the stairs to Harvey's floor when Seymour Hull, MOI's Biology Department chair, rounded the flight on his way up. There was no way to avoid him.

Seymour directed his pointy chin at the life jacket in my hand. "Going kayaking?" He rotated his wrist and glanced at a special-edition sports smartwatch that looked ridiculous on his scrawny arm. "Now? With the Sea Grant deadline so soon?"

The man was exceptionally skilled at pushing people's guilt buttons, including mine. I guessed the behavior grew from insecurity about his outdated research. That his position was endowed in honor of my dead parents, both renowned biological oceanographers, meant he had particular antipathy for me.

If Alise's proposal hadn't required Seymour's support, I would have slipped by with an "Enjoy your day." Instead I plastered on a smile, touched his arm, and lied. "Department of Maine Resources asked me to examine the aquaculture raft floating off Spruce Harbor. I'm sure you've seen it out there.

They need to make sure the mussel density isn't too high."

I left before the man could ask why Marine Resources didn't monitor the raft from one of their own boats.

The door to Harvey's lab was open. I stepped in, looked around, and saw no one. "Harve?"

The voice was muffled. "Back here. Behind the AutoAnalyzer."

I crossed the room and stood before the instrument environmental chemists loved to hate. Harvey mainly used it to study ocean acidification from fossil fuel combustion, a looming problem in the Gulf of Maine for shellfish—including big-business clams, oysters, and mussels. But, like a cat, the AutoAnalyzer could purr along nicely one minute and let you know who was really boss the next.

The top of Harvey's head appeared behind the analyzer before she stepped out into the lab. Whether she's fixing pesky instruments or hosting a visiting scientist, Harvey always looks well turned out and unflappable. Besides that, her high cheekbones, classic nose, and gray eyes give her an aristocratic look, not far from the truth since she grew up in a wealthy family. Confident in her abilities as a marine scientist, Harvey isn't afraid to be feminine in a male-dominated profession. I couldn't wait until she challenged Seymour when his stint as department chair was up for renewal in a couple of years.

Today Harvey's layered, blond bob kissed the collar of a lab coat that would've made Mr. Clean proud. As usual, my ponytail had transformed itself into an unruly mess. I tucked wayward locks behind my ear.

"Hey, girlfriend," she said. "Did you get my email?"

"Figured you needed a little break from the horrid machine." I pointed at the screwdriver in her hand. "The monster's acting up again?"

"Yup. One of the tubes is leaking. I just started to work on it."

I pictured the AutoAnalyzer's guts—yard after yard of clear plastic tubing with bubbles that separated samples from one another. An aqueduct tangle in a metal box.

"How about stopping at the house after work and maybe staying for dinner? Connor would love to see you," she said.

I considered Connor Doyle, Harvey's live-in partner, a special friend. Funny, generous, and Irish to the core, Connor was the uncle I'd never had. He didn't hesitate to tell me when I was full of crap or that my auburn hair and green eyes left a "trail of Irish magic" behind me—sometimes in the same sentence.

Harvey and I blinked at each other for a few awkward seconds. The last time I'd had dinner at Harvey's house, I'd gone with Ted, another MOI scientist and Harvey's half-brother. That was before my relationship with Ted fell apart. Harvey hadn't wanted to pry back then—or now—but it felt, well, lonely not talking to my dearest friend about my confusion, resentment, and all the rest.

"Dinner with you both would be a treat," I said. "Let's see how the day goes. Good luck with the monster. I'm off to paddle to the aquaculture raft I promised Gordy I'd check out weeks ago."

"Be careful. There's an unidentified shark reported out there."

Compared to what I encountered, I would have happily hugged the shark instead.

A half hour later, I slid into my sea kayak, pushed off from the public boat launch, and glided by the stern of MOI's research vessel *Intrepid*. Two days earlier and dozens of miles offshore, I'd watched our half-ton observation buoys dangling from the ship's massive A-frame off the rear deck. Now, the hinged metal frame was pulled toward the bow like a mighty mousetrap ready to spring. I hurried by.

Humming, I paddled quickly as my seventeen-foot-long, twenty-inch-wide kayak sliced neatly through the water. Not bad for a thirty-one-year-old who spent way too much time in front of her computer. While my spirit always soars when I'm on the water, today it skyrocketed. September is my favorite month on the Maine coast. The water was plenty warm for paddling and the days perfect for hiking. Along the roads and on the hills, maple and oak leaves tipped with red and gold foretold a fall riot of color.

I hadn't told Harvey—or even Angelo, my godfather and stand-in parent—that I'd recently started meditating on the word "gratitude" as I picked my way along the beach in front of my house or leaned against the granite boulder on top of Spruce Harbor Hill to take in the sunset. The practice had grown out of a harrowing event. A month earlier, I'd been kidnapped and left for dead in the Haida Gwaii archipelago out in the Pacific off Vancouver. After I'd figured out how to make a fire, keep warm, and cook mussels, my panic had subsided. I felt instead that I was not alone—that something or someone was watching over me.

For a scientist who believed that every so-called mystical event had a physical explanation, the Haida Gwaii experience was unnerving. So I'd translated what happened into something I could understand. National Institutes of Health research showed that gratitude—in my case for food and warmth—fostered feelings of wellbeing and connectedness. I put that understanding to good use when I got back to Maine and Ted announced he wanted to be "just a colleague." After weeks feeling hurt and angry, I decided to focus on my good fortune—Angelo, Harvey, Gordy, Alise, and a career I was passionate about.

So far, the tactic was succeeding pretty well. My fury toward Ted made working on our shared research projects awkward, to say the least. I'd decided to take each day as it came and appreciate what I had. I'd even dropped by Ted's office to go over some water temperature data. The exchange had gone well.

Thank goodness, angst was a thing of the past.

Gordy had anchored his raft between two islands where a fast-flowing current carried an abundance of microscopic plankton to the filter-feeding mussels. The kayak slid to a stop just as the tide turned slack. Up close, Gordy's contraption was pretty impressive. Fifty-odd feet square with a steel I-beam frame, wooden cross members, and oversized polyethylene floats, the thing could easily weather a major blow.

I circled the raft a few times, looking for a way to explore beneath the platform. That's where the excitement was—for a marine ecologist, that is. I had all sorts of questions. What were the mussels attached to? Were they big or small? How many were there?

One place looked as good as another to begin my investigation, so I maneuvered my boat parallel with the raft and secured the paddle under a bungee. Still in the kayak, I leaned over the boat's deck and peered into the gloom below the platform. Slits of light from above danced across row after row of swaying rope that looked creepily alive. Each rope was attached to the bottom of the platform, and I could just make out a foot of exposed line before it plunged down into the water out of sight. Seawater sloshed over mussels the size of my fist encasing the visible rope. *Mytilus edulis*, the blue mussel, had been cultivated by the French way back in the thirteenth century. Now, aquaculturalists were giving it a try in Maine's cold, clean marine waters. I reached out and touched the closest one. Smooth and blue-black, the mollusk slowly closed.

Hand over hand, I traveled down one side of the raft, stopped at intervals, flattened myself across my deck, and peered into the gloom for a better look. Water slapped against the platform—and my face.

At the corner I straightened up, ran a hand across my eyes,

patted the raft, and said aloud, "Gotta give it to you Gordy, this is one wicked piece of engineering."

I really, really wanted to examine the mussels. Maybe they were bigger on the outside edge because they grew more quickly there with better access to seawater. Or maybe the inner ones were fouled with barnacles or invasive sea squirts—not so good for an aquaculture business. I blinked at the sky. There would be more light on the opposite western side. I tried the same flatten, crank my neck, and squint routine over there but still could see squat.

I pushed back from the raft to consider a different maneuver. "Time for a frontal attack," I announced to the gulls overhead. I released the paddle from its bungee hold, and a couple of quick strokes sent me bow first under the platform. The skinny boat slipped between two rows of drop lines. Leaning over the front of my vessel, I plowed further in. Surrounded by a tapestry of dangling, dancing mussel-rope, I closed my eyes and let other senses take over. Pop, slosh, and gurgle enhanced the slap-slap-slap melody. Sharp, briny perfume tickled my nose, sea life exhaling.

I reached out to gauge the thickness of mussel growth. Stacked atop one another, they completely surrounded the lines, so many that my two encircling hands didn't come close to touching. Hardly any barnacles or other encrusting critters disfigured the mussel monopoly.

Just beyond the tip of my bow, something out of place bobbed in the water. Squinting, I tried to make out what it was. An errant lobster buoy? Cast-off bucket? The bulky object didn't belong in the middle of a mussel farm, that's for sure. Gordy would want it out of there. I reached out and tapped the object with the tip of the paddle. It felt bulky, big. I pushed harder. The thing submerged out of sight. Peering into the murk, I scanned the spot where it had been. Where was the goddamned thing?

Suddenly, like a sea monster rising from the depths, the sunken object bobbed straight up out of the water. Its eyes held mine for a moment before the head slipped back down into the black.

My scream ricocheted off the platform into an uncaring sea.

2

THE MARITIME POLICE RESPONDED TO MY 911 FASTER
than I could have imagined. I was still fumbling with the
phone's waterproof case when a good-sized motorboat
rocketed out of Spruce Harbor and headed right for me. The
twenty-five-foot Hydrosport sidled alongside the raft, her dual
200 hp outboards gurgling. A square-built, sturdy guy with a
buzz cut stepped out of the cabin and pulled a pair of Ray-Bans
from his chest pocket. I back-paddled a few strokes to get a
better look at him. The label above the left pocket of his khaki
shirt said "Marine Patrol." The one on the right announced his
name as "LeClair."

"You the lady made the emergency call?"

"Yes. I can't believe how fast you got here."

"Officer Larry LeClair. We were pulling away from the
town pier when you called. Please, ma'am, tell me your name
and restate the problem here."

"Mara Tusconi." I tipped my head toward shore. "Dr.
Tusconi. I'm a scientist at MOI. I found…that is, there's, um, a
body under this aquaculture raft."

Suddenly, the horror of what I'd seen hit home. LeClair
and his boat tipped sideways. I balanced my paddle crossways
and leaned on it. Bile bubbled up. I spit it out.

Voice from above. "You all right?"

I blinked. "Give me a minute." I sucked in a few breaths of
cold sea air. Blew them out. Coughed. "Okay. A little while ago

I was under the raft's platform looking around. I saw something. Could've been a lobster buoy. I tapped it with my paddle. The thing went under." Deep breath, exhale. "When it came up, I saw, um, the head and shoulders."

"Take your time, ma'am."

I met LeClair's gaze. Navy-blue eyes, kind and patient. This was a man who'd seen too much.

"You okay to keep goin'?"

"Yeah."

"You said you were *under* the raft looking around?"

"In my kayak. It's small, you know. I'm a marine ecologist and wanted to see the mussels up close."

Beat. I guessed LeClair was processing the image of me and my kayak beneath Gordy's raft.

He pointed toward the raft. "There's no head space under there. Why would you do that?"

I sighed. It was hard for some people to comprehend that a person could get a kick out of seeing the natural world up close and personal, even under a sloshing, rocking platform. "Later when we have time, I can describe what mussels look like underwater."

LeClair let it go. As a Marine Patrol officer he'd probably dealt with scientists' eccentricities before.

"Okay," he said. "How long ago were you under the raft?"

"Ten minutes or so."

LeClair rubbed his nonexistent beard. "About ten minutes ago in your kayak you were under this mussel raft. You thought you saw a dead body."

I shook my head. "No. I *saw* a dead body."

He wet his lips. "You saw a dead body."

I nodded and glanced at the raft. "Yes."

"If what you say is true, we'll have to get our dive team

over here." He tipped his head to the side. "You're sure, ah, Dr. Tusconi, about this?"

I lifted my chin. "Yes, Officer LeClair, I'm sure. Why in the world would I make this up?"

He scratched his forehead. "I don't suppose you would."

A woman in a spiffy khaki uniform with jet-black hair in a ponytail emerged from the cabin. LeClair said, "Dr. Tusconi, this is my colleague Officer Bernadette DelBarco."

DelBarco gave me a quick nod. "Please call me Bernie."

"I'm Mara."

LeClair announced that he needed to make some calls and see if divers were available. I suspected one of his calls would be to MOI's personnel department. The director there was a good friend and ardent feminist who would surely challenge LeClair if she detected skepticism about a female oceanographer. The man disappeared into the cabin.

With more than a few grunts, I extricated myself inch by inch from the kayak's snug cockpit, belly-crawled onto the raft's platform, tied my boat to one of the cleats, and long-stepped onto the Marine Patrol boat.

Bernie and I waited for LeClair on the patrol vessel's spanking-clean afterdeck. Most boats in Spruce Harbor belonged to hardworking lobstermen who left at dawn, hauled aboard hundreds of dripping and fouled lobster traps, and spent the day amid rotting bait. On the way home after long days, a sternman would hose down the deck with seawater, but it wouldn't be anything you'd want to, you know, eat off of.

In contrast, the Maine Marine Patrol boat looked like it had just come from the factory, and I did eat off the deck, sort of. Bernie offered me a piece of stomach-soothing ginger candy to suck on which somehow flew out of my fingers.

I snatched the sweet off the deck and popped it into my

mouth. "Sorry about that. Ah, so you folks were in Spruce Harbor today?"

She nodded. "We met with a group of lobstermen there to see if we could work better together. There's been some especially nasty tit for tat going on."

I wanted to ask what "tit for tat" meant but guessed Bernie had said all she was going to. "I've never been on a Maine Marine Patrol boat before. You're kind of like game wardens, is that right?"

"Yes." She patted the emblem on her chest. "The MMP's the oldest law enforcement organization in the state. You could call us game wardens for Maine's marine waters."

"I'm embarrassed to say I don't know much about the kind of things you do."

"We're law enforcement, search and rescue, and security for the state's coastal waters."

I must have looked uncertain because Bernie added, "Last week, for instance, we arrested a man in Boothbay who was under the influence. He'd run his motorboat twenty feet out of the water. Got stopped by a tree."

The image was stunning. "So you're in charge of everything from enforcing clam-flat closures, to locating missing people, answering distress calls, and monitoring lobstermen and drunk boaters."

"You got it," she said.

"What's the hardest?"

"Besides finding dead bodies, of course, lately it's been dealing with lobstermen. You know, responding to poaching claims, investigating vengeance deeds."

"Vengeance deeds?"

"Not an official name. What I call it."

"Can you give me an example?"

"Last month a lobster boat in Stonington was sunk three different times over two weeks. You must've seen it in the newspaper. Guy would get his boat back in shape and find it under the water again. Had a good idea who'd done it, too. Arrogant kid who got pissed off when he was called out for messing with traps that weren't his."

"Damn. Did you arrest the kid?"

She ran a hand through her ponytail. "We couldn't get any proof. Nobody was talking, if you know what I mean."

I didn't.

Her look suggested I lived a sheltered life. "The other lobstermen didn't want to say anything because they were afraid their boats would be the next ones sunk. With lobstermen, sometimes it's the wild, wild west out here."

In the cabin a squawking marine radio went silent. Running a hand through his buzz cut, LeClair joined us.

"Dive team's not available until tomorrow," he said. "Afraid I'm stayin' right here tonight to secure the site."

"You're kidding," I said. "You'll be here *all* night?"

"Sure. Unless the victim got himself under that raft, this is a crime scene. Part of the job. The boat's pretty comfortable. There's plenty of food. I can arrange for Bernie to be picked up and brought back first thing in the morning."

Looking at me, Bernie said, "I've got a little girl who'll need her mommy."

I gestured at the raft. "It'll be a tricky dive with all those lines dangling down into the water. I sure wouldn't want to do it."

LeClair nodded. "Got that right. There'll be two teams in full gear. That way, if something happens to a diver in the first team, two guys will be ready to help out."

The gruesome image of a bloated, waterlogged corpse dragged underwater by two scuba divers floated through my mind. I blinked and said, "I assume it's okay if I leave now?"

LeClair explained that I could sign my statement at the Rockland MMP office up the coast from Spruce Harbor. I shook his hand and Bernie's, straddled the Hydrocraft's gunwale, and stepped onto the raft. "Thanks, both of you for all your work. Um, what about the raft owner?"

LeClair said, "Bernie can look into that in Spruce Harbor." He gestured at the platform. "After all, this is his mussel aquaculture enterprise."

"But you can't possibly think...?"

"I've got some calls to make. Thanks for your help, Dr. Tusconi."

On the way back I sprint-paddled and counted strokes in an attempt to block out the appalling image of the corpse rising up from the depths. I thought about stopping alongside an exposed rock to call Gordy and tell him what was going on. But the idea of my cousin listening to a message about a dead body under his raft was ghastly. I'd look for him in Spruce Harbor.

In town, I checked the usual places—the Lee Side bar, Neap Tide Café, town pier. No Gordy. I even checked the town library, which was closed. My discomfort grew as I lumbered back to the public boat ramp to get my kayak. What if Bernie found Gordy before I did? Did he have anything to do with the corpse under his raft? Could he possibly be so foolish as to hide a body among the ropes dancing below his platform? If he didn't, who did and why? Did the body explain why Gordy had been so anxious for me to check out his project? If this was a horrible accident, what was the guy—I assumed the body was male—doing beneath the raft?

By the time I'd secured my kayak on top of the car, the knots in my stomach would have made a sailor proud.

Alise's proposal to study how increasing acidity could

impact Maine's nascent mussel aquaculture industry didn't need much work. In precise, understated prose she had explained that the Gulf of Maine's cold water readily absorbed carbon dioxide from fossil fuel burning. That dissolved carbon dioxide could make Maine's water too acidic for mussels struggling to build shells from dissolved calcium carbonate in seawater. Alise proposed to work with growers to monitor water chemistry in the Gulf and in mussel hatcheries. I added my comments to the manuscript, changed a word here and there, tacked it to my door, and emailed Alise that the revision of her terrific proposal was on my door.

Usually, something catches my eye along the windy, pine-bordered dirt road down to my house on the ocean's edge—the flash of crimson on a red-tailed hawk overhead or the white rump of a deer scampering into the woods. Today, if a she-bear and her cub had sauntered alongside I wouldn't have noticed.

I parked in the driveway, trudged up the deck stairs, pulled open the kitchen door—and stopped dead. Beer in hand, Gordy was just closing the door of the fridge.

"Damn, Cousin," I said. "You scared the bejesus out of me."

"Sorry." He took a slug. "Wish this was strongah."

My antennae stood at attention. "Ah, why?"

"Somethin' bad is goin' on at my mussel raft. The VHF's abuzz with it. Marine Patrol. Somethin' about a sea kayak?" He eyed me.

"You had to know it was my kayak."

"Damnation. I gotta sit down for this." He fell into a chair on one side of the kitchen table. I took the facing chair and re-counted the story from my arrival at the raft to my futile search for him in town.

When I'd finished, my cousin leaned forward, put both large, square hands on the table, and stared at them. A long minute later, he looked up and shook his head. "It's a horrah—and a pissah it was you who found the thing."

"Have to say I agree with you, Gordy. I'll be okay. But it's *your* raft. Why aren't you out there talking to the Marine Patrol people?"

Gordy pulled off his Maine Fisherman's League baseball cap with one hand, smoothed his hair with the other, yanked the cap back down, and took another slug of beer. "Figured they'd be lookin' ta find me, so I stashed my truck in the woods a ways down your road an' walked ovah."

Not what I wanted to hear.

Deciding I could use something wet myself, I pulled a bottle of club soda out of the fridge, half-filled a glass from the cupboard, joined Gordy at the table, and leaned forward. "Gordy, what the hell is going on? Why hide? You've got to talk to the police sometime."

"There's a lot you don't know, Mara."

"So tell me."

"There's been some real bad stuff goin' on with lobstamen out on Macomek Island."

I took a sip. Put down the glass. "Stuff?"

"More than the usual trap poachin'. Lots of buoy lines cut. Guys dumpin' bleach in motors. Things like that. Puts guys on edge so they say an' do dumb stuff."

I cringed. Cut lines meant expensive lobster traps stuck on the bottom and no way to find them. Bleach in a motor sounded pretty nasty as well. "That's terrible, Gordy. But you don't trap near Macomek. And what does the island have to do with the body I found?"

Gordy got another beer and returned to his chair. He slid the bottle back and forth between his palms so many times I was afraid he wasn't going to answer.

Finally, he said, "I've been goin' out there lots lately. You know, ta see someone."

"Really? Who?"

He shrugged. I knew that maneuver too well and didn't bother to press him.

He popped the lid and took a swallow. "I've a bad feelin' about who you found undah my mussel raft."

My hand tightened around the glass. "You do?"

He shook his head.

I regarded my cousin. Always joking and teasing, Gordy was one of the most upbeat people I knew. The man across from me could have just lost his brother. The hairs on the back of my neck stood at attention.

I pushed my drink to the side, leaned across the table, and put my hand on his. "Gordy, something is going on with you and Macomek Island that you don't want to talk about. I get that. We've all got personal stuff. But I *really* need you to tell me if you had anything to do with the pour soul trapped under your mussel raft—and if you knew the body was out there."

He slipped his hand from under mine, put it on his heart, and held my gaze. "You've my word. I knew nothin' 'bout anybody. Whatevah happened to that person, it wasn't me that did it."

3

THERE WAS EVERY REASON NOT TO BELIEVE GORDY. LIKE many fishermen, when describing his haul he could be economical about the truth ("So-so" if he pulls up lots of lobsters, "Doin' okay" if he hardly catches a thing). Besides that, he's through-and-though Irish, a nation notorious for tall tales about wee folk and wide-ranging bull in general.

On the other hand, Gordy was the most loyal, just, generous man I knew. He simply would not lie about something as consequential as a dead body.

I leaned back in my chair and studied my cousin. He was my only close blood relative, and for that reason alone I had to stand by him. Besides that, my intuition told me he was telling the truth. "All right. I believe you. Tell me what you're up to now and how I can help."

Gordy patted his heart. "I 'ppreciate that, Mara. I truly do. My plan is ta lay low a couple days an' find out what's what. Then I'll go find Marine Patrol. Promise."

"Gordy, that doesn't make sense. How can you learn anything if you're hiding out?"

"That, Cousin, is where you come in—and anothah reason why I'm here."

I leaned back against the chair and crossed my arms over my chest. "You want me to snoop around for you?"

"Yes," he said. "Out on Macomek."

I shook my head. "Oh sure. I'll take off work a few days and hang out on a tiny island twenty-five miles offshore which just happens to be the tightest, most infamous lobster community in the state Maine. And where I don't know a soul. Nobody will tell me squat. They probably won't even talk to me."

"I got answers for all that."

Gordy chose to ignore my whopping eye roll.

"I know you're super busy with work," he said. "But you've been sayin' for months you oughta visit Macomek ta meet with that guy who puts monitors on his lobstah traps."

Gordy was right about this. The National Oceanographic and Atmospheric Association—NOAA—ran a program called eLobster. To monitor warming waters, lobstermen along the New England coast attached sensors to lobster traps that recorded temperature and other variables over days, weeks, even months. Since Macomek Island was home to some of the fiercest climate-change deniers in the state of Maine, I really wanted to meet the one guy willing to risk ridicule to join the program.

I wanted Gordy's take on the eLobster program. "That's correct. I'd *love* to meet, um, can't remember his name. I'm really curious to learn whether access to that temperature data could make a difference in how many lobsters end up in his traps."

"He's called Dupris. Malicite Dupris. Odd name. And fer god sakes, Mara, take some time fer yourself. You've been working seven days a week since you got back from that island off Vancouvah. You got vacation time comin'."

Gordy was right. Research scientists, including marine ones, typically did not stick to Mondays through Fridays nine-to-five. On oceanographic cruises, scientists and crew often worked all day and night deploying buoys, sampling equipment, and the like. Research on the open ocean was very expensive, one reason why getting grant proposals was so critical. At sea, if you didn't get your work done you might not get another chance. Many oceanographers I knew sustained that work ethic at home.

I ran a finger around the rim of my glass. "You're right. I could take off a few days. It'd probably be good for me to get out of Dodge as well. So back to Malicite. How useful is that water temperature data to him?"

Gordy stuck a finger under the back of his baseball cap and rubbed his neck. There were streaks of gray at the temples I hadn't noticed before. Gordy was in his forties, but that my vital, bombastic cousin would turn into a white-haired old man was hard to imagine.

His answer to my question interrupted my musing. "Would havin' knowledge 'bout temp'rature where you trap matter? I'm sure no expert on this, but maybe it could. You know that bugs go down deep offshore in the wintah?"

"I do."

"So, he said, "when the watah warms up close ta shore in spring, lobstah walk back there an' stay through fall. But, ya know, there's a whole lotta difference year ta year. This year, bugs might suddenly appear in shallow watah in June. Next year, it could be July. Hard ta say why."

I stopped him. "Let me get this right. Let's say Dupris tracks seasonal movement of lobsters he's actually catching in relation to bottom water temperature. And maybe he finds out that his, um, bugs only head to shore in spring when bottom water gets up to fifty degrees there, regardless of the date. Since a key to successful lobstering is keeping one step ahead of migrating lobsters, would predicting his lobsters' movement in a given year give Dupris an advantage?"

Gordy pulled off his cap with one hand, scratched his head hard with the other, and pulled the cap back on. "If Dupris was good at other things like what the bottom is like where he put his traps, messin' with the traps ta make 'em catch more, and bait—how much, what kind—things like that. Then knowin' the temp'rature could help I suppose. But, like I said, I'm jus' guessin'."

"Given all that, I'd love to talk with Malicite Dupris about how it's working out and why he's participating in the NOAA project. He must get a fair amount of ribbing from the other lobstermen out there."

"Ribbin's not the word. If he weren't such a good guy, my guess is someone would've pulled up his temp'rature measurers an' flushed 'em down the toilet."

"So Macomek lobstermen don't want information about bottom temp?"

"They know it's important. But it's only one thing—and besides, workin' with the NOAA guys'd be admitting there's global warming. That's why scientists want the temp'ratures."

On more than one occasion, Gordy had proclaimed that climate change was "baloney cooked up by Democrat eggheads lookin' ta get money from the government." Since much of my oceanography research focused on warming off the Maine coast, I would be included in this greedy group. But knowing the man, I guessed his ideas about climate change were actually very different from those he shared publically.

"Okay, so I'd really like to meet Dupris. But there are big problems with me going." I stuck out my thumb." First, I don't know a soul on Macomek. Nobody is going to say a whole lot to an outsider, especially if they find out what I do for a living." First finger. "Besides that, there's no hotel, B and B, or campground out there." Second finger. "Then, there's work. I'm absolutely swamped."

Gordy rubbed his chin. "No problem where you stay. Abby Burgess is as nice as they come. She rents out a room, ya know, on the side. She's lived on the island her whole life, knows everyone.

Bettah still, she loves ta talk. You could be her cousin's daughtah for all anyone knows an' Abby won't let on who you really are. You'll love it on Macomek, Mara. It's an outstandin' place fer an outdoorsy type like you."

Gordy was right. Macomek Island was famous for more than cantankerous lobstermen. With no stores, paved roads, or other modern conveniences, it was old, long-gone Maine. Besides that, puffins—birds I'd only observed in Nova Scotia—nested nearby. If I brought my sea kayak, maybe I could take it and go puffin-watching. That would be a blast.

An image of my office flashed through my mind—the to-do list on the white board. Harvey's graduate student's thesis chapter I'd promised to critique. Two grant proposals waiting to be reviewed. With a shake of my head, I pushed the rest of the list aside.

"Gordy, I'm really not sure I can take off for a whole weekend right now."

Gordy looked down at his hands. I felt awful letting him down.

I reached over and laid my hand on his. This was my bighearted cousin who kept me honest and would do anything for me. "Let me think about it and get back to you Friday morning. Okay?"

Both hands on the table, he leaned toward me. "I'll be waitin' on your call."

"Tomorrow's Thursday," I said. "If I work extra hard and get caught up, I can get the ferry Friday afternoon. It'd be terrific to paddle off the island, and I can take the kayak on the ferry."

Grinning like a little boy who'd managed to wrangle a cookie from his mom, he waved a hand. "Nah. I'll take you out. The kayak too."

"But everyone knows your lobster boat, Gordy. You can't be

out on the water in *Bulldog*."

"I'll borrah a boat an' pick you up at the beach below your house."

"We haven't discussed who I should talk to — and about what."

"Ayuh. Assumin" I'm right about the poor dead soul undah my mussel raft, I need ta think on that. On the way out, we'll make a plan."

My throat constricted at the memory of a waterlogged corpse emerging from the depths. With our back and forth about lobsters and temperature, I hadn't thought about, as Gordy put it, "the poor dead soul" I'd discovered hours earlier.

I reached for my glass and finished what was left. "I hope the police quickly figure who died and why."

Gordy stood, drained his beer, and said, "If I'm right an' he's from Macomek, the cops'll get nowheres on why. That island is sinkin' undah a whole lotta secrets."

Gordy wasn't gone five minutes when my cell rang. It was Harvey.

"Does dinner work tonight?" she asked. "It'll be quick. Just you, me, Connor, and some grilled fish he caught."

It was hard to believe she'd mentioned a meal only a few hours earlier. I glanced at my empty refrigerator. "Love to, Harve. Sorry I didn't get back to you about dinner. So much has happened since we talked this afternoon. You'll be amazed."

"Like I've said many times before, Mara, nothing about you amazes me."

Harvey lives in a spotless cape-style house minutes from MOI. Side by side, two trucks claimed the driveway. Harvey's was ruby red. Connor Doyle, her significant other, was a proud Irishman. So his, naturally, was green.

I parked on the street.

Connor pulled open the front door before I reached it. "Mara—a sunny sight for tired eyes. Come on in."

With ringlets of dark hair just going to grey and lively blue eyes, Connor always reminded me of an aging altar boy.

I kissed him on the cheek. "Last time I saw you was right after Ted, ah, decided to go his own way. You gave me your favorite baseball cap to remind me I wasn't alone. I'm a whole lot better now. Do you want it back?"

"Nah. Keep it for good luck. Harvey's in the kitchen."

Connor led me through the living room. With its comfy sofa and chairs facing the fireplace, shining pine floor, and soft lighting, the room spoke of good taste and comfort. I stepped into the kitchen and took in the aroma of basil—gastronomic perfume to a half-Italian like me.

Chef's knife in hand, Harvey looked up from her cutting board. "Hey, girlfriend. I'd give you a hug, but my hands reek of garlic and onions."

"I know you love me," I said. "It smells amazing in here. What're you making?"

"Connor caught some stripers today." She nodded toward the open cookbook on the counter. "Thought I'd try bass with tomato scampi. Garlic, shallots, capers, white wine, lemon, tomatoes, chopped basil. Sautéed, then baked for a bit."

"Huh. Always thought scampi was a shrimp dish," I said.

"Something to drink?" Harvey asked.

"Some white wine would be perfect."

Connor half-filled a glass and handed it to me. "Scampi means cooked in olive oil, garlic, and lemon." He winked at Harvey. "Or so I learned five minutes ago."

Since dinner preparations were well along, I settled onto a stool at the granite counter to enjoy my wine and two of my very favorite people. Harvey and Connor had hit it off the previous spring when they'd teamed up to help me identify the killer of a dear friend and colleague.

They were an unlikely match. Harvey's wealthy parents had sent her to boarding school and an expensive college, and Harvey saw no need to hide her patrician upbringing from down-to-earth Mainers. But god bless her, she'd fallen for a retired cop from Augusta who'd moved to Spruce Harbor because he loved saltwater fishing. They did share a passion for hunting deer and bear and, as Connor put it, "the glorious Maine coast." Connor was also my godfather Angelo's fishing buddy, so I saw him a lot.

Connor pulled up another stool, emptied a bottle of beer into a glass, and sat down. We clinked glasses.

"May good luck be your friend in whatever you do," he said.

"Thanks, Connor." I eyed the empty beer bottle. "What's that? Not a Guinness?"

"I'm tastin' Maine beers. There's more than fifty little brew'ries heah. Can't believe it."

"Why not? Seems like beer goes well with lobster."

"It does. But *these* beers? That's what southunahs drink down in Taxachusetts."

I rolled my eyes. Once, I'd teased Connor about his Maine accent, which only made him lay it on thick now and then. For native Mainers, a "southunah" was anyone in the US who lived south of Kittery, Maine's southernmost town. Taxachusetts was, of course, Massachusetts.

Harvey put down her knife and washed her hands in the sink. "I'll cook the fish in a bit, but first I'm dying to hear what happened to Mara this afternoon. Let's go into the living room."

Connor said he'd join us after he checked on the grill. Harvey slid onto the living room couch while I took a soft chair facing her. She jiggled a silver ballet flat that complimented her grey cashmere slacks. As usual, I hadn't bothered to change out of my jeans.

I ran a finger around the lid of my wine glass. "It's funny," I said. "I only talk at any length with people like you, Connor, and Angelo over food. Does everyone do that?"

She said, "Moms chat with other moms during kid's sports games, things like that. But neither of us has kids. And actually, Mara, eating and talking makes a lot of sense for you. First of all, you're Italian, and Italy's a country where everyone does everything over food, far as I know. Also, you work all the time. That doesn't leave much room for casual chit-chat."

I shrugged. "Can't argue with any of that."

When Connor was seated next to Harvey, her hand in his, I relayed my story from when I'd reached Gordy's raft to my paddle back to Spruce Harbor. Harvey gasped, and her gray eyes widened when I described the body popping out of the water, but she didn't interrupt me. Connor, the retired cop, simply nodded now and then.

"So where's Gordy?" he asked.

"Um, well, I can't say. I looked for him in town but didn't find him until I walked into my kitchen. He'd heard about what happened on the VHF and stashed his truck in the woods. He's hiding out someplace now. Honestly, I don't know where."

Harvey shook her head. "Disappearing like that looks suspicious. Why doesn't he talk to the Marine Police?" She bit her lip. "Unless he's involved in what happened."

Connor leaned forward on the couch, arms on his knees, hands clasped. "I've known Gordy a long, long time. He'd nevah harm a soul except to save himself or someone else."

"You're right, Connor," I said. "And he plans to talk to the police in a few days but says he needs to find out a few things first."

Connor's bushy eyebrows came together. "How's he gonna do that if he's hidin' out?"

I let out a sigh. "He thinks Macomek lobstermen are behind what happened and wants me to go out there and poke around. Macomek's such an iconic Maine island. It would be great to visit. There's also a lobsterman who's in the eLobster program. I'd love to talk with him."

Harvey frowned. "What about all the work you keep worrying about?"

"Right. If I get up real early tomorrow and Friday and barrel along, I'll get it mostly done. Alise can revise the proposal while I'm gone, and we can give it to Seymour right after I get back. You'll be around to answer any questions she has."

"I will but bet she won't need it. You got a winner with her, Mara. Alise is the smartest grad student I've worked with. Nothing throws her—not the chemistry, the AutoAnalyzer, not even Seymour."

"Harvey told me Seymour walks in the other direction if he sees Alise," Connor said.

I snorted. "Don't know if it's her fish tattoos, her "*Love Your Mother Earth*" T-shirt logos, her smarts, or what. But it's terrific."

Harvey sat back and crossed her arms. "Let's get back to you visiting Macomek. That's where lobstermen shoot each other in the street."

"That was only once," I said.

Significant eye-roll. "What about the lobster wars in the Penobscot Islands when fishing docks burned to cinders and a warden raced back to the mainland as bullets were flying by his boat's windshield?"

"I think that was back in the nineteen-thirties," Connor said. "Things have settled down a whole lot. More to the point, how will an outsidah like you learn anything?"

"Sure. I asked Gordy that. He said I could stay with a woman named Abby Burgess. Apparently, she knows everyone and everything and will help me. At the very least, I'll spend a couple of days in Maine-the-way-it-used-to-be, go birding, and talk to that eLobster guy."

Harvey stood and put a hand on my shoulder. Her eyes searched mine for a moment. "I don't like it, but I know you'll go. Please, please be careful, Mara."

Connor's advice was more specific. "See what's what before you go out at night."

4

I WAS AT MY DESK BY SIX THE NEXT MORNING. FUELED WITH caffeine, I plowed through work—research papers got read, data sets crunched, a grant proposal draft flew through cyberspace to a colleague's computer.

Every hour, I got up and looked out the window to check on Gordy's aquaculture raft. Around nine, two boats approached the Marine Patrol vessel, but I couldn't make out what anyone was doing. I tried not to dwell on the horror divers would drag onto their deck. An hour later, the boats were gone.

After that, my window visits were more peaceful. I breathed slowly and focused on happy thoughts. By lunchtime, I was one calm, centered woman.

Feeling pretty good, late in the afternoon I marched down the hall and knocked on Ted's partly open door. To his "Come on in," I took two steps into his office, and stopped dead, my "Time for coffee at the Neap Tide?" stuck in my open mouth.

Seated next to Ted at his desk—knee-to-knee I noted—was a woman with lustrous, black hair draped over a soft, ivory sweater. She turned, appraised me with long-lashed, chocolate eyes, and pursed her lips.

I instantly disliked her.

"Mara Tusconi, meet Penny Russell. Penny's been chief scientist on several HOV missions. Last time on a hydrothermal vent in a Pacific seamount chain."

"HOV?" I asked.

Penny blinked. "Human Occupied Vehicle."

"Of course," I said.

Ted beamed. "We're talking about a HOV dive in the Gulf of Maine to one of the deep-sea coral gardens."

Few people realize that the Gulf of Maine is home to dense "gardens" of lush, diverse corals hundreds of feet below the surface. Exploring these barely studied, spectacular habitats in a submersible would be a Maine marine biologist's dream.

"Is that so," I said.

Ted raised an eyebrow in what I recognized as a "What's with you?" gesture. Normally, my response to a deep-sea expedition in the Gulf of Maine would be wildly enthusiastic.

I gave it a go. "Yes, well, happy to meet you, Penny. Ah, where in the Gulf?"

She launched into a detailed lecture about various dive sites and ended with, "We're most interested in Mount Desert Rock and the hanging coral gardens near Schoodic Ridge. The Fishery Management Council is considering protecting these areas from fishing and needs more information."

"Outer Schoodic Ridge and Mount Desert Rock are prime offshore lobster grounds," I said.

Her head snapped back just enough to notice. Perhaps the HOV chief scientist didn't expect me to know a whole lot about Gulf of Maine corals.

She cleared her throat and said, "We have evidence that fishermen's gear has damaged coral communities in these areas."

"That's true," I countered. "But the damage is primarily from trawlers, not lobstermen. The footprint of a lobster pot is very much smaller than a trawl dragged along the bottom."

She stood and crossed her arms. "Deep-sea corals are vulnerable to any disturbance, however small the footprint. They grow slowly and must be protected."

I mimicked her crossed arms. "Naturally, I'm sensitive to your points. But the lobstermen who fish Maine's waters must be considered in any action like this."

She dug in. "We can't be talking about that many lobstermen."

"Where're you originally from?" I asked.

"Virginia."

"Right," I said. "The lobster industry is the biggest economic driver in northern Maine's coastal region. Hundreds of lobster boat captains and their crew drop traps in the areas you listed. That's a lot of families."

She opened her mouth to respond, but Ted cut her off. "Okay. Good discussion, folks, which we'll have to finish later. Mara, Penny's not here that long and we've got lots of work to do."

I marched back to my office, slammed the door behind me, and fell into my desk chair. What the hell had just happened? Minutes ago I'd been humming along feeling terrific. Now I was clammy with sweat, my heart thumped inside my chest, and I wanted to punch someone or something. The nails of my clenched hands dug into my palms. I relaxed and shook them out.

Calm centeredness had flown out the window like a November robin with the last ticket south.

I needed to vent, talk to someone, step back and assess. At times like that I turn to Homer. He's patient, an excellent listener, and nonjudgmental. My arthropodal friend resides underwater. Homer—short for *Homarus americanus*—is an American lobster.

Of course, where I live, we call this critter the Maine lobster.

Homer hangs out in the basement of Maine Oceanographic Institute's biology building. He's got lots of company—fish, crabs, jellyfish, squid. There's even the occasional octopus, although those smart cephalopods usually manage to climb out of whatever they're in, slink down a pipe, and escape into the ocean.

When I'm upset, just walking through the basement's double swinging doors lifts my spirits. I slipped out of my office, took the back stairs, and did just that. Two steps into the cavernous room I stopped, closed my eyes, and inhaled the briny balm of seawater-saturated air. Ocean water thundered through pipes into a hundred tanks and aquaria on its way back out to the ocean.

The liquid cacophony drowned my anger the way rain cools granite boulders baking in July's sun.

My feet crunched decades of accumulated salt crystals as I wove around various-sized tanks, including one the size of a small swimming pool. I stopped to pay my respects to two marine animals unrecognized by most for their vital importance to humanity—horseshoe crabs and squid. Horseshoe crabs, which aren't crabs at all, have blue-colored blood that can detect human bacterial contamination in the one-part-in-a-trillion range. Its medical application has saved uncountable lives. The squid's giant axon, a nerve fiber twenty times bigger than a human's, won several marine scientists Noble Prizes for their research on electrical activity in the nervous system.

I peered into a tank of lumbering horseshoe crabs and another with zipping squid and said, "Hey you guys, thanks for everything you've done."

Homer was nestled on the bottom in the back corner of his tank kingdom, a favorite spot. I tapped gently on the aquarium's glass, aware that such a tap would sound very loud underwater to a human. Homer doesn't have ears, of course, but tiny sensory hairs on a lobster's body appear to detect pressure waves.

Homer tiptoed toward me on his eight walking legs and touched an antenna to the glass. I matched the gesture on my side with an index finger. After this greeting, he backed up and settled down on the swimmerets between his tail and legs.

"You're looking handsome as always, Homer."

He bobbed his antennae and rotated his round, ebony eyes upward.

"Be right back." I returned with a handful of blue mussels, crushed them one by one, and dropped the pink flesh into the tank. Homer grabbed each piece before it hit the bottom, tore it apart with his ripper claw, and moved the food to his mouthparts with his foremost walking legs. After dealing with the last mussel, he settled back on his swimmerets again. I took this as a sign that he was ready to listen.

I began. "Remember how I told you how much better I was? No more anger and resentment, just gratitude and thankfulness?"

Homer waved an antenna up and down, which I interpreted as yes.

"Well, I've had a setback. At the moment, I'm really pissed at Ted and angry with myself for feeling that way."

Homer didn't stir. He was such as good listener.

"A little while ago I walked into Ted's office. There was a woman there, a very attractive woman. She and Ted are going down in a tiny submersible to look at deep-sea corals." I started pacing back and forth. "I can *just* see it. The two of them crowded together in that tiny space, *ooh*ing and *aah*ing at gorgeous sea fans, fish streaming by." Hands on hips. "It'll be pitch black of course, just the floodlights outside the vessel. They'll probably turn off the inside lights and be there in the dark. Together."

I stopped, dropped my arms to my side, and tried to slow my breathing. The image I'd created out of thin air had turned me into a crazy woman.

Homer noticed, of course. It was embarrassing. After a minute, he rotated his body in a full circle and settled down again.

"You're right, I know. I'm jumping to conclusions, making assumptions. All the things I say scientists should never do. And I don't when I'm doing science. But it's different when it's me and…Ted." I bit my lip.

Homer kind of tipped his head-body.

"What am I going to do?" I leaned forward, put both elbows on the table, rested my head on my hands, and peered in at the lobster. "I guess it's time to talk to Angelo. He's always so good with stuff like this."

Homer backed up, turned, and headed toward to his corner.

"Thanks little guy," I said.

He rotated his body and dipped an antenna.

My godfather Angelo's home commands an outstanding view of Spruce Harbor from the tip of Seal Point, one of two bluffs at the harbor's entrance. It's my home too. Angelo took me in after my parents, both marine biologists, died in a submersible accident when I was nineteen. That's what godfathers do, and Angelo threw himself into the role of dad, mom, and best friend with Italian verve and passion. It was hard to believe the accident was only twelve years earlier. So much had happened to me—college graduation, PhD from MIT, post-doctoral fellowship, the ideal job at Maine Oceanographic Institute—that Mom and Dad knew nothing about.

They would have been so proud. That loss was an ache never far from the surface.

I climbed the granite steps, tugged open the oak door, paused in the foyer, and eyed the top step. How many evenings had I perched up there, listening to Angelo, my mother Bridget and father Carlos, and a guest—fisherman, scientist, or old-time Mainer—debate all things marine? No topic was too esoteric. I'd learned about the sex life of *Crepidula fornicata*, the common slipper shell, a sequential hermaphrodite that changed gender with position in the stack of shells. Of course, there were consequential issues too, like the conservation status of humpback whales and whether climate warming could possibly impact the vast ocean.

The voice came from the other side of the house. "Mara, I'm back here."

My godfather's kitchen was often a sensory delight. Homemade tomato sauce with basil, wine, garlic, and onions simmering in olive oil greeted me. Angelo, at the gas stove, stirred the bubbling ambrosia.

On tiptoe, I pecked him on the cheek and asked, "What've you having tonight?"

"Squid marinara."

"Perfect. At the moment, I'm squid for brains."

He chuckled. "Want to stay?"

I shook my head. "I'll take a rain check but would love some of that sauce."

"Sure. Have a little wine. White wine's in the fridge, red on the counter. Help yourself."

I went for the white. Red felt too hot.

The chat with Angelo at his venerable wooden table in the kitchen was light on angst and heavy on upbeat talk—about how well bluefish were running, whether puttanesca sauce tasted different with anchovies from Peru or Japan, the latest ocean-going technologies.

A retired marine engineer, Angelo described new plans for ships that wouldn't dump much or any ballast water.

"Ships that don't take in unwanted marine organisms from one part of the world and discard them in another. That'd be huge," I said.

Angelo reached for an olive on the plate between us, popped it in his mouth, and washed it down with a bit of wine. "It would be, but I'm guessing you didn't come over here to talk about ballast water. You sounded pretty upset on the phone."

I told him the whole thing. "I'd been doing so well with the whole gratitude thing, then totally lost it in a minute. I'm angry with myself, and embarrassed too."

Angelo reached over and put his hand—at once rough-weathered and soothing—on mine. "Like I've said before, Mara, with an Irish mother and an Italian dad, you've inherited a double dose of spirited emotions. Be easy on yourself. You can get back to that peaceful place again."

The soft kitchen light enhanced specks of blue in Angelo's grey eyes, blue that warmed me. I let out a long, slow breath.

Angelo patted my hand. "Want to say anything to Ted?"

"Like an apology?"

"Hmm."

I drummed my fingers on the table, looked to the side, fell back in my chair. "You're right. I should apologize. I certainly owe him that, and it'd make me feel me a little less like a jerk."

"Good. Should we talk about Gordy's mussel raft?"

"So you heard about that."

"Gordy called last night. Actually, I assumed that's what you wanted to talk to me about," he said.

"Yes and no. I'd rather not relive finding the body right now. But Gordy's convinced somebody on Macomek Island is behind what happened. He wants me to snoop around out there and see what I can learn."

"Ah, so that's what he's up to. I told Gordy to talk to the police, but he said he wanted to wait a few days to get some 'important'—Angelo air quoted the word—information. I didn't understand what he was talking about."

I rubbed my neck. "That'd be me. But there are very good reasons why I shouldn't go. Work's top of the list. Also—and excuse the pun—I'd be a fish out of water. Maine fishing communities are usually pretty tight."

"Fishing *is* in your blood."

I tipped my head. "Say that again?"

"Italians have been an essential part of New England fishing for centuries," he said. "*And* you've got a family connection you don't even know about."

5

I LEANED TOWARD ANGELO. "UM, COULD YOU REPEAT THAT?"
"Let's start with the history lesson. That'll help you understand the other part."

I was super curious about the family link but had to be
patient—not my strong suit. "Okay. Ah, Italians? New England?
Fishing? I'm a marine ecologist and know nothing about this."

Anyone else would have given me a believe-it-or-not-you-
don't-know-everything look. Angelo's kindness prevented him
from doing that.

"Sure," he said. "Before World War Two, immigrants from
Italy's coasts settled in Boston and fished the Grand Banks.
Remember the Fishermen's Feast festival in Boston's North End?"

A childhood memory flashed by. Crowded, narrow streets.
Dad holding my hand tight. Aroma of fried dough, sausage,
pizza. Men carrying a lurching statue of the Virgin Mary on
their shoulders.

Nodding, I blinked back tears. Angelo didn't need to ask
why. "Yeah. Dad took me when I was a kid. But I don't remember anything about fishermen."

"Blessing of the waters happens before the street festival.
After that, it's mostly about the Madonna and celebrating being
Italian."

Anxious to hear about my family, I decided it was time
for the history lesson to wrap up. "Anything else about Italian
fishermen in New England?"

"Well, some of the history's sad. During the war, Italians were designated enemy aliens. The Boston Navy Yard guys finally let them leave the harbor to fish, but their radios were locked and boats inspected by the Coast Guard to make sure they weren't carrying provisions for the Germans."

"Proud Italian fishermen treated like that. Awful. But German subs were right offshore. People were scared," I said. My impatience finally bubbled out. "Is that the family connection? In Boston?"

"There's an Italian wine, a Gavi, I'd like you to try. Let's go into the living room."

Angelo slid a cold bottle of Gavi onto the coffee table, wrapped a dishtowel around it, inserted his favorite corkscrew, and slowly twisted it.

I'd settled into my usual armchair in front of the fireplace (not in use, since it was early fall), kicked off my shoes, tucked my feet under me, and tried to convince myself I was interested in the wine ritual. It didn't work.

The cork finally came out with a satisfying pop. Angelo swirled wine around the bottom of his glass, sniffed, took a sip, and paused. "Good. Excellent white." He filled both our glasses and handed me mine.

"To unknown Italian ancestors," he said.

I lifted my glass and waited for him to settle into his chair.

"All right," he said. "I'll explain what I know, which isn't much. Once when we were alone—your mother was off some-where—Carlos told me a family secret. He never mentioned it again, and I didn't ask."

Angelo stared at his glass of wine as if he were looking into the past. "I'd just built this house and a team of Italian masons were constructing the stone wall around the patio. We were inside watching them. Maybe something about those guys made him want to tell me. I don't know."

"Tell you…?"

"That his father—your grandfather—left Boston in disgrace and moved up here."

I spilled half my wine on my jeans, tried to rub it in with one hand, and dropped the glass on the table with the other.

Angelo handed me the dishtowel. "Let me think so I get his exact words." He closed his eyes for a moment. "Um, he said that his father moved away because everyone on his fishing boat except him died at sea in a storm."

I frowned. "Fishing's one of the most dangerous occupations there is. People die in storms. It doesn't mean the captain's responsible."

"That's right. But the storm cleared quickly and another boat picked up your grandfather. He was intoxicated. I mean, really drunk."

I put my hand to my throat. "Ah."

"You can imagine what it was like. The guilt, accusations, anger. So Carlos's dad and mother decided to leave. They crossed the border into Maine and settled up in Presque Isle."

"Hours away from the coast," I said.

"That's right. He got a job in the lumber industry, and Carlos was born and raised in Presque Isle."

I twisted the dishtowel around my forefinger. "A sad story, that's for sure. I feel bad for Dad, but it's not surprising he never spoke about it. Italians are notorious for keeping secrets."

"That's true, and it comes from our history," he said. "For centuries, Italians had to deceive people who had authority over them—princelings, papal legates, the Austrian military. Do you know the expression 'acqua in bocca'"?

I shook my head.

"Literally, it means 'Keep the water in your mouth.' You can guess the real meaning."

"Something like, 'Don't spill the beans'?"

"That's it. Anyway, now that you know about your fishing ancestor, I hope you won't feel quite so much an outsider out on Macomek."

The drive home gave me time to think about Angelo's prediction. Would knowledge that my grandfather had been a fisherman translate into feeling like a kindred soul on the island? Maybe it was my desperate need for family, but I thought it would. Even if nobody else in the world—except Angelo—knew about my Italian grandfather, *I* did. Fishing was really and truly in my heritage.

My mother always said I loved the sea because there was extra salt in my blood. Now I realized there was an actual lineage she knew nothing about.

I pulled into Maine Oceanographic's parking lot at five-thirty Friday morning—just as the sun poked out of the sea and painted Spruce Harbor's horizon blood-red. By noon, most items on my "to-do" list were done. I called Gordy to tell him I was good to go to Macomek. He sounded relieved and said he'd pick me up at my beach in three hours.

"Tide'll be high," he said. "Grab yer wellies so you can wade out an' keep dry."

One crucial task remained. Ted deserved an apology from me. I ran through my speech a couple of times, walked down the hallway to his door, and stopped. If I were still a practicing Catholic, I would have crossed myself.

The knock was so feeble it was barely audible. My hand was raised for a second try when Ted called out, "It's open!" I stepped in and shut the door behind me.

He swiveled his office chair away from the computer. "Oh, Mara. Um, nice to see you."

I glanced at the chair next to his desk—the one Penny had bogarted two days earlier.

Ted gestured toward it. "Want to sit down?"

I wrapped my arms around my chest, shifted my weight to one foot, then the other. "That's okay. I'll just be a minute."

He blinked. "Right, sure."

I shifted back to other foot. "Ah…that is…um." The words spilled out. "I want to apologize for how I was with Penny."

A single nod. "Ah."

I eyed the offered seat. "Maybe I should sit down." I pulled the chair away from his desk and settled into it, feet squarely on the floor. "She's your colleague. I was, ah, ungracious. Really, really sorry." I studied my hands.

"Mara." The tone was kind. I looked up. For a moment, I was hypnotized by him—the sly smile, hint of dimples, steel-blue eyes. Loss flowed through me, aching and deep.

The loss I'd brought on myself.

Ted's fingers twitched, and for a moment I thought he was going to reach over and touch me.

Instead, he cleared his throat. "Penny can be a little, um, forceful. But I do appreciate your saying that."

We sat in silence. Someone walked by the door. In the harbor, a horn sounded twice. The ping from Ted's computer announced a new email.

Hands gripping both armrests, I pushed the chair back and stood. "Thanks. That's it then. Right. See you later, Ted."

In the doorway, I glanced back. Hand on his chest, Ted stared at me. I stumbled back to my office.

I'd just shut down the computer, straightened the piles of paper on my desk, and rubbed the last tears off my cheeks when the knock startled me. Only one person announced his unwelcome presence in this loud, obnoxious way.

Without waiting for my okay, Seymour Hull yanked open the door. His wiry, twitchy body filled the frame.

I didn't invite him in. "Yes?"

Glasses perched at the end of his ski-jump nose, Seymour glowered down at me. "The Sea Grant proposal. *Really* going to get it to me this time?"

Seymour knew perfectly well why I'd had to scrap writing the proposal the previous spring. I'd witnessed the suspicious death of a dear colleague on a research cruise in April. When MOI declared Peter's death an accident, his wife had begged me to discover what really happened. With luck and Harvey's help, I'd learned that Peter had been targeted by powerful climate change deniers connected to the oil industry. The investigation had left no time for things like writing grant proposals. Seymour finally agreed that Peter had been murdered but took every opportunity to rub the half-written proposal in my face.

I stared up at him just long enough to increase his twitch level. "Of course, Seymour. Like I said already, Alise and I will get it to you right on time." I didn't elaborate on the proposal's focus, and he didn't ask.

Seymour licked his lips, turned, and slammed the door.

I walked over to the window and looked down on the harbor. Sea Grant proposals could include an education component, and Alise had come up with a great idea. Fascinated by the e-Lobster project, she proposed to expand its membership with a series of "lobster town halls." Lobstermen already participating would show cool stuff like underwater videos and real-time temperature data from their own lobster traps and explain how the data might improve their catches. With the fish tattoos on her muscular biceps and a no-nonsense attitude offset by a quirky sense of humor, Alise was ideal for the project.

For the tenth time that day, I mentally ran through the

requirements for the proposal—narrative, references, tables and figures, budget. In addition to the prose, Alise would work on the rest with Harvey's help if she needed it. After Alise revised the proposal, I only had to proofread the whole thing. Then she and I could deliver it to Seymour.

Still, I felt guilty taking off. MOI paid my salary and provided an office and laboratory, but that was it. The rest was on me. Everything about marine research was expensive—field equipment purchase and repair, time on oceanographic vessels, lab supplies and apparatus, salary for a lab technician if I needed one, and graduate student support.

Alise and I, of course, would compete with other scientists in our field who needed money. In the close-knit world of oceanographic research, I knew most of these brainy, ambitious, hard-working people. Since only about ten percent of our proposals would be funded, I doubted many of my competitors would be taking the weekend off.

To assuage my guilt, I told myself that the connection with e-Lobster partner Malicite Dupris would be worth the trip. At the very least, I could describe Alise's proposal, get his input, and ask if he'd help us recruit other lobstermen.

6

MY HOUSE SITS AT THE END OF A PINE-FLANKED DIRT road a few miles from Spruce Harbor village. A sloping bank of huge granite boulders protects the cottage from crashing waves and whatever else the Atlantic throws at my piece of the Maine coast. Gordy motored up to the pebble beach at the foot of the boulders in an expensive new lobster boat appropriately named *Money Pit*. It looked nothing like his venerable *Bulldog*, I was happy to see.

Backpack above my head, I waded up to the transom or "back" of the craft. As with most lobster boats, the open aft design helped fishermen easily slide traps back into the ocean after they'd been emptied of lobsters and loaded with new bait.

"Pretty fancy craft, Captain. Good cover. Nobody'll expect *you* in this wheelhouse."

He reached down and grabbed my gear. "Ayuh, she's a beauty. Full keel, flat after sections, sea-kindly—perfect Down East lobstah boat. Way too rich for me, 'course." He straightened up. "Float out your kayak. We'll slide it right up."

Sea kayak and other waterproof gear on deck and pack in the wheelhouse, we soon turned our backs on Spruce Harbor. Next stop Macomek Island, twenty-plus miles, straight shot southeast. Clangs from Juniper Ledge's bell buoy, steadfast sentry for incoming boats, were still ringing in my ears when *Money Pit* climbed a ten-foot wave and threw me onto my butt.

Gordy tightened his hands on the wheel and glanced down at me. "You okay?"

Swallowing bile bubbling up from my stomach—and my pride—I crawled into the wheelhouse and reached for the backpack. "Yeah, just need some ginger and my seasick patch."

Gordy kept mum and squinted at his GPS screen. He knew very well that a seasick oceanographer had to deal with a lot more than an upset stomach. On research cruises, crewmembers' wisecracks hurt, even if I pretended otherwise.

Sucking ginger candy, I was trying to secure the patch behind my ear when *Money Pit* climbed another wave and slammed into the trough.

"Hey," I yelled. "Thought you said this was a sea-kindly craft!"

Gordy touched his GPS screen, leaned in, and called out, "We hit a squall. Nothin' she can't handle. But you're gonna need foul weather gear for somethin' like an hour." He pointed to a duffle bag within my reach. "Mine's in theah."

Shielded from the driving rain and wind by my trusty yellow slicker, rain pants, and rubber boots, I stood, feet spread, just inside the open wheelhouse. There, I could suck in fresh air, safely relish the wild sea, and talk to Gordy at the same time.

My cousin was in his element. Clad in his own yellow gear, grip on the wheel, he whooped every time *Money Pit* took an especially hard wave.

"You look like the old man in the sea," I called out.

"That old man went fishin' alone in the Gulf Stream in a skiff…."

"That's how Hemingway's story starts?"

"More or less."

"You always surprise me, Gordy."

"Funny how we think we know folks when we really don't."

I wanted to ask what the heck he meant by that, but his

poker face told me it wasn't worth the effort. "There's lots to talk about before we get to the island," I said. "First, I need to know who's who."

He returned the screen to navigation mode. "Ayuh. You're stayin' with a lady named Abby Burgess."

The name sounded familiar. "Do I know her?"

"Lots o' Burgesses on Macomek. Our Abby was named after the girl who kept Matinicus Rock Lighthouse lit ovah three weeks durin' an awful storm. Her father was on the mainland buyin' oil fer those old lighthouse lamps an' couldn't get back. When the storm hit, Abby saved her mother and sisters by gettin' them up into the lighthouse."

"When was that, how old was Abby, and where's Matinicus Rock?"

"Middle eighteen-hundreds. She was only sixteen, an' it's off Macomek a ways."

"From the way you described Abby earlier, I'm thinking she lives up to her namesake," I said.

"Ayuh. She's like, it's hard to explain, old Maine's soul. Times past, the land an' the sea, pride, hard work, family."

Chewing on a cigar he somehow kept lit in the salt spray, Gordy looked like his usual roughhewn self. But there was something in the way he talked that was different. "Not sure I've heard you be quite so, ah, eloquent about Mainers."

The summer tan didn't hide his blush.

"I've been talkin' with some diff'rent folks on the island."

"Different as in female?"

He pulled the cigar stub out of his mouth, studied it, and threw it overboard. "Ayuh."

"What's her name?"

"Patty Burgess. She taught kids on the island."

"Abby's daughter?"

The quick nod both answered my question and announced the end to more.

"Abby'll tell you all about every living soul on Macomek—dead ones too," he said. "But there's one person I 'specially want you ta talk with."

"I'm all ears."

"Tyler Johnson. The guy's a hothead who went aftah a Macomek lobstahman named Buddy Crawford two weeks ago."

"Went after as in…?"

"'S.O.B., I'm gonna kill ya.' I'm not the only one who heard that eithah."

"Gordy, are you saying that you think the dead guy under your raft is this Buddy Crawford?"

He rubbed the back of his neck and shrugged. "Ayuh."

"Don't you think it's an awfully big jump from Tyler's threat to—I air quoted—'It's Buddy under the raft'?"

"Two things. Firs', not one soul on Macomek's seen Buddy fer three whole days. His boat's still in the habah, he's not in his house, an' nobody saw him leave. There's no place ta go on that little island. Besides that, I got inside information. So jus' go with it, okay?"

I let out a long, long sigh. "So you believe that Buddy was killed and the police would be especially interested in this Tyler guy."

"Far as I know, nobody out there is talkin', so Marine Patrol's still in the dark. When they do find out, Tyler'll be tighter'n a clam with lockjaw."

"You can't think he'll speak to me — someone he's never met."

"Hold that. You need ta know why Tyler went aftah Buddy. Crawford was a great guy. Really was. Except Tyler, everyone on Macomek loved Buddy Crawford. A guy who'd help ol' ladies cross the street." Gordy laughed. "If Macomek had real streets."

"So what'd Buddy do to Tyler?"

"Guess."

"Stole his girlfriend?"

"His *fiancé*."

"Ouch."

"What's her name?"

"Angel Burgess. Abby's youngest daughtah. Patty's kid sistah."

"So Tyler was pissed and humiliated because everyone knew."

"He was pissed, fer sure. But hardly anybody knows yet, 'cept Tyler an' Angel. It all jus' happened."

"Patty told you that her sister Angel left Tyler for Buddy. That's how you know all this."

Quick head nod.

I was beginning to follow the series of events. "What can you tell me about this Tyler?" I asked. "Besides that he's a hothead."

Gordy shrugged. "Don't really know the guy, have ta say. Blows hot an' cold. One minute he's got ya laughin' hard, next he'll turn on ya. Weird how he is. I'm guessin' he went aftah Buddy an' things got out o' hand."

"You mean Tyler killed Buddy without really meaning to?"

"Ayuh, maybe. But whatever it was, when Marine Patrol hears 'bout Tyler, the heat's off me. Then, I'll go talk with 'em."

"He does sound like he's a good candidate for Buddy's death. How old is this guy?

"Thirty give or take. Your age."

Gordy stole a quick glance at me, and I suspected I wasn't going to like what was coming next. "I hope your idea isn't that I meet Tyler in a bar or somewhere and come on to him."

"No, no. Nothin' like that. No bars on Macomek anyway."

While we were talking, the waves had settled down. Gordy cut the motor to a slow gurgle, and we shed our raingear to enjoy the gentle sea just as Macomek emerged from the mist off our starboard side. It looked like a respectable-sized island jutting up from the cold Atlantic. Armored by an apron of grey rock, its peninsula-fingers reached out into the ocean like a sea serpent's tentacles.

I'd expected to be excited by my first glimpse of the island. Instead, I was uneasy. Gordy had put me on edge.

He said, "Mara, you gotta understand I'm desperate. Las' couple days I couldn't sleep or eat. I can't go ta jail. I jus' can't."

I took a step back. With sagging bags beneath bloodshot eye, Gordy looked like crap. I was embarrassed not to have noticed his condition earlier.

"What's all this about ja—?"

He cut me off. "Will you hear me out?"

I'd never seen Gordy frantic like this. It weirded me out. "Okay. Sure."

"Drugs are a huge problem on Macomek with the youngah guys 'specially. When lobstering's good, they've got lots of loose cash. Tyler's smokes dope and does othah drugs too. Whatevah he's on, he thinks people're aftah him."

"Paranoid?" I asked.

"Ayuh. Real angry sometimes too. Maybe that's why Tyler lost it with Buddy, who knows."

"Why are you telling me this?"

"I want Marine Patrol ta skip over me and go right after Tyler, 'cause, by Godfrey, I know he's who they want. They'd do that if Tyler splits—leaves the island—'cause he was sure police were ontah him."

"I get your logic, but what's it got to do with me?"

"I'm thinkin' that bein' so nervous, he might take you for a snoop."

"As in undercover cop."

He nodded.

"Gordy, this is absolutely nuts. You've been watching too many detective shows."

He squinted at the island. "I see it in my head an' you don't have ta do a thing. Jus' be there. I'll get it around that you wanna talk with Tyler. You're an outsider he's never seen before. He'll get spooked and take off. That's it."

Gordy's idea hit me like bucket of ice water. "So, Cousin, you want me to hang out there like bait."

He rubbed the back of his neck, coughed, and said, "Well, I wouldn't put it like that."

"So, how *would* you put it?"

"More like a lure or a decoy."

"I'd call it a sitting duck, Gordy."

His eyes pleaded with me. "Mara, I really, really need you ta do this."

The Gordy I knew was funny, energetic, upbeat, sometimes a pain in the rear end—not the haunted, desperate guy before me. Something lay beneath his behavior, and I had to find out what. The whole situation chilled me and left me uncertain how to respond to him.

I walked to the railing and leaned out over the side. The fishes, jellies, and other creatures gliding below just lived their fishy, jelly lives as best they could without decisions to make— or regrets. I envied them.

I turned, leaned back against the railing, and crossed my arms. "Dammit, I really don't know, Gordy. You've thrown a lot at me pretty fast."

Gordy, who'd rather fall overboard and drown than beg

for anything, shot me a look that broke my resolve.

I blew out a long breath. "Okay, Cousin. Go ahead with what you have to do."

1

SOLITARY AND FAR FROM SHORE, ISLANDS LIKE MACOMEK are a marvel of nature. Much as I esteem the sea, I recognize and respect it for what it is—a foreign, often dangerous medium that has snatched the lives of more men and women than I could imagine. My own parents were among its casualties.

In books by Homer, Melville, Hemingway, and many others the sea is a capricious character that feeds you one moment and takes your life the next. Unlike the unstable ocean, islands are solid and safe. Bits of rare earth in a mostly blue planet, islands act as refuges for all terrestrial creatures.

Perched on *Money Pit's* bow, I watched as Macomek grew into a decent-sized island. Good. A thousand acres of habitable land actually did exist on the fringe of Penobscot Bay. The island lay under softening golden light of late afternoon. From a distance, it looked like the landmass was a magnet for irradiance, as if it were hungry for sustenance at the day's end.

Like others who love Maine's coast, I'd spent many hours scrambling over exposed rock at the edge of the sea. As we approached the island, I recognized that its ledges looked different but couldn't say how. Closer to shore, the ah-ha! hit me. On Macomek, the apron of bare rock between shrubs at the forest's edge and the water below was twice as wide as what I was used to seeing on the mainland. That naked granite told a story. On the edge of nowhere, the island was especially vulnerable to storms that attacked with brutal violence. Corrosive seawater thrown high up against the land would lay waste any vegetation within reach. Of course, vegetative fingers tentatively exploring exposed rock were not the only vulnerable life form on Macomek. The ocean killed humans too.

A half hour later, we chugged by a sheltered, tear-shaped harbor where clusters of weathered, rust-colored, shingled shacks stood fifty feet off the muddy, seaweed-strewn bottom. Shrieking gulls grabbed mussels from the muck. The sharp odors of rotten eggs and brine tickled my nose. I closed my eyes. Usually, those smells and sounds made me feel peaceful, safe, at home. So far off the mainland, this sensory remedy didn't work at all.

Just past the harbor lay a deserted, crescent-shaped, sandy beach. Gordy pointed to a gray-shingled cottage set back in a cluster of trees. "That's Abby's house. With the tide this low, you're gonna need help with the kayak an' the rest."

After I'd piled my gear into the kayak's cockpit, Gordy grabbed one end of the skinny, seventeen-foot boat and I took the other. Just beyond the highest row of drying seaweed, we carefully lowered the kayak.

He said, "I'll be itchin' ta learn if you turn somethin' up, Mara. Abby'll know where I'll be."

I watched him wade back to the anchored boat and climb into the stern. A voice behind me hollered, "Ahoy out there, Gordy Maloy!"

I turned to see a slight woman with grey, spiky hair, an impish grin, and bright eyes. She waved at Gordy and, like a little girl, bounced on her toes in worn sneakers.

Gordy called out, "Abby, that's Mara."

Abby took my hand, squeezed it, and called out, "Don't be a strangah, Gordy."

He headed to the bow to raise the anchor, I assumed, and disappeared from view.

Abby reached down for my backpack.

"Please," I said. "I can get that."

She hoisted the pack to her chest and wrapped both arms around it. "No trouble, dearie. You carry up the rest, an' I'll show you where to tie off the boat so she doesn't head off for somewhere like France."

Abby navigated the rocks and boulders so quickly I had a hard time keeping up with her.

"You must've played sports when you were younger," I said. "What was it, running or something?"

She turned and waved a few fingers at the ocean. "Long distance swimmin', deah. Comes in handy out this way."

Abby's was a classic small New England home—gray shingled with two sets of pained windows on either side of a front door painted dark green. As I followed her in, she dropped my pack at the bottom of a flight of wooden stairs just inside the entryway.

"Your room's at the top of the stairs. It's the neat one. Angel's is on the other side up theah."

I grabbed my gear, climbed the steep stairs, and peeked into a neat, snug room with no signs of an inhabitant. Dropping the pack onto an old wooden bench between two windows, I leaned on the sill to check out the view. A splash of salmon low on the horizon above the ocean told me I was looking west. The setting sun complemented the room's decor—a magenta braided rug at the foot of a double bed and spread decorated with little rose, cherry, and scarlet flowers.

Still leaning over, I sensed a presence behind me—something dim, ethereal, shadowy. I straightened, turned around very slowly, and scanned the pine walls, painted ceiling, and floorboards. My time in the bedroom could be measured in seconds, but it seemed much longer, almost as if this were *my* room when

I was a child. That realization should have struck me as odd, but it didn't. I reached out to touch the bedspread, knowing just what it would feel like.

Worn cotton, softened by hours hanging in the sun after a wash. Warm, safe, home.

I ran my fingers across the smooth round bedposts before falling back onto the bed to stare at the ceiling. The intimate balm was receding, and I could not stop its progress any more than I could halt the ebbing tide. I blinked back my tears.

Only few months earlier, I'd experienced something that wasn't supposed to happen. The U.N. had sent me, Harvey, and Ted to the Haida Gwaii archipelago off British Columbia to investigate an international law of the sea violation. My first day there, I'd ended up in a kayak with a broken rudder, which had put me in danger of being swept into the ocean. Out of nowhere, a ten-foot raven specter had zipped by my run-away boat as the cold Pacific Ocean was about to claim me. Moments later, a Haida man motored alongside and helped me reach safety. I learned that his was the raven clan. Given my training as a rationale scientist, the incident had unsettled me, to say the least.

Later, Angelo had proclaimed that anyone with an Italian father and an Irish mother should expect the occasional mystical episode. I decided to believe him.

This time, though, I was on a Maine island and couldn't turn to a rationale like a raven-clan rescuer. Besides that, I had felt, not seen, the inexplicable.

From down below, Abby called, "You all right up theah?"

I sat upright, coughed, and found my voice. "Perfect. Be right down."

I found my hostess lifting a steaming kettle off a gas stove in the tiny kitchen. "Cup of tea, deah?"

"That would be lovely, Abby, thanks."

She tipped her head toward a small wooden table positioned to enjoy morning light from the window above. "Take a seat right theah."

Open shelves that held dishes and glasses along with pots, pans, and other cooking paraphernalia ran the perimeter of the kitchen. Abby reached up, pulled down two white mugs, carried the steaming brew to the table, and sat down with a sigh.

"I splashed in some milk. Hope that's okay."

I wrapped my hands around the mug. Compared to the mainland, fall's chill came weeks earlier on Macomek. "Perfect. Thanks. Um, up in the guestroom I had the strangest feeling I'd been here before. Maybe as a child? Is that possible, do you think?"

She ran fingers through windblown hair standing on end. It didn't help much. "Could you've been in this house as a little girl? Maybe so. You're what, thirty?"

"Thirty-one."

"So thirty yeahs ago, give or take. My dad was still in the house. Mom would've died before then. I was a few years older than you are now. I don't recall a child out heah then. Where would I…?" She ran a hand across her mouth and turned her head toward the window.

I glanced at her, outside, back to my hostess.

Abby stared down at her tea, picked up the cup, slowly lifted it to her mouth, took a sip, and carefully set it down on the table. She wet her lips. "Like I said, Dad was living heah. He did invite visitors, particularly ones who made you think, he'd say. Did your parents work on the ocean?"

"They were marine scientists like I am."

"There you go. It could be they came ovah for a visit when you were little."

I leaned back in my chair. Bridget and Carlos, my mother

and father, in this very house—walking through the front door, sitting at this table, staying upstairs in the guestroom, sleeping in the same bed I'd sleep in tonight.

And me, maybe two or three, with them.

Abby placed her hand on mine. With our own memories and regrets, we sat like that as the sound of waves on her beach drifted through the window.

Up and back, up and back, up and back.

"Abby, since it's getting late, could we walk into town?" I asked. "I've never been on Macomek and Gordy tells me you're the best person to tell me about the island." I rubbed my hands together. "More hot tea when we get back would be great."

"Be happy to show you the place." She pushed the wire glasses higher up on her nose. "And not just tea when we get back. Suppah. Got a nice fish chowdah. And deah, as we walk along, you might as well tell me what upset you so."

We followed a dirt road banked by tall clusters of light purple asters and gaudy yellow goldenrod. The last of the season's monarch butterflies drifted lazily on a breeze. There was not one house in sight.

"How many people live on the island?" I asked.

Abby bent down to pick up a penny. "Winter it's thirty, forty at most. Summertime, it's twice that, maybe a little more."

"Doesn't it feel, ah, too closed in? What do they call it? Island fever?"

"I've heard of that but nevah had it. It's hard to explain what it's like to live out heah. You know, we're literally on the edge. When the weatherman starts talkin' 'bout the Hague line, that's what we listen to."

The Hague Line, I knew, divided US and Canadian fishing waters at the northernmost part of the Gulf of Maine. Cross the Hague Line and you're in the Great White North.

"But what about things like grocery stores, hospitals, restaurants?"

"Yup. We got no regular stores, no doctors or dentists, no restaurants, not even a post office. I take care of letters an' such, but it's not official or anything." She said all this with a good dose of pride and little regret.

"So how do you deal with—I don't know—everyday things like dentists?"

"Humor helps a lot. We've got some sayings like 'You know you live on Macomek if you ask the dentist to do all five fillings at once. And your kids've never been to Disneyland or played on a baseball team, but at eight years old they could drive a truck.'"

As she said the word, the first motor vehicle I'd seen, a truck, bumped down a road away from the harbor. The thing was classic island transportation—old, rusted, missing the passenger door, and probably used for short hauls of heavy or bulky items. It might have a license plate, but I guessed the date would be something like 2003.

We were approaching the lobster shacks I'd seen from Gordy's boat. Rusty-red, the tall weathered sentries overlooking the harbor listed like old men.

"Still, it really must be hard sometimes," I said.

"Spring's the worse. You're finally done with winter. Then the street's a muddy mess, and the fog comes in so thick your hand disappears at the end of your arm."

"So what keeps you all here, Abby?"

"Partly it's the independence, doing for myself. Heck, I can fix a washing machine, shingle my house, and catch bluefish off the rocks. But more than that, it's the people. Out heah, we're like a big family that helps each othah." She gestured at the ocean. "When a lobstahman's in trouble, every boat's out theah to help. If a woman's husband dies, people're with her day aftah day so she's not alone."

The melancholy in Abby's eyes came and went so quickly I nearly missed it.

At the harbor, she stepped around stacked lobster traps and coils of line and peered down to appraise the scene twenty feet below. The pier's pilings were now half-bathed in salt water.

Abby said, "Water's comin' up fast now." She scanned the horizon. "Ayuh, three boats on the way in. There's still a couple more out theah somewheres."

I followed her gaze, couldn't see a thing, and was about to say so when a bobbing speck morphed into the shape of a boat. A titanic ocean for such small vessels. "Does it happen often, Abby, that a lobsterman gets in trouble out there?"

"Twice, maybe three times a yeah. And mostly it turns out good. But when it doesn't, it's truly awful. The worst thing is when you come up on a boat that's going 'round and 'round in circles and nobody's on it."

From behind there was a skittering noise, like scurrying rats in an alley. I whipped around and caught a flash of green vanish behind a pile of traps.

8

ABBY SAID, "LET'S GO OUT ON THE PIER AND WAIT 'TIL the boys come in."

With the ease of someone half her age, Abby perched herself on the edge of the wooden pier and dangled her legs over the edge. Like two kids, we swung our feet back and forth.

"At the Maine Oceanographic Institute I eat lunch outside and sit just like this," I said.

"So tell me what it's like, bein' a girl ocean scientist?"

"I expect it's the same for females who lobster for a living. Some guys're threatened and act like jerks, but most give you a chance. The thing is, you've got to be better than good. I had to prove myself—that I was smarter than most, worked harder than most, got big grants, published lots of papers, all that. Now that I've got a good job, it's easier."

"So your mum and dad studied the ocean too?"

"They did, but both drowned in an accident when I was nineteen. They were studying a coral reef. The sub got stuck."

She reached over and rested her hand on mine. "You poor, poor thing." Tenderness and compassion flowed through me like a balm.

Offshore, the drone of lobster boats announced their approach. Quintessential Maine, for me it was a sunny throb announcing that hard-working fishermen had made it home once more. In one line, three boats plowed thought the water, bows up and proud, sterns buried in their own wake as waves peeled away to each side. Inside the harbor, captains throttled down, and their craft slowed and settled level in the water. Each left behind a smooth, wavy path that would remain long after the boat arrived at its mooring.

Captain and crew on each boat quickly unloaded their catch at the other end of the pier, then scattered and found their moorings. The closet one, *Lucky Catch,* sported a bright red hull and crisp white wheelhouse capped by expensive-looking navigation gear. Water streamed off the aft deck as a guy garbed in a soiled orange apron washed off trap slime, bait guts, and other debris from the day at sea. I assumed he was the sternman, a crewmember who grabbed traps as the captain lifted them aboard, pulled out lobsters, added new, foul-smelling bait, and slid re-baited traps off the open stern. It was hard, repetitive, and dangerous work feet from a frigid open ocean waiting to claim them. None wore life jackets, of course, and many couldn't swim. I'd heard that many sternmen were chosen for their brawn and not necessarily their brains.

On *Lucky Catch*, a guy with an army buzz cut, bright yellow bib-pants, and black T-shirt leaned over the bow to haul in his dinghy. Hand over hand he worked with lightening speed.

"She's a good looking boat," I said.

"*Lucky Catch* belongs to Calvin Ives. That's him in the bow. Best lobstahman on the island, a highliner. Calvin's a smart, hard-workin' guy who's always lookin' at what's next."

Highliners, I'd learned from Gordy, consistently brought in the most lobsters. Typically from generations of fishing families, they were highly respected and seen as leaders in their communities.

The lobster boat farthest away from us was already swinging on its mooring as its dinghy was rowed to shore.

"Who's that?" I asked.

"Malicite Dupris is at the oars, and that's his sternman with 'im. Boat's named *Look to the Future*."

"Dupris is someone I really want to meet."

"Gordy told me that, deah. Malicite's comin' for suppah."

A guy from the third boat stood in its dinghy and extended an arm to the white-haired man still above him.

"The older one who looks like he'll fall in the watah, that's Lester," Abby said with a catch in her voice. "Lovely man, gettin' on like me. Looks like he had a swig or two las' night since it's comin' up on the anniversary."

"The anniversary?"

"Yes, deah. Day when he lost his sternman in a storm a long time ago."

Lester straddled a seat in the dinghy and patted the younger man's arm, a guy probably the age of the sternman who died. I could certainly understand why Lester numbed himself to such a dreadful memory—like the one that had driven my own grandfather out of Massachusetts and into Maine.

On our way out of "town," Abby waved a hand at a grey-shingled structure with a white, paint-chipped side door. "That's our everything building. In the summah when there's more people out heah, that's where one of the ladies on the island sells home-baked bread an' such. There's a bull'tin board with notices 'bout traps for sale, things like that. When the mail comes in on the ferry twice a week, dependin' on the weathah, I put it in a place where everyone knows to get it. And there's one room that can hold twenty-odd folks for a meetin' if somethin' real serious comes up."

"Like what?"

"Last summah, a guy shot ovah the head of another guy. Didn't hurt 'im. It happened right as boats came back in at sunset. A bunch of us saw it. Calvin Ives got us togethah before the Marine Patrol arrived."

"But why? If the shooter was guilty, wouldn't the patrol officer take care of it?"

"Besides no doctors or dentists, there's no law enforcement out heah. Like I said, we take care of our own."

I envisaged vigilantes in the old west. "Um, what did you decide about the shooter?"

"That Tyler did the right thing. He warned a guy who set traps off the island the day before. Nobody traps off Macomek but folks who live heah."

"Tyler Johnson?"

"That's right. Do you know Tyler?"

My stomach tightened. "Gordy mentioned him."

We approached her house where the guest room's pair of windows looked down on me. "Abby, I can't stop thinking about being here when I was young."

"That's really troublin' you, deah. I'll put the tea kettle on and heat up the chowdah. Then we'll have a good talk."

While Abby busied herself in the little kitchen, I sat at the well-used table beneath the kitchen window. Two wide boards spanned the tabletop.

Abby turned to see me run a hand along the grooved surface. "That's an old oak table we use for everything from all our meals to cleaning an' splicing line durin' winter months. My dad brought it down from Nova Scotia."

She slid a mug across the table, and I wrapped my hands around it. The warmth was soothing. "Thanks."

"You miss your parents terrible, an' somethin' with this house makes you think about them. Is that right?"

I bit my lip and nodded.

"You seem like a strong young woman. That's good, but

sometimes even strong ones need to let it go. What we keep inside. Does that make sense?"

"I'm beginning to realize that, Abby."

"Took me quite a while. If you jus' work on the strong side, the othah part might shrivel up. Then, you can't get at it again."

"You're right. It's another thing I'm beginning to understand."

She stood and patted my hand. "Time I worked on suppah."

There were four of us for "suppah." Abby's daughter Patty stopped by for a few minutes and decided to stay. Malicite arrived right on time and helped us move the kitchen table so we could, following Abby's instruction, "properly set it for foah."

The chowder—potatoes, onions, carrots, and seafood—was filling and delicious.

"Wow, Abby," I said. "This is terrific. Besides the fish, what else is in it?"

"Lobstah. Out heah, there's lobstah scrambled eggs, lobstah mac an' cheese, lobstah brownies. You name it."

Deciding not to comment on lobster for dessert, I said, "Patty, I understand you're, um, hanging out with Gordy."

Patty shared several traits with her mother—zeal, devotion to Macomek, and dirty blond spiked hair she kept in line with a wide black headband. The haircut looked better on the younger Burgess.

"What a great guy!" Patty used her spoon for emphasis. "Knows boats inside out, wicked funny, good cook...."

"Gordy cooks?"

She tipped her head and grinned. "Sure. Burgers on the grill, spaghetti, things like that."

Wondering what else I didn't know about my cousin I said, "Huh. So where *is* Gordy?"

"He wanted to talk with Calvin Ives. Don't know why, but he got all serious when I asked."

The little hairs on the back of my neck stood at attention as Gordy's mission came to mind.

Patty stacked the bowls and joined her mother in the kitchen. I turned to Malicite. "Have Duprises been trapping off Macomek for a long time?"

"You bet," he said. "Off the mainland too. Great-great-granddaddy name of Gaspard Dupris came down from Canada in the eighteen hundreds an' ended up out heah. I spent time in Quebec when I was a kid. If we have a party out heah, with my brothahs, uncles, aunts, nieces an' nephews, too many cousins to count, we can only get togethah when it's warm, 'cause there's no place we all fit."

"Sounds like you're a lucky guy," I said.

"It can get pretty wild out heah with the weathah an' all the rest. But family, it's the only rock I know that stays steady," he said.

"Lobster communities along the Maine coast are pretty tight," I said. "People the lobstermen know well and their families are absolutely everything to them. I'd guess it's even more so out here."

"'Tis. It's a funny thing, guys workin' the watah. We compete for bugs at the same time we take care of each othah. Talkin' on the radio all the time we're out. Askin' what's goin' on. Like you said, that's true everywhere in Maine. But on the island all we've got is each othah. It's, I don't know, more intense."

And I'd thought that islanders might more readily welcome me because my grandfather had been a fisherman in another state. How naïve I'd been.

"I assume that intensity includes defending trap territories even more forcefully."

"That's right. I hate the term 'lobstah war' but maybe that's what it is. Guys on Macomek'll do anything an' everything to defend *all* our trap strings."

Besides taking care of each other, what do you especially like about lobstering?" I asked.

"Ya know," he said. "That's a real good question." He drummed his fingers on the table for a moment. "I think it's that we take care of our catch. We might grumble sometimes 'bout throwin' back berried females or makin' sure bugs we keep aren't too small or too big. But all of us know it's keepin' the industry safe an' we lobbied for some of those rules ourselves. We're not gonna wipe out lobstahs like some fishermen did with cod."

"And V-notching one of the female's flippers is voluntary?"

"Ayuh. We notch the inner right one. When traps're comin' up fast, it makes findin' females to throw back a whole lot easier."

Abby walked up to the table. "Either of you want dessert? I got brownies."

I shook my head. "I'm full."

Malicite patted his stomach. "Abby, I love your brownies, but my pants're getting' kinda tight."

"You're too young for that, Malicite Dupris. I'll wrap up a couple so you can bring 'em home for your little one."

"Malicite, before you go, I'd love to hear about the e-lobster project," I said. "What kind of data you're getting, if it's useful, that type of thing. Maybe tomorrow?"

With dark chestnut eyes and a full head of black ringlets, Dupris was a good-looking guy. His eyes lit up. "Be happy to." He rubbed his chin. "Tomorrah I'm out on traps, but it might be poor weathah late. So I'll probably be back early. 'Bout middle of the afternoon, I'd guess. My boat's moored, I'm back. Abby knows where I live."

Adding that he was "gettin' up at four" Dupris stood, thanked Abby, and left. Patty took the seat Malicite had just vacated. "I'd better be going too. Gordy's talks about you a lot, so it's great to finally meet you."

"I'm lucky he's my cousin," I said. "But before you leave, do you mind if I ask why you and Gordy are so sure Tyler…um…."

She blinked. "You mean why he's the one who killed the guy you found?"

"Yes."

"It's got to do with drugs. You know that's a big problem out here, right?"

I nodded. "Like on the mainland."

"Worse. The isolation, not much to do. Lots of money when the lobstering is good, but nowhere to spend it. It was pretty obvious Tyler was addicted. He always had a temper, you know, but it got a whole lot worse. Besides that, he looked awful. Lost weight, got edgier." She leaned forward. "A couple of months ago, he got nasty with Angel. Things like real sarcastic comments, telling her what to do. Angel wasn't about to take that. So she told him to go to hell and took up with Buddy. Tyler and Buddy used to be friends, so Tyler was ripped at Buddy. And he let everyone know it." Patty sat back in the chair and crossed her arms over her chest.

"All that sounds pretty bad," I said. "But we're talking about murder. Do you have any proof?"

Her eyes narrowed. "I didn't see him do it, if that's what you mean. But I'm positive he's guilty."

Tyler, Angel, Buddy. Three young lives in shambles. The situation was raw, and this was not the time to debate the critical importance of evidence. I softened my voice. "Those narcotic drugs, the cost is dreadful. Thanks for the explanation."

Patty unclenched her fists, relaxed her arms, and stood." It was very nice to meet you, Mara." In the kitchen, she kissed her mother on the cheek and left me alone with Abby.

I carried the silverware to the kitchen sink. Abby didn't

comment on Patty's claim about Tyler, and I sensed she didn't want to talk about it. Maybe she was just tired of the whole subject.

"Thanks for dinner," I said. "Seems like you've got two great daughters."

She beamed. "They're the best. Smart too. Angel teaches the little ones out heah. Patty used to do that. Like a female lion protectin' her cubs, she was. She's still that way even though they're grown-up teenagers. Patty's been talking 'bout nursing school. We'll see, but once she sets her mind, not a thing stops that girl. You got brothers and sisters, Mara?"

"Um, no. My parents had me late, when Mom was nearly forty."

"Aunts, uncles, cousins? 'Sides Gordy, that is."

I shook my head. "Both my parents were from small families and their siblings are gone now too."

"But surely, you know your othah cousins."

Knowing where this conversation was heading, I could feel the heat creep into my cheeks. "Actually, no."

"And you're not married."

"No."

She tipped her head and looked at me like I was a creature from Mars. "Don't think I've ever met a person with no family whatsoevah. No parents, brothahs, sistahs, cousins, husband."

"My godfather Angelo is like a father to me."

"Well, that's something."

Desperate to change the subject, I said. "Abby, I'm super tired."

She rolled her shoulders. "Come to think of it, I am too. Lovely to have you heah, Mara. I'm for bed. Bathroom's down the hall."

Upstairs, I changed into my PJs—happy they were flannel

ones—and arranged pillows against the bed's headboard. Hugging my legs, I sat like that for a long time. Abby's interrogation about my lack of family had unsettled me more than such questions usually did. I didn't try to explain that I'd studied my butt off in college and grad school and didn't have time for family. Someone like Abby wouldn't understand that rationale at all.

To avoid weighing Abby's reasoning against my own, I thought instead about Patty's accusation. It troubled me that she was so certain of Tyler's guilt but had no direct proof. On the other hand, she obviously knew the players well. On top of that, I understood little about drugs, addiction, perilous jobs, and life on the edge twenty-odd miles from shore. Given my ignorance about the Macomek community, who was I to question her?

I yawned. It had been a long, long day, and I didn't have the mental energy to reason through the conundrum. I slid down into the bed, rearranged the pillows, and pulled up the covers. But despite my exhaustion, sleep would not come. Wisps of the past floated around the dark room—my mother's perfume, Dad's laugh, peculiar expressions they used. Each time I tried to capture the memory, it vanished before I could grab a hold.

Finally, I got out of bed and padded across the cold floor to the windows. Below, movement caught my attention. A child I knew to be a little girl walked across the bit of lawn, stopped, and turned to look up at me. Our eyes met for an instant before she turned back and slipped into the forest. I squeezed my eyes shut and popped them open. She was gone.

I stared at the spot where the girl had pushed the branches aside and disappeared. I had no doubt that this thing—ghost, mirage, dream, memory—had a message for me. Also, the message was clear.

During the eleven years since my parents' death, I had retreated from the world and buried myself in work. Certainly, there was plenty to do—grad school exams, my PhD research at sea, grant proposals and research papers to write, a job to secure, more proposals and research, more time at sea, professional meetings to attend. I'd ended up with the perfect job at Maine's only oceanographic research institution, so it had all paid off.

But there was a cost I hadn't considered or, to be truthful, even acknowledged. I'd allowed no time or emotional energy for a deep relationship with a man. Sure, I'd had boyfriends. Some may have looked to others like serious loves, but I'd always found a reason why they were lacking. Sometimes they were. Once, a guy I'd been dating for a while had cheated on me. Harvey found me sobbing in MOI's bathroom and took me outside to vent. While her generosity led to our friendship, I quickly realized my distress had more to do with hurt pride than anything else.

Ted's arrival at MOI earlier in the year had challenged my independence. Being with him was easy and a joy. We talked about everything from the latest marine ecology papers to the likelihood that the Boston Red Sox would win the pennant again. Besides that, the sex was terrific. Without thoughts of anything more serious, I was happy to bounce along just as we were. Then Ted changed everything with the word "marriage." I freaked out, backed away, and ran. Hurt, Ted said he wanted more from me, and if he couldn't have it, declared we should just be "friends and colleagues." That was two months ago.

What Abby's questions and home stirred in me were not only memories from three decades ago. The longing for human intimacy was inside me now—crying for attention.

9

AT DAYBREAK, I WOKE TO THE DISTANT LOW RUMBLE OF lobster boats heading out of the harbor. On Macomek, like every other Maine fishing community, the low gurgle hardly registers. It's as much a part of the soundscape as traffic noise in New York City or cows mooing in Wisconsin's dairy lands.

Abby fed me scrambled eggs, hot-from-the-oven oatmeal muffins, and strong coffee. As I ate, she warned me about the dangers of Macomek's waters.

"That's an awful skinny little boat," she said.

I licked a bit of butter from my forefinger. "No worries, Abby. I've paddled it up and down the Maine coast."

She frowned. "Alone?"

"Not usually, but I'll stay close to shore. I do need your help with the weather report. My weather radio's at home with a battery that won't charge."

Abby carried the radio to the table and turned it on. The computer voice announced, "Winds ten-to-fifteen knots, seas five feet and rising close to shore." She flipped it off. "Good report. Still, you be careful."

By eight, I was on the beach clad in all my paddle gear. With the ocean a cold fifty degrees, a full wetsuit, neoprene booties and gloves, turtleneck and fleece pullover, waterproof paddle jacket, and fleece hat were essential additions to the usual sprayskirt and life jacket. Ordinarily, my hand-held VHF marine radio would be tucked into my lifejacket front pocket next to waterproof binoculars. The radio had to be within easy reach if I capsized. I didn't like paddling without it, but the report on Abby's radio was pretty good, especially given my location twenty-odd miles from the mainland.

"You be careful out theah," Abby had said. "It's not like the mainland. Water's coldah, winds breeze up fast, waves grow like somethin' fierce. Remembah, you don't have your VHF to call for help."

I'd looked at NOAA's wind and wave data for Macomek's waters and knew Abby wasn't exaggerating. I resolved to hug the shore.

High tide made carrying the fifty-pound kayak down to the water's edge easy. There, I positioned the chart under bungee cords on the front deck so I could read it, adjusted the compass, snapped the two halves of my paddle together, wriggled my bulky self into the snug cockpit, and shoved off.

The first minutes in my sea kayak always remind me why I'm passionate about the sport. Quickly sliding into the meditative rhythm of paddling, I was free to drink in the soft slap of ocean against the boat, wind cooling my cheeks, and sun sparkling off the water. Inches from the sea's surface, I could watch twenty-foot-long kelps wave back and forth beneath me with the grace of ballet dancers. A glittering curtain, silver fish in a school wound their way through the seaweed, scattered, and regrouped in an instant.

Drifting alone in my little boat, I often marveled at the simple wonder of water—so sturdy it holds me up, so gentle it flows, so abundant it covers over half of Earth. I looked toward the open ocean. Out there somewhere—and hundreds of times in a day—Macomek's lobster boats circled traps and slid to a stop as their captains leaned over to pull their prizes aboard.

Boats forty to fifty feet long. So very small in a sea that's awfully big.

Small craft like that are vulnerable in storms. The open ocean, especially twenty miles from the coast, can transform from tame to vicious in minutes. In summer, thunderstorms with winds over fifty knots can turn little vessels into bobbing corks. In winter, the seas sometimes boil with waves that can flip lobster boats and throw captain and crew into an ice-cold grave.

I poked along the rocky coast, circled Macomek's harbor, and poked along some more. A cluster of large marine birds called common eiders kept me company. My father had once explained that the bird's Latin name translates to "very soft" because the eider's nest is lined with eiderdown from the female's chest. Like a little armada of boats, Macomek's eiders rode the swells boiling off a rocky outcrop. Up and down, up and down, they were mesmerizing to watch. I whooped when a large swell carried the squad safely through a fissure in the rock. Off the mainland, I'd have to try that trick in the kayak.

I sheltered in the lee of a hillock on the north side of the island and squinted at birds circling above a tiny island less than a mile offshore. The binoculars gave me a closer look. For a marine ecologist in particular, what came into focus was a glory of nature. Puffins were everywhere—in the sky, on the rocks, floating in the water.

Atlantic Puffins are one of Maine's most popular birds for a reason. The stocky little guys breed off the Maine and Canadian coasts, mate for life, and produce one adorable chick each summer. After breeding, they travel the oceans over a home range of five hundred thousand square miles. Pretty impressive for birds less than a foot tall.

The birds' appearance makes them especially lovable. Puffins could be Disney characters. Like penguins, they are "tuxedo birds" with white bellies and black backs and wings. It's their head, though, that arrests your attention. Huge, triangular, parrot-like beaks—gaudy orange when they breed—give them the nickname "sea-parrot." At the same time, their white faces and small black eyes bring to mind a clown with wings.

Nearly everyone I knew well—Harvey, Connor, Angelo, Ted, and even Gordy—had taken a puffin cruse at one time or another to visit one of the offshore rocky colonies. "Fabulous trip," they all said. "You've got to do it." But I never did, maybe because it was such a touristy thing.

As a result of my tourism snobbery, I'd never seen *Fratercular artica* up close. But now they were right there, an easy paddle away. To kayak among puffins as they popped out of the water and circled screeching above, how could I pass that up?

I squinted at the island. Getting out there would be a piece-of-cake, half-hour paddle. On the other side of my rock outcrop shelter, the waves had increased a bit but were still only a foot or so high. I scanned the sky. A few cumulous clouds formed puffy mounds. Nothing to worry about there. No dark storm clouds darkened the horizon to the east, west, and north. I couldn't see the southern horizon because I was below a knoll that blocked my view in that direction.

What the heck, I thought. The little puffin adventure would be an absolute blast. If the seas picked up, I'd head back and be on shore in less than an hour.

I aimed the boat at the little island, checked the compass reading for a straight shot there (sixty degrees) and back (three hundred), and left Macomek Island behind. Less than a half-mile from shore, I nearly rammed the boat on a rock with a razor-sharp edge just under the surface. Luckily, a telltale ring signaled the rock's presence below. Closer to shore, boaters relied on charts that designated submerged hazards like rocks. On the edge of nowhere off Macomek, local knowledge was the best protection against such dangers.

Paddling as fast as I could, I made excellent time until halfway though my crossing when the waves increased to two feet. Annoying, but nothing I couldn't easily handle. I passed a largish island with a cove on the south side, considered taking a break there, and decided to keep going.

The growing cacophony of screeching puffins drove me on. Panting and laughing like a crazed loon, I slid into a little protected bay on the Macomek side of the bird-covered island.

I named the place Puffin Rock.

Once my breathing had returned to normal, I poked the boat out into the confused sea. Birds were everywhere and didn't seem to be bothered by their visitor. Skyward, hundreds upon hundreds of screeching puffins circled in disarray. Some zipped right over the boat. The rapid beat of wings broadcast the struggle to keep their squat bodies aloft. Puffins dove down into the water only a yard or two from the kayak. The sea was so clear I could see their wings beating underwater until the birds disappeared into the depths. Puffins, I knew, could dive hundreds of feet down in their search for fish.

Careful to avoid the slosh of waves against rocks, I began to circle the little island. Onshore, countless puffins bobbed up and down as they scrambled over slick rock. Their gaudy orange feet splayed out behind when they launched themselves into the air. The puffin show so absorbed me that I didn't notice the sky until I rounded a ledge.

I sucked in a breath. To the west, a wide band of dark charcoal clouds obliterated the break between sky and sea. From one end of the horizon to the other, that black smudge was racing right at me. Ahead of the storm, the sea's surface was a sickening grey-green.

I swung the kayak toward Macomek, fixed my heading at three hundred degrees, and dug the paddle into the water. Rotating left and right with the full strength of my abdominal muscles, I pulled the blade as fast and cleanly as I could. The boat shot forward, but too soon the messy sea made efficient paddling a joke. Closely packed waves jostled the kayak from side to side and threatened to turn me over. To avoid being capsized, I had to lean into the bigger ones using the paddle as a brace. The maneuver slowed my progress to a crawl.

I stopped to catch my breath, squinted at the approaching squall, and didn't like what I saw one bit. A black roiling avalanche, the storm's progress was much quicker than my own.

Ahead of the rain and like a slap across my face, the wind suddenly blew up to thirty knots—a gale. The boat acted like a big magnet and swung into the wind—away from where I had to go. And with the whistling winds came even higher cresting waves. If a wave knocked me over, I could roll my kayak to an upright position in a calm sea but doubted if I could complete the maneuver in a wild one.

More than a mile off a Macomek island, itself twenty miles from the coast, I was alone in a bucking sea kayak I could not steer in a frigid sea that could swamp my little boat in an instant. In all my years kayaking, I'd never faced anything close to this.

My fear turned to anger. Screaming like a banshee, I called those waves, that wind, and the sea every awful name I could think of.

"Goddamn it, you're *not* going to throw me over, you friggin' son-of-a bitch!"

As if obeying my demands, the wind died down a bit. I aimed at Macomek and tried to make forward progress, but the kayak climbed every wave and slammed down hard with a shudder. Desperate to keep my compass heading, I inched along, arm muscles crying for a break. I dared only to flex my fingers.

The wind blew up again and turned into a screaming menace in an instant. I screamed back, lost my bearing, and was on the edge of losing all hope when to my starboard side a shadowy black mound materialized though the pelting rain.

The island with the cove I'd passed on the way out.

I turned in that direction and made for it. If nothing else, I could shelter on the lee side away from the full force of the wind and accompanying waves. I'd huddle there until the gale passed by.

With the wind behind me, I surf-boarded the crest of twenty-foot rollers and advanced toward the island. But as I approached, those enormous waves crashed into island's rock face and threw me back out to sea. For the second, third, and fourth time, I tried to make forward progress, only to be pitched backwards.

Exhausted, soaked, and frustrated beyond words, I backpaddled to catch my breath. Even with an island so very close, my ballgame was heading south and fast. I was weary on the way to being exhausted, shivering violently from the cold, and my reasoning was slogging into slow motion.

That's why I believed the motorboat bucking whitecaps was a mirage. I wiped rainwater from my eyes. No, my rattled brain did not imagine it. A lobster boat was heading right for me.

As he approached, the captain waved from behind his wheel. His white hair stuck out from beneath a baseball cap with a brim that dripped onto his already soaked yellow slicker. The man looked familiar, but I couldn't place him.

Keeping a safe distance in the messy sea, he leaned against his gunwale and yelled over the howling wind. "Do you need a tow?"

"No," I hollered. "Block the wave slosh off the rocks, and I'll keep to your port side."

He saluted, put the boat into reverse, slowly backed up, turned her around, and waited for me to come alongside. Passing the stern, I laughed out loud at the boat's name—*Sea Angel*.

Protected from the backwash, I easily paddled next to *Sea Angel* as she motored alongside the island's rocky ridge. When the captain rounded the end of a spit, I could see that the granite headland we'd traversed was matched by another several hundred yards away. Together, like welcoming arms, the twin headlands reached into the sea and protected a little bay from the ocean's onslaught.

As *Sea Angel* pulled ahead, I whispered thanks to the Catholic god I'd ignored for fifteen years. The lobster boat approached its mooring, and I passed between the twin bluffs and glided into waters that hardly knew the hell brewing on the other side.

My white-haired savior stepped into his tender, untied it from the mooring, settled onto the seat, and picked up the oars. I waited until he slid the dinghy high up the beach before I came ashore and climbed out of my cockpit.

Striding back down the stony little beach in black rubber boots he said, "That's one hum-dingah of a blow out theah. Bet you got knocked around in that skinny little boat."

The voice was at once warm and commanding. I remembered Abby pointing out the clean-shaven old lobsterman in Macomek Harbor, but I couldn't recall his name.

"I was on my way out to search for ya, Mara, when I spotted the kayak off the island. By Godfrey, am I tickled to see you're here in one piece."

Shifting from one foot to the other on shaky legs I said, "Not nearly so happy as I was to see you, ah.…"

"Where're my manners? I'm Lester Crawford." He reached out, enveloped my right hand in both his giant ones for a moment, and stepped back. "Abby's been on the VHF frantic. Let's go up to the shack an' let the ol' gal know you're heah with me."

I pulled a dry bag with a change of clothes from one of my hatches. Following Lester across the cobble beach, I considered his name as we walked along a well-worn path that led to a shingled garage-like building on high ground. Gordy had called the dead lobsterman Buddy Crawford. The old guy seemed to be in good spirits, so surely he and Buddy couldn't be related. Crawford was a common Maine name.

Saying that his radio was in the back, Lester walked across the cement floor and disappeared behind a stack of old wooden lobster traps.

Staring at the traps and still recovering from my ordeal, I was bothered by something buried in the back of my mind that seemed important. Whatever it was didn't manifest itself.

I pulled off my wetsuit, quick-changed into dry clothes, and scanned the room. Lobster fishing paraphernalia was everywhere. Neatly stacked, antique traps lined the back, their gray half-moon sides facing forward. Coiled loops of yellow, red, and blue line shared one wall with banged-up wooden lobster buoys arranged by color and shape, mostly dull reds and blues. Unlike bullet-shaped modern buoys, these antique ones had hard edges and looked like little towers. An odd assortment of gear decorated the facing wall—nets, oars, baskets, gaffs, and poles.

The collection was a museum of sorts—Maine lobstering in the old days. I recognized the traps piled in the back as the old-fashioned ones made with slats. They were about four feet long, two high, with flat bottoms and round tops. Stacked, the antique traps looked liked piles of big birdcages. In contrast to today's Styrofoam ones, the buoys hanging on the wall were also wood. In the old days, Mainers hand-carved a spruce or cedar spindle or maybe a small keg and attached the homemade buoy to a trap with tarred line. Since wood floats, traps were weighed down with rocks or bricks. Every trap was hand-pulled from wooden boats the early fishermen rowed.

That was as age of spruce traps, brightly colored spindle-buoys, and lobster boats rowed to and from shore. Lobstermen back then could not have imagined a day when a boat could cost hundreds of thousands of dollars. Old-timers would be even more astounded to learn that some of today's lobstermen could pull four hundred traps a day and gross more than many of their non-fishing neighbors.

On the wall, a lone photograph beside one of the nets leaned at an angle. Thinking it might fall to the floor, I walked over and lifted the framed photo off the wall to check the wires. They looked secure. There was nothing on the cracked backing that identified people in the old image, so I slid it back onto the nail and leaned in to take a look.

A slimmer version of Lester with dark hair knelt beside a lobster trap. The cluster of children facing him were about nine or ten, and the woman behind them was probably in her twenties. It looked like someone had photographed young Lester as he was explaining how traps worked to some of the island's school children and their teacher. Slim and attractive, she looked vaguely familiar, but in profile it was hard to tell.

I stepped away from the wall as Lester rounded a trap tower. "That Abby is all heart. She started cryin' when I said you were okay."

Picturing Abby's tears, I cringed. Completely focused on getting to safety, I'd failed to realize that she always listened for weather alerts and would have assumed the worst when I hadn't returned to the island.

"Lester, it's awful I made Abby worry. Should I use your radio and talk to her now?"

"Nah. Now she knows you're with me, she's all right."

"You've got quite a collection here." Pointing at the photograph, I said "That's you with kids from the island?"

He walked over and stared at the image. "'Tis." Leaning in, he tapped the glass gently with a finger. "Abby when she was teachin'." Fixed on the image, he was suspended in time and memories. In the back room, the radio crackled.

"Be right back," he said.

As Lester shuffled across the floor toward me, I met him halfway. Denim eyes bluer than his navy shirt, the man stared like he'd never seen me before.

I put a hand on his arm. "Are you all right?"

He blinked. "To be truthful, I'm not. Let's go in the back where I can sit down. I'm a talker an' it'd be good for me to get it out."

Hoping he'd prove me wrong, I suspected what was coming and followed him. The pile of pots hid a door leading to a room just big enough for a table, two chairs, and a counter with a gas burner, dented kettle, and carboy of water.

Lester fell back into a chair and rubbed his eyes. "A terrible, terrible thing's happened."

"Lester, would you like something hot? Coffee, maybe?"

"That would be good, child." He nodded toward several small wooden boxes stacked under the counter. "Coffee's in the box nearest the stove theah with the matches. Kettle's already got watah in it. Tea's there too if you want some."

The stink of stale alcohol hit me as I bent down to search for the coffee and matches. Waiting for the kettle to boil, I found the source of the foul odor. On the floor between the counter and the wall, three empty bottles of Jack Daniels whiskey leaned against each other in a metal pail. Abby had mentioned a terrible anniversary—the day Lester's sternman had died in a storm. Unless Lester had a drinking problem, it looked like the day had recently passed and the man was still wracked by grief and perhaps guilt years after the event. If Buddy and Lester were related, a second horrible anniversary might be too much for him to endure.

I handed Lester the mug of steaming instant coffee and settled in the chair on the other side of the table with my own mug of tea. He sipped the coffee, stared down into the mug, coughed, and raked a hand down his face. "Abby jus' told me some awful news. Buddy, my grandson." Lester coughed again. "He's dead."

Two things raced through my mind. Gordy was right in thinking the man under his raft was Buddy Crawford. But why had it taken so long for the police to contact Buddy's family? Now was certainly not the time to voice the question.

I leaned toward him. "Oh, Lester. I am so terribly sorry. Is there anything, anything at all, I can do for you? Maybe call someone? Do you want company or would it be better for me to leave? The storm's blown over so I can easily paddle back to Macomek."

Lester stared blankly at me for a moment before he got his bearing. "Buddy, he was a good kid, outstandin' lobstahman." He blinked. "Would you like to hear 'bout him?"

I reached out and put my hand on his. "Of course, Lester. I'd love to hear about Buddy."

Lester coughed and wiped his mouth. "He, Buddy is— was—oh God." The old man looked down and shook his head.

I squeezed his hand. "Sure you want to do this now?"

"Pardon me." He pulled a handkerchief from his back

pocket and blew his nose. "Talkin' 'bout him, it's a way of, I don't know...."

"Honoring him?"

"That's it."

I sat back to hear the old lobsterman's story.

Lester blew out a breath. "Crawfords been lobsterin' in Maine for generations. Not even sure how far back. But my son, name's Todd, said he wanted somethin' else. Can't blame 'im. Life out heah, it's hard. But still, that hurt all the same. Like I disappointed Crawfords all down the line. But Buddy, he wasn't like his dad. Said he wanted to be a lobstahman like me."

Lester choked back a sob, picked up his mug, put it back down.

Leaning forward I said, "Lester...."

He held up a hand. "I'm all right. Like I said, it's good talkin' 'bout the boy." Lester went on. "Buddy stared out as sternman with me, then Calvin Ives. 'Couple yeahs ago Buddy got his own boat. Did pretty good an' in the last yeah he did incredible. Traded the old boat for a fancy new one. Got more traps, new GPS, all that."

Lester got to his feet. "I got lots of photos with Buddy in 'em."

Watching as Lester rifled through a wooden crate, I blinked back tears. The man was literally touching decades of family memories—photos with babies and kids at school, of clam bakes and fishing expeditions, at Christmas and birthday parties. And now, in an instant, memories of one cherished grandson would come to a halt. Anguish flowed through me, so powerful I nearly sobbed.

By the time Lester had selected two black and white photos, I'd pulled myself together. He slid the photographs across the table. Holding down the curling edge of one with his thick forefinger, he said, "That's Buddy with me. He was seven, maybe eight."

The younger Lester looked even more like a giant lumberjack than the elder version. A towhead grinned up at him, one front tooth missing.

In the larger photo a row teenagers clowned for the camera. "He's at the end an' was somethin' like sixteen in that one."

I picked up the image for a closer look. To the far right, a longer-haired version of Buddy wore a Red Sox baseball cap. Next to him, a cocky young man who winked at the photographer had his arm draped over the shoulder of an attractive girl who rolled her eyes. I handed Lester the image. "Who is standing next to Buddy?"

Squinting, he said, "Oh, that's Calvin Ives. Always teasin' the girls."

Dropping the photos on the table, Lester fell into his chair, choked back a sob, and said, "Why? Why would anyone want to hurt Buddy? He was a great guy. Everyone liked Buddy."

He buried his face in his hands. I tried to think of something to say, but anything that came to mind seemed insipid.

Finally, he ran a hand through his hair. "Talkin's not gonna bring Buddy back, is it? Mara, there's family things I gotta do on the mainland so I'll guess I bettah get a move on. You'll paddle that little boat back to Macomek okay?"

I got to my feet. "If the storm has gone by, I'll be fine."

The weather radio told us that an "unusually fast-moving gale" had left Macomek's waters. Outside, we stood on the bluff and scanned a flat sea off the little island.

I said, "It'll be a very easy paddle back to Macomek." Lester stared straight ahead. I put my hand on his arm. Below the soft denim, solid muscle attested to decades of dripping fifty-pound lobster traps pulled up out of the water.

"Lester, I'm so very sorry for your news and wish we could've met at a happier time for you. Thanks for calling Abby, I really do appreciate it."

He managed a slight smile. "That Abby."

"There's no way I can thank you for taking your lobster boat out and finding me. You probably saved my life."

"Happy to do it."

"Before I go, can you tell me what this place is? Your collection, why it's here?"

The smile got a little wider, and I guessed that talking about his old traps and the rest was a comforting, if momentary, distraction.

"This shack? When I was really lobsterin,' you know, hundreds 'o traps, I kept my gear mostly here. More room then on the island. Friend of my grandfathah owned it, but everyone calls it Lester's Rock these days. Anyways, when lobsterin' started to change, I got to collectin' old gear. That's pretty much all that's heah now." He gestured toward Macomek. "I'm alone back there. Wife's gone, son lives inland. Abby...." He coughed. "Um, so I guess the gear's like an ole friend that keeps me company."

10

THE PADDLE BACK GAVE ME TIME TO THINK, MOSTLY about Lester. I felt desperately sad for the venerable fisherman who kept antique gear for company and had just lost his only grandson, the one Crawford who had preserved a cherished family tradition. I already considered Lester a friend, and while I didn't press it with him, my protector as well.

I'd traveled to Macomek Island to help Gordy, the cousin who'd saved my life not so long ago. Now I had a second urgent reason to discover who killed Lester's only grandson.

I thanked Lester aloud. "If you and your little island hadn't been right there, I really might be dead."

Dead.

It bugged me that Gordy had been convinced Buddy was the dead man under his raft several days before Lester was informed. Odd, but maybe the delay had something to do with official identification of the body.

I'd just gotten out of the kayak on Abby's beach when she ran down the shingle to my side and threw her arms around me. "My goodness, deah. You gave me an awful scare."

Feeling like a coed who'd forgotten to call her mother, I said, "Oh Abby, I am *so* sorry."

"You're safe an' that's what matters. Let's get this boat up, then we'll have some lunch. You can tell me about it."

We reached the high tide line, lowered the kayak together, and started up the path to the house. I wasn't sure if Abby knew about Buddy and was trying to decide if I should ask when she saved me the trouble.

"Lester called with the awful news. I know you heard all about it," she said over her shoulder. From behind, I couldn't see her face. The catch in her voice said enough.

"I didn't know Buddy, but I can't imagine what Lester's going through," I said.

The stoic islander shook her head but didn't add anything.

I downed one grilled cheese and picked up my second. "Abby, this is perfect. I didn't realize how hungry I was."

"You've had quite a mornin' deah, with the puffins, gale, an' all."

Nodding, I looked for a napkin before wiping my fingers on my jeans. "Lester seems like a really great guy. You must've known him for a long time."

Seated across from me, she ran a hand across the table. "More years then I want to let on. He moved heah when he married an island girl. She died young a long time ago. Cancer."

"But they had a son," I said.

"Jus' the one. Todd's a nice young man who left the island a good while back. He's a lawyer out in Augusta. Not sure what kind."

"And Buddy is, was, Lester's grandson."

"Buddy's real name is Lester. Callin' the boy Buddy made knowin' who was who easiah."

"So Buddy was Lester's only grandson, *and* they shared the same first name. Buddy also carried on the family fishing tradition. It's all so incredibly sad."

"I recall when Buddy said he wanted to lobstah with Lester. Lord, he was so proud. Now this. The man's had more than his share o' grief."

Her gaze shifted to the window and we sat there in silence

until someone knocked on the door. We turned to see Gordy step in.

"Mara, I jus' heard you were out in that blow. Damnation, you could've gone ovah and that ocean's frigid cold. Jus' learned two kayakers got caught in the same gale off Acadia. One capsized an' from what I heard on the radio they might've died."

I jumped up from my chair. "You're kidding. Paddlers *dead* off the National Park?"

He shook his head. "It was one hellish blow. Where were you? What happened?"

I described "Puffin Island," my fight with the gale, and Lester leading me to safety.

"You an' your birds," he said. "Well, now you've met Buddy's granddad."

"Gordy, how did you know who was under your mussel raft days before Lester found out?" I asked

He looked down at Abby. "Would you rathah not heah 'bout Tyler again?"

"It's all right. I'll clean up the kitchen while you talk with Mara. Take my seat."

Gordy pulled back Abby's chair as I fell into mine. He leaned back and crossed his arms over his chest. "Couple reasons. First off, Patty's sistah Angel's been givin' Patty an earful 'bout Tyler bad mouthin' Buddy. I can't repeat all the exact words, but you can guess."

"Did Tyler say he actually wanted to kill Buddy?"

"Said 'kill,' 'drown,' 'wipe out.'"

"Not too smart."

"Well, like we said, Mara, Tyler's a druggie. He fried his brain. Then Buddy goes missin'. Two an' two."

"I see," I said, "Is Tyler still on the island?"

"Ayuh. Sleeps on his boat."

"So does this drug addict who threatens to kill people really think I'm a narc trying to put him away?"

"You scarin' Tyler off the island, that's jus' an idea. If his boat's still heah tomorrow, we're callin' Marine Patrol."

"And you'll go talk to them yourself, right?"

He pushed back the chair and stood. "Jus' like I said."

After lunch, I walked down to the harbor to meet Malicite Dupris. Shielding my eyes against the sun, I squinted at his boat. A voice said, "Down heah!"

Seated in a white dinghy thirty feet below, Malicite grinned up at me, oars in hand. "Take the ladder down."

Given my lack of enthusiasm for heights, I made slow, hand-over-hand progress down a wooden ladder that had seen better days. Malicite reached up to help me step into the little boat.

"Thanks," I said.

The twinkle in his dark eyes told me he'd guessed my fear.

Rowing across the harbor, his black curls bobbing, Dupris bubbled with enthusiasm for the eLobster project. "It's amazin' what they do. Lobstahmen from all ovah workin' side by side with ocean scientists. An' I mean *with*. Those guys, they listen to us, really want our help."

"It's NOAA, right? What do they get out of it?"

The dinghy approached the stern of his boat. "We'll talk about that. Step aboard right heah. I'll keep the dinghy steady."

Look to the Future was one of the tidiest lobster boats I'd ever seen. Everything was in its place. Since Malicite was right-handed, the steering wheel and electronics were rigged on the starboard side just inside the open wheelhouse. Hanging from a hook, his thick orange oil gear—venerable bib pants and jacket for protection against wind and rain—looked brand-new clean. The hydraulic pot hauler was poised for action. Most of the deck was taken up with essential lobstering gear—bait bags, brass measuring gauge, banding pliers, thick claw bands, heavy-duty bright blue gloves, and picking box that would hold lobsters waiting to be measured. The gear would all be methodically arranged and within easy reach as traps were hauled aboard.

Inside the wheelhouse, a small wooden table held a portable computer. A lobster trap lay on the deck.

Malicite brought the computer to life. "These pictures'll give ya an idea about the project. The first one heah, that's a meetin' we had down in Woods Hole."

The Massachusetts village of Woods Hole, I knew, was home to NOAA's Northeast Fisheries Science Center. Right down the street, hundreds of marine scientists and technicians worked at the Woods Hole Oceanographic Institute (WHOI). I assumed that engineers from WHOI and NOAA's fisheries biologists had teamed up to develop the unique program Malicite described.

I leaned in to look at his photograph. It showed twenty-odd guys in jeans and flannel shirts with white nametags stuck to them. Most looked to be thirty to fifty, although there were a few older men as well.

"No women," I said.

"Not that day. But there's a few in the program."

"So tell me all about it. The instruments, what data you get, how it all works," I said.

He knelt down and cradled a round device about three inches across strapped to the top of the trap with a black plastic tie. I squatted next to him.

"This here's the temperature sensor. I attach it to the trap. When I haul 'er up, I can see the temperature right away on that little computah up theah." He nodded to a micro-computer with a half-foot screen mounted next to the wheel.

The sensor fit in the palm of my hand. "You can look at your own temperature numbers on your computer, but how does it get transmitted back to the eLobster people?"

He pointed toward the roof. "There's a satellite transmittah mounted on top of the wheelhouse that sends it."

I pictured a cartoon of a lobster boat sending data to a satellite circling the earth, which in turn passed the numbers along to a NOAA server somewhere. "Amazing," I said. "There's a wireless temperature sensor on your trap and the data is transmitted when you pull it up. You don't have to do a thing."

"Nope," he said. "Nothin' changes for us. We jus' do what we do. No buttons to push or whatevah. Those NOAA guys, they know how busy it gets when we're out workin'. Aftahwards, we give 'em the location and trap depth for each sensor."

"I'd imagine when you're in the middle of hauling traps you don't have time to look at the data at all."

He laughed. "You know it. Traps coming up, keepers flying into the pickin' box, rejects ovahboard, sternman shovin' traps off the stern. It's crazy out theah."

"Can I see some of your temperature data?"

He got to his feet and fiddled with the computer until a graph appeared on the screen. "This here's spring through fall." He ran his forefinger up the scale on the left side of the graph. "That's temperature in Fahrenheit." He moved his finger to the right side. "'N here it's Celsius." Turning toward me he said, "'Course you know all this."

I nodded. "Sure, but I love being on the receiving side of this lesson,"

He positively beamed.

I leaned in and traced my finger along the graph's black line. "Okay, for this trap the temperature on the bottom started out about forty degrees Fahrenheit in June. Then it climbed steadily and got up to something like fifty-five in September."

He squinted at the screen. "Ayuh."

"What does that tell you? I mean, what do you learn from these numbers that's useful?"

"We spent lots 'o time at those meetings in Woods Hole figurin' out what it means. Lobster scientists gave little talks 'bout highah temperature and lobsters. Then some of us sat in front along a table an' said what we knew."

"A panel?" I asked

He nodded. "That's what they called it, a panel."

I tapped the computer screen. "So in the end, does knowing the temperature where you trap make a difference?"

"'Couple things. First off, there was that awful shell disease that killed off lobsterin' south of here."

"The shell disease that caused the collapse of the industry in Long Island Sound and Massachusetts," I said.

He nodded. "Some NOAA scientists did a study showin' that bottom temperature in the low fifties was one reason why the disease happened."

"But not the only reason," I said. "Chemical contamination of the water could've also contributed to the collapse south of here."

He nodded. "No chemicals up heah, thank goodness. But I sure don't want to find out that warm watah by itself causes shell disease in Maine lobstahs."

"Right." I studied the graph on his screen. "For this trap anyway, bottom water reached fifty Fahrenheit in August and climbed up to fifty-five through September."

"Which is why I'm might be puttin' those traps deepah."

I leaned back against the wheelhouse window. "Does going deeper take more work?"

"It does. I gotta go out farthah an' it takes longah for the traps to come up. Adds up. If that's how I avoid that shell disease, hell it'll be worth it. But I got to think on it more."

Malicite showed me a few more graphs and reached around the back of the computer to shut it down. In the process, he slid a notebook aside.

I pointed at the notebook. "Is that some kind of journal?"

He held up the half-foot tall brown booklet. "This heah is gold. It's where I write down important things I can't keep in my head. Things like how many lobstah I get where an' when. What the weathah was like. Now I add eLobstah data."

I completely understood how critically important it was to store data safely. Any scientist I knew had multiple data backups. "Your notebook is super valuable."

"Yeah. Every lobstahman I know keeps one. We all hide it in our cabin where nobody's gonna mess with it." Malicite pointed over his shoulder. "Why don't we go outside an' enjoy the sun."

On the stern deck he turned over a bucket, sat on it, and motioned to a wooden box. "Pull that out. Bes' seat in the house."

I lowered myself onto the box and asked, "Will access to bottom water temperature data where you trap help you catch more lobsters?"

He shrugged. "There's a whole lot to catchin' bugs. You might put traps near ledges where lobstahs like to hide. There's special spots we call honey holes we put to memory. There's bait—why kind, how long it lasts. We fuss with traps. It goes on an' on. Okay?"

I nodded.

"For eLobstah, temperature is the million dollah question. An' jus' like you eggheads, my answer is, 'It's complicated.'"

I laughed. "Good answer. Complicated because of lobster biology, economics, or what?"

"Both and how lobstahmen think 'bout climate change."

I settled down for a lobster lesson. "Go with the biology stuff first."

He leaned forward, elbows on his knees. "You know Maine lobstahs move from offshore to inshore in midsummah, right?"

I nodded.

"Here's what we talked 'bout at those meetin's. In twenty-twelve, spring was warmah than usual an' bugs moved inshore early. Surprised us. Our big catch shifted to June an' July. Usually it's July to August or Septembah. Messed us all up."

"So if you had good data on bottom temperatures—what it starts at and how fast it rises—maybe you could better anticipate where to put your strings when and also what months your big hauls would be," I said.

"Right, but there's more."

Loving this, I nodded again.

"The market also depends on how fast lobstahs grow an' that depends on sheddin' rates. So twenty-twelve was double trouble 'cause warm watah meant more bugs moltin'. We had lobstahs way early an' tons of 'em ta boot."

I snapped my fingers. "Yes, I remember now. We had a picnic with steamed lobsters, and they were incredibly cheap that year. It was because lobsters flooded the market and prices plummeted."

"Ayuh. Lobstermen were gettin' somethin' like half the usual price. The weird thing is down south, like in Long Island, the lobstah industry collapsed with the disease an' all. So there we were swimmin' in bugs, an' all they had was dead ones. Twenty-twelve, that was grim. The Woods Hole scientists, they called it the yeah that drove climate change home for the industry."

"Meaning what?"

"Everythin' is changin' with this climate thing. We gotta

expect the unexpected."

"That's a pretty scary proposition," I said. "With the collapse of cod and the rest of the ground fisheries, coastal communities up and down the Maine coast depend on lobstering. It brings in hundreds of millions of dollars a year. That's huge."

He got up off the bucket and arched his back to stretch. "It's a savage problem. What you're dependin' on isn't dependable no mattah how much you want it to be."

I stood as well, which made my sore butt muscles happy. "That was super interesting."

He shrugged. Well, this eLobstah, it's 'cause of you eggheads."

"How about the other lobstermen out here. What do they think of your working with scientists?"

"'Many of 'em them say if there's warmin' it will change, so who cares 'bout temperature. But they might know what's goin' on an' not want to admit it."

"Because they're worried warming *is* for real, and if they say it out loud it's more likely to happen?"

He shrugged. "Somethin' like that. Guys who work the watah, they're superstitious."

"Are there any Macomek lobstermen who were interested in the eLobster project?"

"Buddy Crawford."

I waited for Malicite to say add something such as how much he missed Buddy or that Buddy was a great guy. But he just crossed his arms over his chest and looked to the side.

"Um, was Calvin Ives interested in the project too?"

"Calvin's smart, so you think he'd get it. But he said it was stupidest thing he ever heard."

"One last question before I go, Malicite. Maine lobstering is good now, but that's not going to last forever. Given what you know about warming out here, what're your plans for the future?"

He rubbed his chin. "We're pullin' in bugs like there's no tomorrah now. There's what, five thousand licensed lobstahmen in Maine? Most I talk to say it's gonna last for a good long time. I think they're wrong. This happened before, then it crashed." He looked over the stern of the boat and stared at the water. "I'm studyin' NOAA charts for the Gulf of Maine to see where the watah's deepest. Maybe that's where the bugs'll go. I need to see what it's like workin' out theah. I could put down a string or two. Ya know, to have a claim." He laughed. "May have to steam all the way up to Canada. Wouldn't that be a pissah?"

When I described Alise's Sea Grant "eLobster town hall" idea, Malicite said it might work and offered to be a presenter. I couldn't wait to tell Alise.

As I pulled my hair into a tighter ponytail, the sun glinted off the steel trap hauler. "Before we go," I said, "Could you explain how the hauler works and what lobstermen used to do?"

"Don't tell me you haven't been out on a lobstahboat," he said.

I shrugged. "When I was a kid. But that was a long time ago."

Malicite walked up to the pot hauler. "Okay. When I come up alongside one of my buoys, I cut the engine an' gaff the line below the float." He pointed to the good-sized metal pulley hanging off the water. "Then I run the line up ovah this snatch block an' down around the pot hauler in the wheelhouse."

"So how does the pot hauler work?"

"It's a hydraulic winch with a rotatin' disk that pinches the line an' pulls it through."

I winced. "Damn. With everything happening so fast, I'd imagine that spinning disk can just as easily pinch your finger." I didn't articulate the dreadful image that came to mind.

"Ayuh. I've seen guys who lost fingers or got the tips pulled off. Where was I? Um, aftah the line goes through the spinnin' hauler, it drops down on the deck an' sends slime an' watah all ovah. All that happenin' so fast makes for dangerous work."

"Before haulers, what did lobstermen do?"

"They pulled 'em up by hand. Imagine how hard it'd be. They reeled 'em up hand ovah hand. Bringin' those heavy wet traps ovah the side of the boat must've been brutal. Haulers came about in the nineteen-fifties. That's when strings of traps an' open sterns on lobstah boats got popular. The traps in a string could jus' slide off the stern into the watah one aftah the othah."

"Thanks for the lesson, Malicite. You're a great teacher."

Given the extent of his grin, it was clear the lobsterman appreciated my compliment.

On our way back to shore, I was leaning over the dinghy to watch a jellyfish pulse by when Malicite said, "I met anothah ocean scientist in Spruce Habah couple months ago. Guy named Ted. We had couple beers an' played darts at the Lee Side."

I jerked up so quickly the boat rocked. "Oh, um, Ted. Yes, he's a colleague of mine."

"Thought so. When I asked if there was any good-lookin' lady scientists where he worked he laughed. Said there was one he 'specially liked. She was athletic lookin', had reddish-brown hair, an' was smart an' funny. Kind of sounds like you."

To change the subject, I said the first thing that came to mind. "Ah, where do you live, Malicite?'

He gestured with his chin. "Jus' a quartah mile that way. Hey, my wife an' little girl'd love to meet you. Why don't you come by in a couple minutes just to say hello."

I did a quick assessment and decided he really did want me to visit. "Sure, that would be nice. But just for few minutes like you said."

I climbed back up the rickety ladder, called down, "Thanks!" to Malicite, stepped up onto dry land, and vowed not to think about Ted. Of course, I did just that. The dart game must've happened soon after Ted and I got serious about each other. Damn, we had a great time back then. We did everything together—worked, ran, kayaked, cooked, drank wine, and had fun in bed.

Reliving the later a little too graphically, I picked my way around a couple of damaged lobster pots and nearly walked into a guy who could have been a trainer with the Marines. Calvin Ives.

"Oh, sorry."

"No problem. I'm guessing you're Abby's cousin." The slightest twitch in his cheek suggested he'd guessed I wasn't related to Abby at all. He probably respected her too much to say so.

"Er, I was just visiting with Malicite. That ELobster program sounds amazing."

He waved a hand. "Dupris, he's a good lobstahman, but that eLobstah's not gonna make 'im bettah."

I had to ask. "Why's that?"

"This climate thing's a scam that gets scientists more cash from taxpayers."

This was not a conversation I wanted to have at the moment. "Calvin, I'm going over Malicite's house to meet his wife and little girl. What's the easiest way for me to get there?"

He pointed to the north. See that path comin' off the main road theah? Follow that, and you'll end up at his house. He pulled at his baseball cap, said, "Well, I got work to do," and strode past me toward the harbor.

I watched until he disappeared behind a lobster shack. Calvin's comment about climate scientists' motivation was nothing new. After all, Gordy had said the same many times. But Irish to his core, Gordy's strong convictions about politics, sports, the environment, and most everything else were often based on emotion, not careful reasoning. From what I'd heard, Ives was intelligent, ambitious, someone people were willing to follow—traits I usually associated with nuanced thinking. Of course, people were always more complicated than I could imagine.

I followed Calvin's directions and quickly came upon a shingled bungalow at the crest of a small hill. A woman wearing jeans and a red flannel shirt was pulling white sheets off a clothesline in the back yard. The strong wind made the maneuver a challenge.

I hurried over. "Please, let me help you."

She shaded her eyes from the sun. "Great. You grab one end and I'll get the othah."

I followed her instructions and introduced myself. "I'm Mara and was just with Malicite. He was telling me about the eLobster project."

She walked toward me, rolling the sheets into a big ball as she went. "Got it, thanks, deah. I'm Elizabeth; people call me Liz. Malicite tol' me he was doin' that. Speak of the devil, here he is."

Malicite strode up and put his hand on his wife's shoulder. "Hah. So I'm the devil. I invited Mara over to meet you and Sybil."

"Just for a few minutes," I added.

She smiled. "You stay long as you like, deah."

We walked around to the front of the house. The weathered, dark grey shingles had clearly seen decades of storms and sun. Between two multi-paned windows, the faded turquoise front door slowly opened. A blue-eyed towhead with bangs and braids stood on the threshold and wrinkled her nose at me.

"I'm Sybie. Who are you?"

Malicite stepped forward, swept up the child, and hoisted her onto his shoulders. She whooped with delight.

Elizabeth looked up at her daughter and tried not to laugh. "This is Mara, Sybie. She's here for a little visit. How about you introduce yourself properly to her."

Malicite put Sybie down in front of me. She extended her hand. "How do you do? I'm Sybil Dupris."

I knelt and took the little hand. "Very nice to meet you."

Sybie led us into a tiny house with a living room–kitchen that constituted most of the first floor. Smelling of biscuits, it was the kind of home where children grew up with dogs, and adults traded the day's stories after the kids went to bed.

The four of us sat around a small, square, wooden table, the only one in the room. Elizabeth put a plate with two hot biscuits in front of me and moved the homemade blueberry jam within reach. Sipping tea made a little less strong with milk, I listened to stories about cousins, aunts and uncles, brothers and sisters who lived on the mainland. Between Malicite and Elizabeth, the number of relatives was mindboggling.

"So none of them live out here?" I asked.

Malicite said, "A couple of my brothers tried, but they couldn't take the remoteness. Kept goin' back to the mainland an' finally stayed."

"How about you, Mara?" Elizabeth asked. "Your family?"

"Um, well, it's a lot different for me. My parents died when I was nineteen, and I don't have any brothers or sisters."

Elizabeth blinked, opened her mouth, and closed it. She cleared her throat and said, "No brothers or sisters?"

Sybie blurted out, "You mommy and daddy died. How did they die?"

Malicite jumped in. "Sybil, where are you manners?"

The child pursed her lips and looked down. "I'm sorry."

"No," I said. "It's all right. Sybie, my parents were scientists who studied the ocean like I do. They were under the water in a little submarine that got stuck."

Big eyed, she said, "They died in a *submarine*. Wow. But if you don't have brothers and sisters, what do you do at Christmas?"

"Oh, I've got a godfather and lots of friends."

I walked back to the harbor feeling melancholy. Generous and kind, Malicite and Elizabeth had no idea that stories about their huge families kindled a desperate longing I'd tried so hard to suppress. Hardly anyone they knew lacked parents or siblings. That I was so different wasn't my fault, but I sure felt like a freak.

"Not a freak," I said aloud. "A deviation from normal."

My little joke didn't help a bit.

Halfway to the harbor, I noticed a path that looked like it headed toward a part of the island I hadn't seen. In need of distraction, I took it and soon found a tiny sand beach which the sun told me faced west toward the mainland. I could imagine the island's would-be residents—people who tried and eventually rejected Macomek as a place they could live—standing there, eyes fixed straight ahead, thoughts on what they'd left behind. They might miss movie theaters, decent cars, grocery stores. Or maybe they were desperate for family and friends. Whatever it was, the longing was a sore they couldn't ignore. Funny. The ones who stayed might stand beside them, consider all the same things, and quickly turn away, glad to be free of all of it.

Back on the main path I passed the lobster shacks and was startled by several men's voices I didn't recognize. I knelt down, pretended to tie my shoelace, and listened.

"Look Richie, we agreed on it an' did what we had ta. What're you, soft as a shed lobstah?"

"Talkin' 'bout it, that's one thing. But doin' it? Don't tell me it ain't gettin' undah your skin. I saw that whiskey bottle...."

The rumble of a boat motor overrode the sound of the argument. If the guys continued talking, I couldn't hear them.

I stood and walked quickly away. Whatever Richie and the other guy were discussing sounded pretty unsavory. Could "it" be getting rid of Buddy? Maybe, but they could also be talking about putting down a beloved dog or worse, letting doctors pull the plug on their dying mother. All I could do was report the conversation to Marine Patrol and let them deal with it.

The unsavory pair also reminded me that I'd focused on someone like Tyler working alone. But Buddy could have been murdered, if that's what happened, by two people or more. Maybe a group of Macomek lobstermen had taken care of business as the islanders were known to do.

Maybe, maybe, maybe.

Farther down the road toward Abby's house, I spotted a deer walking among low shrubs a couple hundred feet away. The doe stood statue-still, her huge ears at attention. Even though she looked right at me, her big chocolate eyes were better designed for distant movement than details. She stomped a foot to get a reaction, and I tipped my head to the side. A quiver rippled across her chest before she bounded through the bushes and was swallowed by the pine forest. A big deer like that was the last thing I expected to see on Macomek. How did it get all the way out here? Besides that, the animal was a sitting duck for hunters, so to speak. But maybe they saw her as a source of future deer meat.

I recognized the unusually uniform vegetation as a low-bush blueberry field the islanders probably burned every other year. Just beyond the blueberries, off-white flat stones tilted this way and that. An old graveyard.

Like many New England hikers, I'd stumbled across small

cemeteries in the middle of the woods—relics of abandoned family members.

In the fourteenth century, Giovanni Verrazzano described Maine's coast as "full of very dense forests." The European explorer would have been amazed by the industry of those who came after him. By the seventeen hundreds, our forefathers had cut down an astounding number of trees, mostly for firewood, and cleared about eighty percent of the land. Every single year, they needed at least forty cords to keep a drafty house marginally warm during the winter. Cutting, hauling, and chopping all that wood—each cord four feet high by four feet wide by eight feet long—was a hell of a lot of work. When railroads made travel west easier, farmers left their poor-soil, rocky, hilly, treeless New England farms for flat Midwest land with ten feet of rich topsoil.

And, of course, they left their dead behind.

Since these cemeteries offer a glimpse into the lives of people who came before us, I never missed the opportunity to stare at the headstones and try to imagine their lives and their deaths—so many of them infants, children, and women of childbearing age. In Maine, lots of men died young too, and on the coast they often died at sea.

A path through the blueberry field took me to a small plot with twenty-odd stones. As usual, Maine's acidic rainwater had partly dissolved the limestone, which made most inscriptions unreadable. I squatted in front of a few before finding one I could read. Below the floating head with wings, the caption for Captain Thomas Exeter, born 1790 and died 1841, read: "HE IS DONE CATCHING COD AND GONE TO MEET HIS GOD. DROWNED IN THE DEEP, DEEP SEA." Beside his father, a tiny stone for infant William Exeter read: "TO MY PARENTS I WAS BRIEFLY LENT, ONE SMILE TO THEM I GAVE BEFORE I DESCENDED TO THE GRAVE."

I wandered among the stones, running my finger along the engravings, imagining the pain of husbands whose wives died so very young, parents who lost child after child, wives who looked to out sea for a husband who never returned.

At the edge of the mowed grass, a cluster of mostly dried flowers leaned against a small granite boulder. Someone on the island had visited the spot fairly recently.

"Makes ya wonder what that's about, them flowers."

I spun around to face the forest as a skinny, unkempt man stepped into the light. His beady porcine eyes darted between my face and our shared surroundings like a pinpoint light searching for the enemy. Given the location, my first thought was that he was an extra in a Stephen King horror movie set on a Maine island.

11

"**D**AMN, YOU NEARLY SCARED ME TO DEATH." THE GUY reminded me of a prehistoric bird—skinny and darkly tan with those squinting restless eyes that flitted around like someone or something was about to grab him. He didn't respond to my complaint, so I tried a different tack.

"Would you mind telling me who you are?"

"Name's Tyler."

Given Gordy's claims made against the man, I should have felt scared. But somehow he didn't strike me as malevolent. More dotty than dangerous. What came next confirmed that opinion.

He flapped an arm toward the blueberry field. "Did ya know Maine grows more blueberries than any other state?"

I wasn't sure what to say, but it wasn't an issue because he didn't give me a chance to respond.

"Besides that, there's only four fruits we eat heah that're native. Wild blueberries are one of 'em."

I was trying to come up with an effective "See you later" line, but his next remark stopped my synapses cold.

"Gordy wants ta know who kilt Buddy, but he's got ya lookin' in the wrong place."

He correctly interpreted my open mouth.

"Killer's off island."

"Um, Tyler, I don't understand."

"Buddy, he was a real good lobstahman. Was gonna give Calvin Ives a run fer his money. But las' yeah Buddy bought some *real* 'spensive stuff. New boat, all rigged up. Best ya could buy. Thing is, he wasn't bringin' in more lobstahs. You gotta ask, where'd all that cash come from? And, assummin' it's drugs, his supplier is who you should be lookin' for."

As he spoke, Tyler became a new person. He stood straighter, looked right at me, and his voice deepened. Maybe the weird wacko was an act. I decided to take him seriously.

"How do you know how many lobsters Buddy caught?"

"We set our strings in the same area an' I watched 'im. We'd go out an' come back 'bout the same time. Had the same numbah traps, give or take. It's like, ya know, a big family out theah. All of us from the island, we're always talkin' on the VHF."

I didn't want to insult the guy but had to ask. "I still don't get it. You said Buddy was a very good lobsterman. That meant he could afford a new boat."

At that moment, anyway, there was nothing wrong with the circuits in Tyler's brain. He understood what I was getting at right away. "If you're askin' if he was bettah than me, you're not lis'nin'. He was always good, but bang, he's got all this dough? Somethin' else was goin' on. Look fer his drug lord or whatevah you call it."

I extracted myself from Tyler's company with a promise that I'd give Gordy this information, didn't turn my back on the man until I reached the blueberry clearing, and speed-walked to the road. Once there I scanned the forest, saw nothing, and set off again for Abby's house.

It was hard to know what to make of Tyler's declaration about Buddy's wealth. On the one hand, Tyler might have heard Patty's claims about his own guilt and invented the story as a distraction. One the other, it was true that lobstermen working the same waters were like siblings in a big family. They competed, bantered, sometimes fought, watched each other's backs, and knew one another's business. And the bottom line for their bread and butter was lobster landings and price. They'd have a pretty good idea who was making what.

So Tyler might well have information that should not be dismissed.

Through the woods, I'd just glimpsed the shingles on Abby's roof when a sole flower demanded my attention. I strolled over and knelt beside an abandoned stonewall to take a look. Flowers in clusters on a single stem, five rose-pink petals the length of my thumb. I pulled off a leaf and rolled it between my palms. The pungent, spicy aroma announced the plant's name—Musk Mallow. It was a bright, happy flower you would notice, and I had seen it a few times in abandoned fields along the coast. But all the way out on the island it was an unexpected find. I scanned the wall. No other mallows graced its length or the fields on either side. I craned my neck to one side, then the other. Dappled light exposed no bits of pink on the forest floor, and there were no mallows along the side of the road. I scanned my botanical memory. I'd not seen any musk mallows on Macomek.

The plant I knelt before had no companions.

Cradling the delicate, lovely flower in the late afternoon sun, I was overcome with a sudden, terrible melancholy. Tears ran down my cheeks as sorrow flowed through me in waves. Of course, I knew why.

Family was everything to everyone on the island. To a person they talked about siblings, parents, cousins, aunts, uncles, nephews, nieces. But I had none of those. Like the mallow, I was utterly alone.

My mother and father had been taken by the sea, the very entity they'd worked so hard to bring to life for others. I'd lost so very much—years of birthdays, their discoveries and mine, vacations in Ireland and Italy, sailing expeditions, the ritual of watching the full moon rise over expanse of sea. None of it had happened.

Gone. The saddest word I knew.

I'd armored myself against that pain and buried myself in work until Ted got a job at MOI the previous spring. He was smart, kind, funny, and good-looking in a Boy-Scout kind of way. After I finally realized he was Harvey's half-brother, not her boyfriend, we'd hooked up. And we had a great time until he mentioned the M-word. I backed off like a lobster facing a dog shark—not one of my most generous moves—and lost the closest thing I'd had to a soul mate.

My armor had gone back up and stayed that way for months. Now this island, these people, this flower, Abby's home had fed my starved soul. On my feet, I extended both arms toward her house as if it were an animate thing I could hold close.

The voice behind me was soft. "You think you got it tucked away, then it's there again somethin' fierce."

Dropping my arms, I slowly turned. Abby was looking across the field toward the graveyard as she said, "I didn't know a broken heart kept on beating."

I followed her line of sight. She was fixed on the old maple tree. "The dead flowers next to the rock. They're yours," I said.

The nod was slow, deliberate. "It's a keepsake. There's nothing there."

"Baby?"

Still fixed on the tree she said, "That's right, deah. Mine and Lester's. Found somebody off island who took care of it. My husband was dead. Lester, he was married."

I reached over, put an arm around her shoulder, and steered her toward the house. "Let's go sit on the beach and listen to the ocean."

Gentle waves carried stones up the beach slope and dragged

them back down. Again and again and again.

Voice gritty, she broke the trance. "My Fred was two yeahs gone. Lester's wife had the cancer. But Lester an' me, we had so much life in us, so much love. There was an old shack by the watah. Long gone now. When I told him 'bout the baby, he was horr'fied. Made it too real, ya know. Aftah it was gone, Lester felt guilt jus' terrible. So that was the end of it."

"Abby, it's obvious he cares a great deal about you.

She patted my hand. "I know that, deah." After a minute she said, "What's his name, the one who hurt you and put a hole your heart?"

"Ted. And I did the hurting."

"Ah. You love each other?"

"I love him. Not sure what he's thinking now."

Pebbles rose up and back, up and back.

"I was afraid and couldn't...."

"Give yourself up," she said.

I stood, picked up a stone, and hurled it at the water.

She got to her feet. "I'd bet it's not too late, deah. But sometime, it will be."

My gear was packed and ready to go when Patty walked into the house with Gordy right behind. He had, I was astonished to realize, opened the door for her. Abby had set out a "some snacks" so Gordy and I wouldn't starve on our trip back to the mainland. The four of us sat around the kitchen table eating while I relayed Tyler's assertion.

Gordy finished his beer and set the bottle down hard. "Lemme get this right. Tyler says Buddy's money was dodgy an' we should be lookin' inta that."

Patty shook her head. "Yeah right. Tyler's makin' this up so we don't think its him." She spat out the rest. "Does he *really* think we're that dumb?"

"Gordy," I said, "let's say another lobsterman you knew well suddenly bought a real expensive boat and all that goes with it but wasn't pulling in more lobsters. Would you wonder what was going on?".

He rubbed his chin. "If I really knew the guy, 'spose I might."

Patty turned to him and barked, "Damn it, Gordy, I thought you were on my side heah. Tyler's guilty an' we both know it. This 'what if,' it's bull."

I waited for the Irish temper to emerge. Instead, Gordy just said, "Patty, take it easy."

I added, "It was just a hypothetical question."

She swiveled in my direction and slapped a hand on the table. "Right, an' from someone not from heah who knows squat 'bout a soul on Macomek. You—"

Abby broke in. "Patty, stop this right now. That's no way to treat a guest."

Patty shoved back her chair so hard it fell over, marched to the front door, yanked it open, and slammed it behind her.

Three sets of eyes stared at the door.

Abby reached across the table for my hand. "Mara, I've never seen Patty act like that. I am so sorry. 'Course with what happened to Buddy, we're all on edge. But still, it's not like her one bit."

After Gordy left to get his boat, Abby and I waited on the beach while he motored around the point from the harbor and reached shoal water.

"It's been real, real special, you bein' heah, Mara. Please come back for anothah visit."

Blinking back tears, I hugged her. "It's been more special than you can know. Being here with you is like, um...."

She stepped back, her grey eyes twinkling. "Apple pie at Thanksgivin'?"

"Close enough, Abby. Close enough."

Gordy and I kept to boat basics like "Keep your eye on that bottom sounder" and "Mind the block pulley" until Macomek was well behind us. At that point, the winds had picked up to thirty knots, so I settled onto a bench in the wheelhouse and stayed there.

"Cousin, I feel bad," I said. "We're leaving the island with no better idea what happened to Buddy than when we arrived."

He glanced at the compass and adjusted his course a tad. "Maybe we know more than we think. There's somethin' ya do when you're studyin' the ocean if things get real confused. Let's try that."

"You mean when the data are so confusing, I can't see a pattern at all?"

"That's it. What do ya do?"

I ran my fingers through my hair, got stuck on a couple of tangles, and gave it up. "Let's see. Well, I go back to the beginning—what I know as factual, what seems clear, no second guessing. Then I ask questions and follow where that leads to."

"So let's do that," he said. "Start with you finding Buddy."

Wishing I had a white board to write on, I said, "Okay. I found him under your raft Wednesday. That's four days ago." The image of the face with lifeless eyes flooded my brain. I pushed it away. "He hadn't been, you know, eaten by a bluefish or anything, at least what I could see. So he probably hadn't been there that long."

"That's the facts. Okay, so where do we go from there?"

I looked up at the cabin's overhead as a hitchhiker fly scurried across it. "I ask the most obvious question. In this case it's why was he under the raft in the first place?"

"Good," Gordy said. "That's jus' what I'm thinkin'."

"And?"

"Firs' thing, whoevah did Buddy must've had a boat. Or they knew somebody who had one. So I'm thinkin' they kilt 'im on the island, or nearby, an' headed fer the mainland."

I jumped in. "And they probably didn't have a plan for what to do with the body, panicked the closer they got to Spruce Harbor, spotted your raft, and saw their opportunity." I frowned. "I still don't get how they got Buddy under the raft. Moving a dead weight like that's not easy."

"I'm thinkin' there's more than one of 'em. You know, one ta keep a look out while the other one slides the body undah the raft."

"When you kill someone, disposal of the body is hard," I said. "Stashing it under an aquaculture raft is pretty smart. Nobody would ever think to look there, it wouldn't go anywhere, and pretty soon the dead person would be fish food."

"Unless you're unlucky and a nosy scientist goes and finds it," he said.

"Gordy, the word's *curious*, not nosy."

As the Juniper Ledge bell buoy's clang announced our approach to Spruce Harbor, I pulled out my cell phone to call Angelo. "Gordy and I are nearly back," I said. "Just wanted to let you know."

"Welcome home," he said. "Bet you don't have much in your refrigerator. Come over for dinner. You can tell me how it all went out there."

"You're right. There's just a lonely bottle of seltzer in my empty fridge. But I haven't cooked for anyone in days. I must owe you a half dozen dinners."

"For goodness sake, Mara, I'm Italian. You know I love cooking, especially for you. See you at seven."

Gordy helped me upload the kayak and rest of my gear onto my beach. "Monday, I'm drivin' up ta the Marine Patrol office. I'll tell 'em what I think 'bout Tyler killin' Buddy," he said.

"Take me with you so I can explain what Tyler told me."

"All right," he said. "Jus' don't let Patty know."

It only took me an hour to lug my kayak and gear up to the house, rinse everything off with fresh water, jump into the shower, wash my hair, and change. I stepped into Angelo's kitchen just as the old schoolroom clock ticked to seven.

He was wrapping a strong-smelling fillet in aluminum foil. "Grilling bluefish?" I asked.

He turned and held up his hands. "If I give you a hug, you'll smell like I do. Connor and I caught some blues today."

Outside on the patio, Angelo slid the bluefish onto the hot grill and closed the lid. "Be right back with your wine."

I settled onto one of his cushioned chairs, leaned back, and closed my eyes. Angelo's home sits atop a bluff on Seal Point. It's a spectacular spot where ospreys and gulls circle overhead, all manner of boats announce their entrance into the harbor below, and you can watch the big dipper ever-so-slowly revolve on a clear night.

Neatly dressed as always in pressed chinos and an oxford shirt, Angelo strode back with two glasses of wine. Stately, with thick silver hair, I'd often thought he could've been an Italian movie star. Instead, he'd made his mark in the world of marine engineering, a worthier profession.

As we clinked glasses he said, "*Cento di questi giorni.*"

"And a hundred of these days for you too. Remember when I was little how we'd lie out here at night and watch the constellations move? Or appear to, anyway? We should do that again."

We both watched a red-tailed hawk zip through the tree

canopy with the speed and grace of a racecar driver. "Can't imagine how those birds do that. Sure, I remember. You were such a great kid to have around. Interested in anything and everything in nature. Birds, sea animals, rocks, whatever."

"Speaking of me as a kid, I had another, um, odd experience on Macomek."

He settled into the facing chair, crossed one long leg over the other, and searched my face with slate-blue eyes. "Are you okay?"

"I'm fine. You helped me a lot when I experienced"—I air quoted the words—"'all that weird stuff' a couple of months ago. It'd be good to talk about this now."

The lines across his brow disappeared. "So what happened?"

"I told you I was staying with Abby Burgess, right."

"I've met her. Smart lady."

"She is. Um, I walked into to her guest room and just knew I'd been there before. Everything about it was so familiar—the light, colors, how it smelled, feel of the bedspread."

In his experience, mine wasn't a bizarre incident. "Last year, I wandered around the Church of San Giorgio Maggiore in Venice for the first time since I was a boy. It was the scent of warm candles, damp plaster, and sweet white lilies that did it. In an instant, I was a child holding my mama's hand. A very powerful experience."

I leaned over and squeezed his hand. "I knew you'd understand."

"Were you able to confide in Abby?"

Angelo knew I'd long considered being depressed or worried weaknesses a strong person had to overcome alone. I'd never expose such feelings to anyone else.

"It's getting a little less painful—admitting my, um, worries to people. And she's so easy to talk to. When I asked if

I might've been there as a kid, she told me her father invited interesting people to the house. So Mom and Dad could have visited with me in tow."

"Well, Carlos and Bridget Tusconi certainly were delightful guests. Carlos, he told the best stories about men who took ships through U-boat patrolled waters, early days of oceanographic research, all that. And Bridget Shea, with that red hair and green eyes you inherited, she lit up the room when she walked in."

I grinned. Angelo's descriptions of my mother always made me wonder if he'd been a little bit in love with her.

He finished his wine and put down the glass. "People loved Bridget's talks about everything from whales to the tiniest shrimp. She had a way of getting folks into the water with her stories about scuba diving, oceanographic ships, whatever it was." Standing, he added, "So your mom and dad could've gone out to Macomek and stayed in Abby's house. Give me a minute. I've got to check the fish."

I watched as he pulled up the grill lid, peeled up a bit of aluminum foil, and leaned over for a look. Angelo was my link to my past, the only person alive who could tell me stories about my parents.

"Angelo," I said. "*Ti voglio bene.*"

He looked over and winked. "I love you too, Mara. And it's done. Let's eat inside. It's getting chilly out here."

Over dinner, I narrated the rest of my visit on Macomek—talking with Malicite, Gordy and Patty's claims about Tyler, my encounter with Tyler in the cemetery. I described my interaction with Lester but downplayed the near wipeout with the gale.

"I've met Lester a couple of times," Angelo said. "Real nice guy. Can't imagine him losing Buddy after what happened in that storm a while back."

"You know about a storm?"

"Let's do these dishes. I've got some almond cookies that'll be good with coffee. Then I'll tell you all about it."

I was dunking my second cookie in espresso when he said, "It was the tail end of a hurricane up from Cape Cod. Eighty-mile-an-hour winds, thirty-foot sea. Blew his lobster boat right over. That Lester got rescued was a miracle. But the sternman, can't recall the name, didn't make it."

"So when was that?"

"Probably August or September since that's hurricane time in New England. Maybe ten years ago?"

"Abby said something about an anniversary, and I got the idea it was a sad one." I tapped my cup as the image of a child looking up at the guest window floated through my mind. I blinked. "There's something about that island that's, I don't know—haunting—like unsettled ghosts walking around."

"I'll bet the *Rockland Free Press* has Macomek news. Not sure you'll read about ghosts, but it might be interesting to poke around and see what you find about Macomek history."

"Good idea. Gordy and I are going up there Monday to talk with Marine Patrol. While he's off doing errands, I can go to the library and find out if everything is on line."

"So Gordy's convinced that this Tyler killed Buddy, but you're not."

I shrugged. "Patty's got Gordy convinced. Tyler strikes me as a little off, but Macomek's got a reputation for unconventional folks. I kept asking Patty if there was evidence linking Tyler to the murder, but she didn't want to hear it." I pictured her glare and the feeling she wanted to reach across the table and slap me. "Fierce doesn't describe the woman."

"Well, somebody did it."

"On our way back to Spruce Harbor, Gordy and I came up with some good ideas. First, given where I'd found Buddy, whoever killed him probably has a boat. Besides that, it would've been a lot easier to get the body onto the boat and under the raft if there were two of them. And I've been wondering why in hell anyone would put a dead person under an aquaculture raft in the first place. But maybe they didn't plan that at all. They could've seen the raft as they approached land and realized it was a pretty good place to stash a body."

Angelo nodded. "You're right. If Marine Patrol agrees, that probably gets Gordy off the hook." He pushed back his chair and crossed his arms across his chest. "So I've heard about lots of people except one."

I looked to the side. "You mean Ted."

"Uh-huh."

I shrugged. "I haven't seen him in days. There's really nothing to say." I pictured Ted in his office with smart, stunning Penny Russell at his side. In an instant, tears flooded my eyes. "Damn."

Angelo leaned over and handed me his handkerchief. "Want to talk about it?"

Dabbing the corners of my eyes, I shrugged. "I don't know."

"When you described feeling so melancholy about your parents, I wondered if Ted had anything to do with that."

I sniffed. "Maybe."

"Being so lonely makes you more susceptible to strong emotions like that."

"I'm super busy with my own work and helping my grad student. I see Harvey and Connor a lot."

"It's not the same, and you know it. You've got a hole in your heart."

I sighed. "That's exactly the same expression Abby used."

"Like I said, she's a smart lady. Did she say anything else?"

"Yeah. If I didn't do something soon, Ted might not be there."

12

I'D JUST TURNED OFF SEAL POINT ONTO ROUTE ONE WHEN the sky opened up. Sideways sheets of rain forced me to crawl the last few miles to the turnoff for my dirt road. As I bumped along under a canopy of tall pines, it felt like I was in a tunnel driving into a fire hose. I leaned forward, squinted, and switched between high and low beams with little effect—which is why I didn't see the deer jump out of the shrubs until it was in the middle of the road staring into the headlights. I slammed my foot on the brake and stopped within what must have been inches of her flank.

The expression "deer in the headlights" exists for a reason. The doe—I guessed she was a female yearling—stood mesmerized by car's lights for a full minute. Then, with a flick of her white tail, she jumped back into the shrubbery and was gone. I rested my forehead on the steering wheel until my heart stopped pounding and soon splashed into my driveway where the wind off the water had turned the storm into a gale.

As usual, I'd forgotten to turn on the porch light and in the driving rain couldn't even see the house twenty feet away. Rain pounded my windshield as wind rocked the car and made an unearthly howl.

Hand on the door handle, I hesitated giving it a push and jumping out. I peered into the gloom, feeling nervous and silly at the same time. There's nothing out there, I told myself. It's just a storm. You're jumpy because of the deer. Finally, silly won out. I gave the door a shove, sprinted for the porch, took the steps two at a time, yanked the kitchen door open, and dove in. Breathing hard, I groped for the overhead light switch, flipped it on, and looked around. No bad creature—living or dead—greeted me. Relieved and a little embarrassed, I locked the kitchen door, grabbed a hand towel from the bathroom, rubbed my hair, and walked around the house to make sure all the windows were down tight and the front door was locked.

My computer was on the kitchen table, and I weighed the call of my comfy bed against curiosity about the storm. As usual, curiosity won. I flipped the laptop open and scanned the NOAA weather site. The storm was a hurricane remnant that models predicted would have swung eastward out to sea from Carolina's Outer Banks. Instead, it had barreled up the coast, flown across Cape Cod, and smashed into Maine's shores, and catching everyone off-guard.

NOAA quoted a back-peddling weatherman who blamed models based on historic data. I talked to the computer. "While you meteorologists denied climate change, climate scientists were developing their own models that anticipated stronger, more frequent, unpredictable storms. Go talk to them."

The weather was bad news for mariners, be they commercial fishermen or vacationers on sailboats and other craft. I pictured fishing boats in Macomek harbor thrashing wildly, straining on their moorings, and hoped my new friends were okay.

Overhead, the light flickered. Waiting, I mentally ran through the location of flashlights and candles. Luckily, the power gods did not plunge Spruce Harbor into darkness. Grateful to be home, dry—and with electricity—I took a hot shower and slid under the covers with a sigh. Rain pelted the bedroom windows, but I didn't hear it for long.

By seven o'clock Sunday morning, I was sitting at my pub

table overlooking the deck, mug of coffee in hand. Given the lack of anything healthy in my fridge, including milk, it was a good thing I could drink it black. I peered out at a grey, wet world. Trees, laden with water, slouched like old men. A barrel positioned beneath the gutter to collect rainwater overflowed onto the sodden grass. And it'd be raincoats and rubber boots for at least a few more days because, as NOAA informed me, "an unusual rain event stalled over the coast of Maine would likely deliver significant precipitation."

I'm a marine biologist, so water is one thing I'm prepared for. Outside, clad in red rain pants, green wellies, and a yellow slicker, I splashed about like a little kid.

MOI's parking lot was empty, not surprising given the time and day. I parked my car, trudged up the hill to the Neap Tide restaurant, and stepped into the usual early morning cacophony—lobstermen at the counter quarreling with one another, crew members throwing barbs across wooden tables, the racket of dirty dishes on their way to the kitchen. Passing the row of lobstermen on stools, I realized they were talking about our harbor and the storm.

"Jeezum crow, it was bad out theah."

"You're tellin' me. Swear ta god, I thought it was gonna be bumper boats in the habah. Lobstah boats strainin' on moorings like them chunks o' granite on the bottom was gonna come right up."

I winged a prayer for the Macomek families and took my usual little table in the back corner. Sally, Neap Tide's owner, slid a mug of black coffee toward me and wiped her forehead with her sleeve.

I took a sip. As usual, it was hot, crisp, and chocolaty, "Sally, you make the best coffee. Hey, you live on Spruce Harbor River. What's it like with this storm?"

She rolled her eyes. "'Twas worse with Hurricane Floyd. Gawd, that was awful. But she's runnin' pretty good this mornin'. Bet our basement's gonna be flooded. Okay, hon. What's it gonna be?"

My stomach had growled as I walked up the hill so I ordered the whole shebang—eggs, toast, hash browns, fishcakes.

Sally patted her substantial chest and winked. "Be careful, Mara. Bettah put on them runnin' shoes or you'll look like me."

After breakfast I turned down River Road to check out the torrent. Descending, I walked faster and faster. Some people chase tornadoes, others rainbows. Swirling, rolling, pounding, dangerous, deadly—it's the awesome power of water that makes my heart beat faster.

I reached the bridge and looked down over the rail. The reach was normally littered with Volkswagen-size boulders, but no rocks were visible in the turbid torrent below. Trees sailed by like they were made of Styrofoam.

"Goddamn."

The voice I knew so very well had come from behind. As I spun around, my hand flew to my heart. "Ted. I, ah, didn't hear you walk up."

He stepped onto the sidewalk next to the railing and hollered, "With this racket, I can see why. Lord, it's amazing! Where'd all this water come from?"

"Eventually, all things merge into one," I said.

Ted finished the sentence. "And a river runs through it."

We stood there side by side as the swirling, churning river raced down to the sea. I glanced at my former lover—the chiseled profile softened by dimples, soft lips, and wavy, straw-colored hair buffeted by the wind. My finger twitched as I longed to push a lock up off his eye.

What do you say to the lover you backed away from but desperately wish you hadn't? I went for safe—and lame.

"Um, well, guess I'll head up to the lab."

He turned and studied my face so long I could feel my cheeks reddening. Finally he said, "Think I'll hang out here for a while."

I trudged up the hill, my emotions as chaotic as the river behind me. I could have said something, anything, that signaled my feelings for Ted. Even, "Ted, it's great to see you" would have been better than nothing. Why didn't I?

"You're afraid, that's why," I whispered. "You can buck five-foot waves in a long, skinny boat, but you can't tell Ted you made a big mistake, love him desperately, and want to be with him."

I yanked open MOI's back door and was halfway up the granite stairs to my floor when I stopped and slowly turned around. Something was different, not right. Closing my eyes, I let my other senses take over. The air was damp brine but more biting than usual. Eyes still closed, I strained to listen. The sound of seawater flowing through pipes briefly echoes up the stairs when someone opens the double doors to the basement, but what I was hearing was different—constant and much, much louder.

I ran down the stairs and stopped short of the basement's bottom step because it was underwater. Then I stepped down into water halfway up my calves and peered through the double door's window.

Dull sunlight spilled through rows of casement windows onto an aquatic maelstrom. White plastic pipes along the walls—the pipes that carried seawater in and out of aquaria and tanks—were submerged. Walkways between tables had become swirling streams. And scariest of all, rows of oversized aquaria normally four feet off the concrete floor on the wooden tables were inches from being submerged by the flood churning around them.

I ran a finger through the water and touched it to my lips. The taste was brackish, not full-strength seawater like it should have been.

Those aquaria held marine animals—fish, crabs, starfish, squid, mussels and clams—all of which would die in brackish water. And in one of the aquaria was Homer. I didn't know how long a lobster lasted in half-strength seawater but guessed it was minutes.

I sloshed through the water back to the stairs, yanked the cell phone from my back pocket, and called MOI's emergency number. The phone rang once, twice, three times, four.

"Come on. Come on."

Pause. "If this is an emergency, dial nine-one-one...."

I jabbed my finger to end the call. "Of course, it's an emergency!"

Spruce Harbor dispatch answered the 911 right away. "This is Dr. Mara Tusconi at MOI. The basement's completely flooded and nobody's answering the institution's emergency number."

I didn't recognize her voice. "Are you in any danger?"

"No. No, I'm fine."

"Where are you, Dr. Tusconi?"

"In the back stairwell near the basement."

"Okay. Stay right there. Emergency personnel will arrive very soon."

I lowered myself onto a dry step and stared at the double doors. Homer was in that flooded basement. If the swirling water poured into his home, my buddy would be swept out into an underwater hurricane. I pictured him tumbling into aquaria, nets, and other paraphernalia typically left lying about.

"That's not gonna happen," I said.

Dropping the phone on the step, I got to my feet, splashed over to the double doors, and gave one a shove. The sudden deluge nearly threw me back against the stairs, but I managed to slide through the half-foot opening and let the door slam behind me. The cavernous room I knew so well was utterly unrecognizable. As a kid, I'd often crunched across the salt-encrusted floor and pressed my nose against aquaria to watch barnacles wave their lacy food collectors and baby lobsters zip about with their claws outstretched like tiny supermen.

Without a thought, torrents of storm water had swept aside manmade order along with a child's precious memories.

Stunned by the assault of the thundering inflow, I held onto the closest table in numbing cold water halfway up my thigh and forced myself to focus. Okay, Homer's aquarium was about thirty feet in front of me. That wasn't far, but I'd have to buck the current to get there. After I scooped him out of the tank, I'd need something to put him in for the trip back. A red bucket bobbed into an aquarium on next table over. Still holding on, I shuffle-waded over and floated it within reach on the way back.

Jeans offer no protection against the cold, and my stinging calves and thighs were already on their way to uncontrollable numbness. As a sea kayaker, I knew how astonishingly fast hypothermia led to mental confusion. Quickstepping, the edge of the table at my belly and bucket in the crux of my arm, I pushed through the current.

By the time I reached Homer minutes later, my legs were dead stumps. He lay in the bottom of his tank as usual but certainly knew something was amiss. Antennae raised and moving back and forth, he elevated his carapace off the bottom with his walking legs and shifted to and fro.

"Come on, baby. I'm getting you out of here."

I dipped the bucket into the tank to partly fill it with seawater. Then, as gently as I could manage, I reached in and lowered the lobster into the bucket. He settled at the bottom and waved his eyestalks at me. "Buddy, I'll take good care if it kills me."

My arms started to shake so violently I could barely hold onto the table. If I didn't get the hell out of the water within a couple of minutes, I could slide into unconsciousness as Homer slid into deadly brackish water. Taking a couple of deep breaths to push down panic, I considered my options again. Rushing water in the direction I was going meant a faster return trip, but the current was also a hazard. I'd have to hold onto the table with uncontrollable digits and keep Homer's bucket from drifting away. Swirling water made both bad options.

I'd tried to walk a few feet toward the exit when I knew that wasn't going to work. My senseless limbs wouldn't obey commands from my brain.

I glanced down at the lobster. He peered up at me. "Guess I'm going for a full body experience."

In one quick movement, I slid onto my back, stuck my legs out toward the doors, and grasped Homer's upright bucket with my thighs.

"Never had a lobster this near my privates before," I announced.

Homer and I rocketed toward the exit. We were nearly there when one of the double doors opened a bit. Ted poked his head through, stepped in, and stopped my accelerating arrival with his outstretched hands.

13

I DIDN'T REMEMBER TELLING THE EMERGENCY FOLKS I WAS only mildly hypothermic, but the nurse checking my blood pressure assured me I did.

"Yes, ma'am. You came in like a wet dog, all wrapped in blankets tellin' us that. We got you out of those soggy clothes and into bed with warm compresses on your middle. You warmed up pretty good."

Blinking, I turned my head on the pillow. I was lying in a hospital bed surrounded by a sliding white curtain.

"Where am I?"

"An urgent care facility just north of Spruce Harbor."

"The place on Route One?"

"That's it."

That I'd often driven by my present location was reassuring. Voices drifted through the curtains. "Sounds like there's other people here."

"Yes, ma'am. This storm's made all sorts of trouble for folks an' you're not the only one who got hypothermic."

"By the way, what was my temperature when I came in?"

She patted my leg. "I know you're an MOI scientist, deah. Ninety-five degrees. On the cusp of moderate hypothermia." She pulled off the cuff. "Blood pressure's very good. You should be able to go home soon. Your godfather Angelo is waiting to see you. Ready for him?"

My smile answered her question.

Angelo pulled back the curtain a bit and stepped in. "How're you feeling?"

"Good. They wanted to keep me here for a while but will release me in a little while. What time is it?"

"Mid-morning, about ten."

"Fill me in on what happened. I'm still a little fuzzy."

Somber, he sat on the edge of the bed.

I slid my hand toward him. He covered it with his own, warm and roughened by decades working on and around the sea.

"I'm sorry to make you worry again," I said.

He gave my hand a little squeeze and released it. "You did a very good thing. With nobody in the building on a Sunday morning, who knows what could've happened if the water kept coming in."

"I assume it was the storm, but what *did* happen?"

"MOI guys are still working that out. It looks like the main seawater outflow pipe got clogged at the same time storm drains outside overflowed into the basement. But the water's got to go way down before they know. And before you ask, the lobster is fine. He's in that big display aquarium on the first floor."

"Thanks for the update and, um, for not telling me that saving him was a harebrained idea."

He stood. "Of course it was harebrained. But you've done worse. I'm just happy to see you're doing so well. They'll tell me when can leave."

More tired than I wanted to admit, I said, "If you can give me a ride to my car, I'll head home."

I closed my eyes to rest when the voice, his voice, drifted through my thoughts. Was I dreaming?

"Mara?" Ted said. "Okay if I come in?"

My mouth was so dry it was hard to talk. "Sure," I croaked.

He pushed the curtain aside and stepped in. I patted the bed.

Ted chose the spot Angelo had just left. "You look pretty good. Feel okay?"

I reached over for the glass beside the bed and sucked up some water though a straw. "That's better. Yeah, I'm fine and can leave in a little while." My hand itched to slide over his, but I didn't move. "Hey, thanks for the help."

He laughed and shook his head. "I didn't do much of anything, just opened the door a crack and got real surprised by an accelerating oceanographer with a bucket."

Ted's positive attitude was a relief. After my kidnapping on Haida Gwaii, he'd complained that "trouble followed me around." Since I didn't go out of my way to find trouble—not usually, anyway—I considered the observation unfair. Was it my fault I happened to stumble across dead people a time or two? The difference of opinion hadn't helped our relationship any.

"Well," I said, "the emergency crew arrived right after that, things got confusing, and I barely said 'boo' to you."

He stood. "You were kind of out it then. Just wanted to check that you're okay." He turned toward the curtain.

"Ted?"

He looked back. "Yeah?"

"It's really nice to see you."

The grin was shy. "Me too you."

I got home late in the day, stashed groceries in the fridge, and headed outside for a stroll along the beach. Crises have a way of helping you realize what's really important. Writing grant proposals, reviewing research papers, and everything else on my to-do list could wait. I felt good, Homer was safe, MOI's basement was draining, and the afternoon sun warmed my face. Everything I witnessed made me smile—bright red clusters of beach rosehips shining against the dune's green foliage, beach hoppers that defined pandemonium when I lifted the dried seaweed they hid under, terns that rocketed straight down into the sea and came up with a tiny fish.

Even thinking about Ted didn't hurt. Our interactions had been friendly if brief. Maybe things…I shook my head. That was too much to think about now.

After a dinner of grilled salmon and salad, I watched a little TV, read my latest mystery until I was restless, and picked up an old newspaper lying on the coffee table. The date, September thirteenth, tugged at my brain. Of course, I thought, Lester said Buddy died on the thirteenth, an unlucky number, especially for fishermen. Someone on Macomek had mentioned another terrible event that took place on the thirteenth of some month. I closed my eyes for a moment and Abby's voice drifted into memory. "Lester doesn't go out the thirteenth of August, September, October, any month. That's when he got caught in that awful storm and Cody, his sternman, died."

Before the basement flood interrupted my day, I'd planned to go online to read an account of that event. I flipped open the computer and searched with "Lester Crawford," "Macomek," and "storm" as keywords. I didn't learn anything new, but the account led me to an obituary.

Cody Booth September 13, 1975–September 13, 1995

The family of Cody Booth sadly announce Cody's untimely death, the result of a boating accident off Macomek island. Cody was born October 13, 1975 to Alice and Harold Booth and graduated from Rockland High School in 1993. Funeral services.…

I didn't read the rest. A young man gone in an instant on his twentieth birthday was just too ghastly. Shaking my head, I set the computer to sleep mode.

My watch said it was just short of ten. Despite starting the day borderline hypothermic, I knew Lester's horror and Cody's dreadful end would make sleep difficult. But a distraction might help.

I walked out onto the deck. The big dipper lay low in the sky. What was the saying for Maine? Spring up, fall down for the dipper's position. Yes, that was it.

Below, water sloshed back and forth on the beach. A lovely evening, warm for September, not much wind. An evening ideal for my annual check-out-the-bioluminescence venture. The perfect distraction.

Bioluminescence happens when a chemical reaction releases light energy. Organisms that glow—fireflies, fungi, deep-sea fish, and the rest—share the same chemical mechanism but not necessarily the same purpose. Fireflies use the light to attract mates, deep-sea fish to catch prey, and some squid to confuse predators.

The source of my bioluminescent quest could be tiny floating dinoflagellates or larger comb jellies. For once, I'd try to switch off my science brain and just take in the phenomenon's beauty.

I carried my kayak and gear down to the beach, pulled a scribbled version of Charles Darwin's description of bioluminescence from my pocket, flipped on a flashlight, and read it aloud. The young Darwin had spent four long years at sea on the HMS Beagle collecting specimens around the world. He'd also left flowery accounts of the voyage.

"The vessel drove before her bows two billows of liquid phosphorus, and in her wake she was followed by a milky train."

Excited to see my own "liquid phosphorous" and properly fitted out in my wetsuit, lifejacket, and spray skirt, I climbed into the kayak and drifted away from the beach. The first sweep of my paddle left behind the most brilliant sparkle-swath I'd seen in Maine waters. Elated, I took a few more strokes, rested the paddle across the cockpit, and let the gentle current take me where it would through the shallow water. A halo of shimmer bathed the long, skinny boat. I splashed a hand across the surface of the water, grinned as bits of blue-white light appeared on command, and did it again. Paddling back to my beach, I created a riot of sparkles with each stroke.

After the boat was safely above the high-tide line a half hour later, I walked back to the water and waded in. It wasn't overly warm, but the wetsuit was enough for a quick immersion. Floating on my back, I made like I was a kid lying in snow making snow angels. Each sweep of my arms and legs enveloped them in a swirling glow. A spectacular "bioluminescent bay" on the island of Vieques off Puerto Rico has something like a 100,000 dinoflagellates per liter. At night there, I've stood on a boat looking down on kids doing the snow angel thing. That's fantasyland for real.

After a hot shower, I was definitely ready for bed. Grateful to have witnessed one of the ocean's spectacles, I slept peacefully through the night.

At sunup Monday morning, I stood at my office window and watched lobster boats chug through a harbor turned crimson by the gaudy red-yellow sky. Before returning in late afternoon, the guys in those boats—Spruce Harbor has no female lobstermen—would have pulled up hundreds of traps, saved keeper lobsters and returned the others, re-baited each trap, and slid it off the stern. It was dangerous, back-breaking work, and I admired the hell out of them for doing it day after day.

I'd just erased number four on my whiteboard's to-do list when Laurie Culligan knocked on my door. Laurie was well known for her research on juvenile lobsters, and I was delighted to see her.

Clad in green twill pants and a red and black checked flannel shirt, she looked like an off-duty game warden. Knowing Laurie, she might have been one in her early days. The scientist straddled the wooden chair beside my desk, pushed dirty-blond hair off her face, leaned back in the chair, and crossed her arms. "Hi there, Mara. How's it going? What's it been, two years?"

"Something like that," I said. "I know you helped organize the lobster meeting. That's great."

"Lobstermen are asking about warming and lobsters. This is a small meeting, maybe fifty total."

I nodded. "It's so important that they're learning what's known and what's not from the experts. So how's the research going?"

"Several of us are studying how temperature impacts juvenile lobsters."

"Sure. I've read your papers."

Quick nod. "That's why I'm here, actually. There's a new field site I'd like to check out on scuba and my usual dive partner is sick. Do you have any time later today to dive with me? The site's in Friendship."

I glanced at my wristwatch. "Gordy and I are driving up to the Maine Patrol office in Rockland in a bit. You know what happened to Buddy Crawford, of course. We've got information they might be interested in. Gordy can drop me off in Friendship when we're done."

She shook her head. "Poor Buddy. He was a really, really good guy." She stood. "Can you meet in Friendship at the public boat launch at eleven? I'll have all the dive gear and can drive you back here."

"It'll be terrific to see what you do up close and personal," I said.

As Laurie shut the door behind her, I glanced at the

whiteboard. I'd made progress, but half the list was still up there. Everything but Alise's grant could wait and a research dive with legendary lobster researcher Laurie Culligan was something I simply couldn't pass up. Knowing Laurie, we'd be in wetsuits, not drysuits, and I'd come out blue-lipped and shivering. Harvey and I joked about the scuba dives in warm places like Hawaii or the Caribbean that never seemed to happen.

Alise arrived as I was organizing the papers sprawled across my desk. She pointed at the tallest pile. "What're those?"

Grant proposals and scientists' research papers I promised to review."

"How many?"

"Um, five. Maybe six."

"Ouch."

"What you have to look forward to when you finish your degree. What time is it?"

Alise pulled a phone out of her denim jacket. "Eight"

"Good Just enough time to go through any questions you have with your proposal."

14

A T 8:45 I SAT ON MOI'S GRANITE FRONT STEPS EATING A bagel while I waited for Gordy to pick me up. The weather was perfect for September—bright sun and a cool breeze that hinted at the fall chill on its way. The front door slammed behind me as one of Betty Buttz's army boots tapped my thigh.

"Shove ovah, Mara, so we can chat a bit."

Betty, a legendary retired oceanographer who'd broken the gender barrier on oceanographic research vessels before I was born, lowered herself onto the step with a grunt and straightened out her legs one at a time. "Goddamn arthritis. It's awful getting old, Mara."

"My mother used it say it beats the alternative."

"I do recall Bridget saying just that." She turned and examined my face with such intensity it was hard not to look away. "You're more and more like your mother every day."

My eyes tightened. Would this pain ever diminish?

Betty didn't appear to notice and said, "Heard about you finding that flood in the basement. Last time that happened was in the ninety-nine hurricane. Also heard you came across Buddy Crawford's body under Gordy's mussel raft. Busy lady."

"Yeah. Gordy and I are going up to the Maine Marine Patrol office to talk with them about that. That's why I'm sitting here. If those guys have made progress finding Buddy's killer, they're keeping it quiet. Hey, weren't you involved in that investigation of a crewmember who died on an oceanographic ship a couple of years ago?"

"Yes, I was. A core-drilling cruise. Poor guy was done in by another crewmate."

"Any advice for finding Buddy's killer?"

"Just the usual."

Gordy's truck came into view at the end of the street. I popped the last bit of bagel into my mouth, licked a dab of butter off my lip, and stood. "I've got to go, Betty. What's the usual?"

"You know. Power, money, love—or all three."

Gordy and I made small talk until he turned north on Route One. "Okay, I said. Let's figure out what we're going to say."

He passed a slow-moving car with an out-of-state plate. "Damn, it'll be good when tourists stay home for the wintah."

"It's says 'Vacationland' on our license plates, Gordy. Money in lots of locals' pockets."

"Ayuh, well, Marine Patrol. We're gonna talk with Larry LeClair. Good guy."

Always the good old boys, I thought. "Sergeant LeClair stayed with the body under your raft overnight. An officer named DelBarco was also on the Marine Patrol boat, but she had to go home at the end of her shift."

"I'll tell LeClair all 'bout Tyler," he said.

Pushing down my irritation, I sighed. "Like I pointed out a couple of times, you and Patty have no proof about Tyler. You can't just say he's guilty because you think he is."

He adjusted his rear view mirror. "Patty's positive."

"That doesn't make her right. Naturally, you should explain what you think about Tyler and why. Just don't go barreling in there claiming he's guilty, okay?"

He tapped a finger on the steering wheel. "What else?"

"Your idea that someone, or more likely at least two people, killed Buddy on Macomek and left the island with him in a boat. That makes good sense."

We passed an ice cream place that already looked closed for the season.

"Someone like LeClair would've figured that out already," he said.

"That they planned to dump the body somewhere onshore but saw your raft as great place to stash it—it's an interesting idea he may not have thought of."

"I'll tell 'em that. No, wait. Why don't you? LeClair might think I was makin' somethin' up 'cause it's my raft."

"Okay, I'll explain the raft idea. What else?"

"Tyler's the big thing."

Tyler, Tyler, always Tyler. "Gordy I know she's, um, a good friend, but Patty seems...I don't know, a little *too* sure Tyler did it. Does she have something against the guy?"

Gordy frowned. "Don't think so. She never said if she does. Tyler's got a bad side you don't know about. That's what Patty meant by—"

"Me being an outsider?"

"Yeah."

"So tell me."

Gordy glanced to the side, pulled out, and passed a slow-moving car. "'Nother outta-state. As a kid, Tyler was pretty wild. Drinkin', goin' with girls too young, throwin' money around."

"He's a skinny little guy," I said. "Could be he was trying to make up for his size."

"Maybe. Tyler lef' Macomek. Lobstahmen don't just take off like that."

"He did? Well, I have to agree with you there. So besides Tyler, who could it be? I've only met a few of the lobstermen out there, but they seem like pretty good guys."

"They are. But if one of 'em offed Buddy, it's for a good reason an' nobody's gonna say one word."

"So Marine Patrol will have a heck of a time solving this murder."

"Ayuh. That's why I asked you ta snoop around. Somebody might let somethin' slip 'cause you're like a tourist."

"Didn't you hint around that I was an investigator?" I asked.

"Ayuh. I tol' Calvin Ives I was tryin' ta spook Tyler inta takin' off. Calvin thought that was a real interestin' idea an' passed it around."

That Macomek's lobstermen discussed who I was and wasn't pissed me off. "Goddamn it Gordy, it's like I was specimen on display out there."

"'Course you were, Mara."

We passed two gulls fighting over a bag of chips in an empty parking lot. I said, "So bottom line is Marine Patrol's got a heck of a job figuring out what happened to Buddy."

"Ayuh. It's why I took my sweet time talkin' with them. Gave 'em a chance ta poke around an' not jus' jump on me when they're stuck."

"We haven't discussed that. I assume LeClair's pretty angry with you."

Gordy shrugged. "He wasn't real happy on the phone."

The Marine Patrol office was classic institutional architecture. Concrete, Formica, linoleum in gray and puke green. LeClair met us at the front desk and led us back to a small, spare room with a rectangular metal table bordered by a half-dozen wooden chairs that bore nicks, scratches, and scars. He gestured toward the two chairs closest to the door and circled around to the other side, an oversized notebook under his arm

LeClair flipped the notebook open, thumbed a few pages

with the eraser end of a pencil, and cleared his throat. "Nice to see you again, Dr. Tusconi." He nodded at Gordy. "Mr. Maloy."

I stole a glance at Gordy. He stiffened in his seat.

"As you know, we've got a real serious situation here. It's nearly a week after Dr. Tusconi found Buddy Crawford's body under the aquaculture raft, and this is still an unsolved homicide." Slow pivot toward Gordy. "It didn't help that you disappeared for two days."

"Like I said on the phone, we went out ta Macomek ta see if...."

LeClair cut him off. "We prefer to do the investigating ourselves."

Gordy studied his hands.

LeClair lifted a pen from his shirt pocket. "Having said that, I'd like to hear your thoughts and ideas about who killed Buddy."

For the next hour, Gordy and I laid out everything we'd talked about in the car. To his credit, Gordy backed off a bit on Tyler's guilt. LeClair had already come up with the idea that the stashing the body under the raft was a last-minute decision.

LeClair was very interested in what Tyler had said to me about Buddy. "Can you remember Tyler's exact words?" he asked.

I looked at the ceiling and imagined myself standing in the cemetery listening to Tyler. "Something about Buddy spending a lot of money on a new boat and other things. Tyler wondered where the money had come from since Buddy's lobster catch hadn't increased."

LeClair rubbed his forehead. "Hard to know what to make of that. This Tyler doesn't seem like a reliable source of information. Also, if he's got something to hide, he'll shift the blame elsewhere." He looked down at his notebook. "Let's see. Besides Tyler, what lobstermen did you meet on Macomek?"

The question surprised me. "I only talked to a couple—Calvin Ives and Malicite Dupris. Why?"

"Just give me your impression."

"As I'm sure you know, Calvin is the highliner out there. Abby Burgess, the woman I stayed with, told me that people looked to him for leadership. I talked to him very briefly. He struck me as intelligent, personable. I spent more time with Malicite because he's involved in a NOAA project in which lobstermen attach temperature monitors to their traps. He was very generous with his time. I liked him a lot."

LeClair tapped the end of his pen next to what he'd just written like he was deciding something. "Dupris has dual citizenship, US and Canadian."

My response was quick. "He told me he spent time in Canada."

"Hold up. This might not be relevant, but he was in and out of juvie up there for a couple years."

I'd watched enough cop shows to know that "juvie" referred to a juvenile detention facility. "Some guys have a hard time as kids. What of it?"

"We're looking into the background of anyone who knew Buddy well. Part of what we do. I'm telling you about his history to see if the information rings any bells."

I shook my head. "Malicite seemed like a smart, great guy. At the harbor I did overhear a conversation that sounded fishy. A couple of guys whose voices I didn't recognize said things like 'We agreed on what we had to do' and 'Talking about it is one thing but doing it is another.'"

LeClair wrote something in his notebook and looked up. "Hard to know what to make of that. Do you know their names?"

"One of them was called Richie. I don't know about the other one."

LeClair asked, "Okay. Anything else you want to tell me?"

"That's it. I am wondering if Buddy drowned or what."

He shook his head. "Can't tell you anything about that. Ongoing investigation."

LeClair scanned his notes, closed the book, and looked at Gordy. "There's an angle we're working that I'd like your take on. We've been told that Buddy may have sold drugs to teenagers on the mainland. Do you know anything about that?"

I expected Gordy to say he didn't. Instead, he just sat there biting his lip.

"Mr. Maloy?"

"Patty Burgess out on Macomek said something about that. You should talk to her."

LeClair said he'd like to speak with Gordy alone, so I left the room and closed the door. A minute passed. Two. Four. I looked up and down the hallway. Nobody was around so I pressed an ear to the closed door. Muffled voices, one louder than the other. When the Gordy and LeClair finally emerged, I was leaning against the wall studying my nails.

We climbed into Gordy's truck and turned south on U.S. Route One.

"Drop me off at the Friendship boat launch," I said.

"Ayuh. That's what you tol' me."

We were nearly there when I couldn't stand it any longer. "So what did LeClair want?"

"Let's see. We talked about trap poaching."

"Be serious."

"We did. And he said if I ever took off like that again, he'd pull my license."

"What was that business about Buddy selling drugs?"

He tapped the wheel with his finger. "Patty said somethin'. That's all I know."

"I don't suppose you learned anything about how Buddy died."

He pulled into the boat launch parking lot right on time. "Nope, but I will."

I stepped onto Laurie's dive boat and turned back, but Gordy and his truck were already gone.

Finned feet squarely planted on the inflatable's deck, fingers gripping a handle, Laurie sat poised on the gunwale opposite me a half hour later. In a wetsuit, weight belt, dive mask, scuba tank, regulator, and buoyancy compensator, she was unrecognizable. The woman was all business.

"Let's go through this again."

I shifted on the bouncy gunwale and pushed the mask up off my face.

"We usually monitor juvenile lobsters in real shallow water." She said. "But with the Gulf of Maine warming, they may be settling in water that's deeper and colder than where I've been looking for them. Not good if you're trying to predict how many lobsters will be out there for lobstermen to catch in the future. So like I said, this is a scouting trip for a possible new sampling station. We'll start at roughly seventy-five feet, and move closer to shore and shallower water. Thirty feet is what I'm most interested in, but I figured you'd like to see the deeper habitats."

On the way over to the dive site, a protected area well away from boat traffic, Laurie had warned me that the most of the dive wouldn't be too exciting. I didn't care. Being underwater—the hidden domain of the biology I studied—was always a treat, no matter what I saw. Starting the dive in stunning deep-water kelp beds, habitat for organisms I didn't often see in their home territory, would add to the adventure. I very much appreciated the thought.

Regulator in hand, she said, "That's it. Any questions?"

"Houston, I am good to go."

"Great. I'll start down the anchor line. The visibility is probably poor. Keep me within view at all times, and I'll do the same with you." Then, with one practiced move, she leaned back and disappeared over the side.

Still balanced on the gunwale, I settled the mask over my eyes, saw squat, yanked the thing off, and delivered a mouthful of spit onto the faceplate. A quick rub cleared the condensation. Mask properly in place, I popped the regulator into my mouth, looked skyward, fell back into the water, and rolled upright underwater.

The first moments of a dive are always magical for me. In an instant, ambient everyday sounds I'd barely noticed—waves sloshing against the hull, drone of distant boat motors, harsh laugh of gulls overhead—were gone in an instant. I'd entered the dense, utterly foreign world of watery creatures that extract oxygen from seawater through specialized organs like gills. It's a domain instantly deadly to terrestrial air breathers who disobeyed the rules or pushed them beyond the limit.

Fatality rates for divers matched motor vehicle deaths. Nearly ninety percent of dead divers broke a cardinal rule and went down alone.

As Laurie predicted, abundant floating microscopic plankton, derived from the Greek word for "wanderer," reduced visibility considerably. Still, I could easily see her holding onto the bowline ten feet below. I glided down and hovered next to her.

She made a circle with her thumb and forefinger and extended the other digits up—the divers' way of asking, "Are you okay?"

I repeated the gesture. "I'm okay."

Next she made a fist with one hand and extended her thumb downward. "I'm going down."

I nodded and repeated the okay maneuver.

Holding onto the line, hand over hand I slowly descended. When the weight of the water above pushed uncomfortably on my eardrums, I had to stop and clear my ears—create pressure inside my ear canal to match the outside water pressure. The tricky procedure required me to pinch my nose and gently blow air into my Eustachian tubes. The welcome "pop" told me I'd succeeded.

Laurie, who descended more quickly, hovered above the bottom until I reached her. She signaled again with the okay maneuver, and I returned the gesture. Laurie pointed in the direction I knew was shoreward. Side by side, we leisurely glided toward a kelp bed where golden-brown seaweeds, about ten feet long and a foot in diameter, streamed sideways with the current.

The seaweed, what scientists call algae, had scientific names that rolled off a marine biologist's tongue: *Alaria esculenta* and *Saccharina latissima*. As the name "saccharina" implies, animals from sea urchins to humans eat that particularly sweet alga. Thankfully, some of Maine's maritime farmers now grow sugar kelp, which takes pressure off nature's kelp communities.

A cluster of Maine kelp is called a bed, although forest would better portray the scene we floated above. But to creatures from the air world, this was a bizarre forest indeed. Swaying idly this way and that as they surrendered to the current's will, amber seaweed "trees" were bathed in otherworldly green light. And like birds zipping through dense trees, clusters of tiny fish flashed silver as they wove in unison between swinging kelp blades. I dove down to the bottom and traversed the forest's edge to explore how the kelp stayed put. Like a tangle of tree roots in appearance, each kelp blade has what's called a holdfast. I tried to poke a finger into the structure, but its grip on the rocky bottom was so fierce I failed. Not surprising since this anchor, which doesn't carry water or nutrients up the blade, has to withstand swirling currents that would toss my body about like a rag doll.

I was happy to see a scattering of green sea urchins, a little larger than golf balls, clinging to the kelp blades. Kelp is a preferred food for these herbivores, and large masses of them can decimate a bed with their sharp pointy teeth. Usually their numbers are kept in check by predators including lobsters, crabs, and several fish species. That changed in the late nineteen-eighties when Maine humans—in search of the urchin's orange-yellow reproductive tissue called "uni"—became their top predator. As a result, urchin numbers plummeted.

Urchin roe is a delicacy in Japan and elsewhere and a good urchin diver could make $5000 and more a week, depending on the season. Total landings in the state reached $40 million in 1992. Unfortunately, the boom quickly went bust as the unregulated industry decimated the urchins. We humans never seem to learn.

I was tempted to glide through the forest and investigate dozens of animal species it sheltered from current and predators—wonders like purple sponges, sea slugs, wave whelks, sea squirts, blood stars, and scallops. But I didn't. My last dive in British Columbia's magnificent kelp forests had nearly ended in catastrophe when a sudden current hurled me into a tangle of kelp. Wrapped like a mummy, I managed to slice through the binds with my dive knife and the encouragement of a sympathetic seal. The experience was not something I wanted to repeat.

Beyond the kelp bed where Laurie waited, there was still plenty to see. Below and on the water, the Gulf of Maine is astoundingly diverse. The most recent marine census yielded a whopping three thousand species including over six hundred kinds of fish, a hundred eighty birds, thirty mammals, and over seven hundred different types of algae. The numbers surprised scientists because people have fished, crisscrossed, and thrived on the productive waters that stretch from Cape Cod to Nova Scotia for hundreds of years. It was humbling to recognize how little biologists knew about this historic body of water literally in their back yard.

Clearly eager to examine the gravelly shallows ahead, Laurie flicked her fins and glided on before I reached her. I matched her speed and tried to register each new creature below. A flower-like pink anemone waved its frilly tentacles, trying to entangle and stun prey foolish enough to come within reach. Words from Jules Verne's *Twenty Thousand Leagues Under the Sea* popped into my mind—that the ocean is a "curious anomaly…where the animal kingdom blossoms, and the vegetable does not!"

Beyond the anemone and humped over a clam, a starfish wiggled hundreds of little tube feet and pulled apart its prey. A sea urchin grazed algae from a rock face, leaving a barren swath in its wake. What looked like a codfish darted away and scared the crap out of me.

The good-sized lobster was too alluring to pass by. I caught up with Laurie and with hand signals managed to covey my desire to stay put and lobster-watch. She nodded, pointed to her destination, and showed me all five fingers. The shallows she wanted to see were within view, and she only needed five minutes to check them out. Good. I could keep an eye on her and enjoy the lobster at the same time.

Twitching its antennae as I approached, the good-sized crustacean backed into its hidey-hole between two rocks. Unlike a human shackled with scuba gear, the lobster is beautifully adapted to its environment. Its two long antennae act as sentinels for vibration, and sensory hairs covering its ten legs can "taste" the waters for chemical clues. Having no need for heavy weight belts, lobsters are neutrally buoyant and can tiptoe along the bottom on their walking legs.

Dead and red, a lobster draped across a dinner plate looks nothing like the live animal a foot from my dive mask. For one thing, live lobsters are neither red nor all the same color. A varying mix of brown, dark blue, and green, lobsters can be as distinctive as human blonds, redheads, and brunettes.

They're also amazingly agile. Tiptoeing like a graceful ballerina one moment, the animal could blast itself across the bottom with a flip of its tail. As lobstermen with missing digits can testify, a lobster is an aggressive bugger that can get you with a swift, fierce snap of its pincer. Even wearing dive gloves, I wouldn't reach out to touch a live lobster. Extend a stick, and the animal will grab it and simply not let go.

Put all that together and you've got an animal that everyone loves to eat but hardly anyone truly loves. Unlike pandas and eagles, lobsters are not the least bit cuddly, majestic, or noble. Thankfully, the success of the lobstermen's conservation measures such as size limits mean the animals aren't likely to be threatened by extinction anytime soon.

On the way back to the boat, a foot-long fish that looked very much like a cod glided beneath us on the bottom. Given the cod's endangered status, I was surprised to see one so close to shore. When we reached the inflatable, I broke through the surface, let the regulator fall out of my mouth, and pushed the mask up off my face. Laurie clung to the boat's bow line.

"Wow, Laurie. The dive was terrific. That wasn't a codfish, was it?"

"Tomcod. The darn thing swam right in front of me earlier, but I was too busy checking out the bottom to pay attention to much else."

"Does that area seem like good juvenile lobster habitat?" I asked.

"It did look promising, but I won't know until they settle."

On the way out of town, we stopped at a house owned by Laurie's "friends of a friend." Nobody was around, but Laurie said they wouldn't mind if we used the hose to rinse seawater off the gear and ourselves. Much as I love the ocean, salt-encrusted skin is something I never got used to, so I was grateful.

Since Laurie was a walking lobster library, I quizzed her about the *Homarus americana's* future in the Gulf of Maine.

"I'm pretty careful about making predictions," she explained. "You know how lobstermen complain that scientists' dire warnings don't materialize. We're in a boom now many researchers didn't expect. Events like that keep me humble."

"I'm not a lobsterman," I said. "So give me your guarded opinion."

"Well, like I said earlier, I'm pretty worried about the mismatch between our low counts of juveniles and what lobstermen are getting in their traps. We don't know what it means, and that's pretty unsettling."

"Here's something else I'm been wondering about," I said. "If you were a lobsterman who understood that the Gulf of Maine is warming, where would you plan to set your strings in the coming years?"

"That's exactly the question Calvin Ives has been asking me," she said.

"Huh. Interesting."

"Actually, *ask* is putting it mildly. It's like the man's obsessed with the issue."

"He's a smart guy, and folks on Macomek look to him for leadership. I guess he understands that warming will be a big deal for lobsters sometime."

"I guess. He's coming into Spruce Harbor for the meeting this afternoon."

"Anyone else from the island?"

"You mentioned you talked to Malicite Dupris when you were out there. He'll be there." She downshifted as we approached a hill on the outskirts of Spruce Harbor. "Hey, we're meeting at six at the Lee Side for beers and burgers. Why don't you stop by?"

"Thanks," I said. "I might just do that. In any case, I'll see you at the meeting in a couple of hours."

15

HE POSTER TITLED "IMPACTS OF CLIMATE CHANGE ON
Maine Lobstering" directed me to MOI's smaller auditorium. I pulled open one of the double doors and walked
into an uncommon scene. In front of the row of seats, small
groups of sunburned lobstermen gestured wildly at significantly
paler scientists who interrupted them. Seated attendees flipped
through handouts or turned to others who'd just settled in next
to them. On the small stage, MOI's Director Frederick Dixon
called out without success for people to sit down and be quiet.
Someone walked across the stage and handed him a microphone.

Dixon's authoritative voice filled the room. "Please, everyone be seated so we can begin this important meeting. We have
a very full schedule."

The hubbub died down as people who were standing found
seats.

Dixon introduced himself and thanked everyone for coming. "As you all know, this is an unusual event. MOI has long
encouraged exchange between our scientists and Maine's fishing
industry, but this is the first time we have devoted a meeting
solely to lobstering. You will hear from scientists who study lobsters as well as from working lobstermen. As the meeting's title
signifies, the focus is on the future of Maine's lobster industry
in the context of climate change. Now I will hand things over to
Gordy Maloy, President of the Maine Lobster Alliance."

Gordy walked toward Dixon. The two shook hand and

traded places. Except for one time at a wedding, I'd never seen Gordy looking quite so put together. In place of his usual fringed canvas shorts, boots, and white socks he wore a clean pair of jeans and a tan chamois shirt tucked in.

Gordy pulled down the brim of baseball cap with one hand and held up the microphone with the other. "You hear me okay without this thing?"

Several guys called out that they could. Gordy walked to one the side of the podium. "That's bettah. Guys in this room lef' their strings early today so they could come ta this meetin'. That's a big deal. They're doin' it partly so scientists remembah that they're out on the watah every day. No machine or water test matches that kind of learning. On the othah hand, we know the Gulf o' Maine is changin' fast, even though sometimes we don't want ta admit it." Laughter rippled across the audience. "We don't know how fast or what's gonna change, so we need ta keep up with what scientists find out. Our livelihood, kids, communities—all of it—depends on one thing." He gestured toward the audience. "I know folks in this room. They had dads, granddads, even great-granddads who caught bugs for a living. It's our life."

I'd never heard Gordy speak so powerfully about impacts of warming on Maine's lobster communities. Given the hush in the room, his message had hit home.

Laurie Culligan took Gordy's place and reviewed the schedule of speakers and coffee breaks. It was an ambitious agenda that included a dinner break at the Lee Side followed by an evening session. I wasn't sure how that would go after Lee Side beers, but the lobstermen couldn't take off more time. I scanned the schedule, noted when Laurie was speaking, and slipped out.

At the break, I left my office to take advantage of the free coffee. Cup in hand, I waited for Gordy to finish a conversation and tapped him on the shoulder. "Cousin, that was a terrific introduction to the meeting."

Gordy glanced to the side and, for the first time in my memory, the man blushed.

"Um, thanks."

"So how many Macomek lobstermen are here? It's a long trip for them."

"Malicite, Calvin, an' a couple other guys you didn't meet. Hope they don't make any trouble."

"Trouble?"

"They've been loud an' clear 'bout climate change. Money grab for scientists an' all that."

"Not too long ago, you said the same thing."

He shrugged. "Mos'ly I was givin' you a hard time. I know the Gulf 'o Maine is getting' hottah. What's causin' it, that's anothah thing. Big question is how it changes lobsterin'."

This was significant progress. "Wow, Gordy. I'm impressed. Do you know how many other lobstermen are coming around?"

He glanced at the big clock on the wall. "Laurie's speakin' after Barbara Poole talks about some kinda fishermen survey."

"I want to hear both of them, but who's Barbara Poole?"

"A lobsterman from Stonington."

Smiling at the irony of female and male bathrooms when women were called "lobstermen," I visited the women's facility, then slipped through the auditorium door and took a seat in the back.

Brown ponytail bobbing against her navy T-shirt, lobsterman Barbara Poole strode across the stage as if it were just her usual walk down the pier to her boat. Her lumberjack physique revealed that the woman hauled hundreds of fifty-odd-pound traps each working day. From the smiles and enthusiastic applause, it was obvious that her fellow fishermen liked and respected lobsterman Poole.

Smiling, Barbara acknowledged the response with a little wave. "Thanks everyone. It's great to see so many of us heah. The American Fisheries Center did a real interestin' survey an' asked if I'd present it in this meetin'."

Barbara went on to explain bullet points projected behind her. I learned that the American Fisheries Center had polled a thousand ground-fishing and lobstering permit holders. Since there were so many, they had to take a sample for some specific questions.

She faced the screen and directed a laser pointer on one of the bullets. "As you can see, about two-thirds checked the politically conservative box." She turned back toward the audience. "What we'd expect, right? But look at the next thing." She paused for effect, turned, and pointed at the next bullet. "Even though they're mostly conservative in their politics, four times as many fishermen said climate change is happening compared to those who said it's not."

A low murmur rippled through the audience.

"People who did the survey separated out lobstermen from different states. When asked if they'd noticed that waters where they trap are warmer now, more than six outta ten lobstermen from Maine said yes." She pointed the laser at the next line. "And, about eighty percent of them said climate change is the cause of the warmin' they see."

A guy in the middle of the audience wearing a green baseball cap shot to his feet. "What you're sayin' 'bout Maine lobstahmen an' global warmin'? That doesn't add up."

Nonplussed, Barbara said, "Explain what you mean."

"Not one single lobstahman I know thinks that. And I know a whole lotta lobstahmen."

Here and there, men in the audience nodded.

"Sure," Barbara said. "I get that. You need to understand that the people doin' this study couldn't get opinions from every single lobstahman 'cause there's too many. It's a sample, like they do for political elections."

Still on his feet, the lobsterman said, "That went real well in the president's election, didn't it?" He turned left and right for effect.

Hands on hips, Barbara fixed a killer stare at the lobsterman. "That's enough out of you, Richie Woodman. Sit down and lemme finish this talk."

Without another word, Richie did what he was told.

Barbara outlined some next steps, answered several questions, and returned to her seat in the front tow. Laurie Culligan strode across the stage and waited as her talk's title—"Repeated, Year-round Sampling of Juvenile Lobsters in the Intertidal Zone."—appeared on the screen behind her. Then she stood away from the podium and spoke directly to the audience with the confident and unhurried cadence of an experience presenter.

"For this talk I'll focus on how my team and I assess the number of recently settled juvenile lobsters and show you some recent data. For over ten years, our goal has been to identify lobster nurseries so we can protect them. The juvenile lobster data are also useful for predicting numbers of adult lobsters that could be trapped in the future."

Laurie went on to explain that throughout the year she and her field team returned to the same sampling sites at the very lowest tides. "We turn over rocks and count the juveniles in the same one-meter-square quadrants in each month. That way, we avoid all the difficulties of trying to count lobsters in the subtidal zone with scuba gear."

About halfway into her talk, Laurie showed a graph that

made many in the audience gasp. With the laser pointer, she drew a long downward line as steep as a ski slope. "As you can see, the number of juvenile lobsters in all our sites has dropped dramatically over the last ten years."

She faced the group again. "This is real puzzle because this steady downward trend in juvenile settlement has taken place when both lobster egg production and commercial catch are high. So what's going on?"

A photo of tiny lobster in the palm of a hand appeared on the screen. The miniature lobster looked about a half inch long.

"Here's a fourth-stage lobster, the juveniles we count. We think food availability for earlier stages may be the problem," she said.

Laurie went on to the next graph. "As you know, for several weeks newborn lobsters float near the surface and go through several molts. During this time they must eat and avoid being eaten, and it's the fourth molt survivors that settle on the bottom and hide. Some of our colleague's plankton tows show a sharp decline in copepods that closely mirrors the decline in fourth-stage lobster larvae. Tiny planktonic crustaceans named *Calanus finmarchicus* are the staple of the lobster larval diet. We don't know why the copepod numbers declined or whether that trend will continue.

Laurie pushed a bottom on her remote and the screen went blank. "I think I'll stop here folks and take your questions."

Hands throughout the auditorium shot up in the air. Both lobstermen and scientists were anxious for answers. "Does this mean that our lobstah catch will go down sometime soon?" "Could increase in predators explain the decline in lobster larvae and copepods?" "What about other places? Maybe you're just not lookin' for baby lobsters in the right spot?" "Could decline in juvenile settlement be related to rise in water temperature?"

Laurie addressed each question as clearly as she could, but she didn't have the definitive answers many wanted to hear. I left the auditorium and headed back to my office as people stepped onto the stage to talk with her.

"You still working?"

I rubbed my eyes and looked up from the computer. Harvey stood just inside my office door.

"Hey. Didn't hear you come in."

"I knocked, but you were in concentration mode."

Harvey teased me about my ability to tune out the world and completely fix my attention on work. Rolling my shoulders I said, "Think I'm finally caught up. What time is it?"

"Nearly six."

"Laurie and some lobstermen here for the meeting are going to the Lee Side for dinner. Think I'll go. Want to come along?"

Harvey shook her head. "The Auto Analyzer continues to takes its toll. I'm pooped and heading home."

"I'm pretty tired myself but don't have the energy to go food shopping or cook."

"When was the last time you ate at home, Mara? I thought Italians liked cooking."

I shut down my computer and stood up. "Ever since I found Buddy's body things've been, I don't know, batty."

"Batty?"

"You know, weird, funky, dotty."

"I could use any of those words to describe you at one time or another, Mara. Especially the last one."

The Lee Side bar didn't bother with marine bric-a-brac because its customers, people whose livelihood depended on the sea in one way or another, gave the place its identity. Crewmembers from MOI's research vessel *Intrepid* sat in booths along one of the walls. In howling wind and dripping with sea spray, those guys had stood right by me, more times than I could count, as we deployed instruments off the ship's stern. Just as important, they knew when we needed to get the hell off the lurching deck. One of the crew tipped his black cap. I waved back.

Joey, Lee Side's longtime owner, was polishing the already shiny long slab of oak that was the bar. I climbed onto a stool.

"Haven't seen you in here for a while," he said.

Ted and I sometimes stopped in the Lee Side after work. For obvious reasons, I didn't explain my absence.

"Got any white wine, Joey?"

"Not many requests for that. Gimme a minute." He ducked down behind the bar and quickly came up with a bottle of Pinot Grigio. "Good?"

"That's great." I looked over my shoulder while he poured. "Has the crew from Macomek gotten here yet?"

"Some of 'em are out on the deck an' two guy are in the back are playin' darts."

Joey had wisely set up the dartboard in a back corner where stray missiles were unlikely to hit an unsuspecting customer. Wine in hand, I walked the length of the bar, rounded the corner, and stopped. Calvin Ives held a dart in his right hand and stared at the board, unblinking. Utterly still, the man looked like a statue. To Calvin's side and back a step, Malicite regarded Calvin with raised eyebrows. When he saw me, he winked.

Like a cat ready to pounce on an unsuspecting bird, Calvin's complete focus was on that board. Then, with a lightning fast snap of the wrist, he released the missile and followed through until his arm was fully extended. The dart landed solidly in the middle of the board.

He applauded himself and yelled, "Ha! Got ya."

While Calvin gathered darts for another game, I took a seat at an empty table against the wall. Sipping my wine, I watched the game and ordered and ate a burger and fries. If Calvin noticed I was there, he didn't let on.

I was used to competitive guys who worked out, bragged about how fast they'd run the weekend's marathon, and let everyone know when their grant proposal had been funded. But Calvin's behavior—fist pounding his palm, hoots when he won, all of it—put him at the far end of the cutthroat line Since he was Macomek's highliner, maybe I shouldn't have been surprised. Even so, I was.

The dart game was still going strong when I decided to thank Laurie again for the scuba dive and head on home. Malicite caught me before I left.

"Tomorrah's Buddy's memorial at the Macomek's school. There's a get-together for Abby on her beach aftah. Her seventieth birthday. She was gonna cancel but thought people could, ya know, celebrate Buddy too."

"Thanks, Malicite. I probably won't make it but appreciate the invitation."

The Lee Side's deck, which faced the harbor, was cold even with the windows closed. I rubbed my arms and scanned the tables.

"Well, look who's heah."

I turned around and for a moment didn't recognized Patty. Mascara was smeared around her eyes like she'd been rubbing them, and her greasy hair stood straight up. The slack jaw told me what was wrong. Patty Burgess was stone drunk.

She elbowed the man next to her and waved a finger at me. "Richie, this lady heah," she slurred. "She keeps tellin' me it's not Tyler who offed Buddy. But she don't know squat."

Two guys sat on either side of Patty and a third directly

across. I assumed they were all Macomek lobstermen. Each one sized me up like questionable bait. Richie put an arm around Patty's shoulder and snarled, "Out on Macomek we don't like outsidahs tellin' us nothin'. 'Specially 'bout what happened ta our good friend, Buddy. Get the message?"

Backing up a step, I said, "Excuse me," turned, and returned to the bar area. I stood next to the cash register by the exit to pay my bill when Ted and lovely Penny Russell walked in. After Ted and I exchanged extremely awkward hellos, he ushered her toward the bar. She gave me a hesitant smile before she left.

Outside, I shuffled down the hill to my car. What the hell had just happened? One moment I was enjoying my dinner watching a dart game, and the next I was being ridiculed by Abby's drunken daughter and her lobstermen pals, then forced to acknowledge Ted and my replacement.

At home, it took another glass of wine to moderate my mental state to only mildly feverish. As a distraction for my emotional side, I decided use my brain to review what I'd learned in the last few days and see if any insights into Buddy's murder emerged.

When field or lab data made little sense, I often sketched ideas, questions, and words on the whiteboard in my office. For some reason, the visual display helped me recognize patterns and put together seemingly disparate pieces. Lacking a whiteboard, I spread a big piece of white drawing paper across the kitchen table. In black marker, I listed factual information items such as the day Buddy died and where I'd found him. Questions like "Why is Patty so insistent it's Tyler?" and "How and where did Buddy die?" I listed in red.

Next, I wrote, "Why would someone on Macomek kill Buddy?" Under that question, I listed Betty's words: "power," "money," "love." Leaning over the table, I realized that two critical reasons needed to be added. Next to "money" I wrote "greed" and to "power" the word "ambition."

I stepped back and frowned. Something was missing. I went out on the deck and studied the stars. The Pleiades—the Seven Sisters—were clearly visible, including the star Electra, who in one Greek legend, was killed in an act of revenge.

"Of course," I said aloud.

Back inside, I wrote "revenge" at the bottom of the list.

For the next hour, I stared at the sheet, paced around the kitchen table, returned to the deck, walked to the living room and back, lay on the couch, and got up again. The kitchen stove clock read 10:49 when it came to me. I wrote the name next to "ambition," turned off the kitchen light, and climbed the stairs.

16

THE PHONE RANG ONCE, TWICE, THREE TIMES.

"Hello?" Harvey sounded like she had marbles in her mouth.

"You up?" I asked.

"I am now." The phone made muffled crackles. "Christ, Mara. It's just five."

"You're an early riser."

"Sure." She yawned. "But this is a little extreme. Is something wrong?"

"I'm fine. Actually, I wanted to talk to Connor."

"He's still asleep. Wait, his eyes just popped open. I'll have him call you back."

I poured a second cup of strong black tea, splashed in some milk, and climbed onto a stool by the pub table overlooking my deck. In the early morning light, fog had transformed trees, rocks, and ocean beyond into a wet, grey, sameness. Cradling the mug, I sipped the comforting brew until the phone rang.

A retired cop from Augusta, Maine's capital city, Connor Doyle had also been a first responder. A five a.m. call from a friend was nothing to him.

"Top 'o the mornin', Mara. What's up?"

"I've got a pretty good idea who killed Buddy, and I'm hoping you'll take me out to Macomek to poke around."

After digesting this for a moment with a "hmm" he said, "If you're really onto somethin' Mara, won't who you're talkin' about get suspicious? You only left the island a few days ago."

"I've got a good excuse. Yesterday, Malicite Dupris—he's a lobsterman out there—invited me to a double-do on Macomek. People want to do something to honor Buddy, and it's Abby Burgess's seventieth birthday. An odd combination, but we are talking about Macomek. It's this afternoon."

"I guess that sounds okay. My boat's too small so lemme work on borrowin' one. I've got an idea on that. We're comin' back this evening?"

"Yeah. What I need to look into won't take long. We should be able to head back to the mainland around sundown."

"I'll call you in a couple hours."

I stared at the silent phone in my hand. I'd set the wheels in motion, and it was up to me to keep them running smoothly. My business was deadly serious. A mistake or two and things could go very badly for me. Besides that, a dear and lonely man who'd saved my life might well never know what happened to his only grandson and why.

No way could I screw this up.

I returned the landline phone to its cradle—cell phone service was spotty this close to the ocean—with a "Thank you, Connor." What a terrific guy. He didn't question my sleuthing ability or demand to know what the hell I was talking about. The previous spring, Connor and I had worked together on a complicated case. A colleague and friend had died on a research cruise in what MOI claimed was an accident. Since the victim had been an outspoken climate scientist, I'd suspected otherwise and found evidence that supported my assumption.

Connor now trusted my instincts for which I was deeply grateful. It was also a huge plus that he'd be out on Macomek with me. Given the island's reputation, an experienced ex-cop with an uncanny ability to interpret people's behavior would be the perfect partner.

As Connor sidled *Money Pit* up to Spruce Harbor's town dock, I threw my backpack onto the stern deck and jumped aboard.

Space in the harbor was tight, so I waited until he had woven through a cluster of moorings before speaking. "What's with *Money Pit*? It's the same boat Gordy borrowed when we went out to Macomek."

Connor grinned. "Poker game. Guy's rich but a terrible player."

He waited until we were well past the harbor's headlands before he gave the boat her head. *Money Pit* shot forward like a frustrated filly. Grinning, Connor said, "This boat's got lots of pep. In a former life she ran drugs, so I hear." He reduced the speed to just below fifteen knots and checked our bearing. "We gotta a good day. Should be at the island 'round ten."

I'd settled onto one of the cushy bench seats in the wheelhouse. "I really appreciate you taking the time to do this, Connor."

"You kiddin'? I'm runnin' a fine boat out on the watah, and you laugh at my jokes." He checked the bottom sonar and nodded. "Good. Okay, now tell me what this is all about. Take your time. We got it."

"I assume Gordy filled you in after we got back from the island?"

"Ayuh. Had a couple beers with 'im in the Lee Side. He hadn't talked to the Marine Patrol guys yet."

"What'd Gordy say?"

"He couldn't stop talkin' about this Tyler guy."

"Right. Gordy's fixed on Tyler Johnson because his girlfriend Patty Burgess is."

Connor scanned the waters ahead and to port and starboard,

making sure we weren't about to run over debris he hadn't seen earlier. One hand on the wheel, he partly turned toward me. "And what do you think?"

"When someone's so positive they know the killer, you have to wonder why."

"I get your meanin' Mara, that's smart. But let's back up. Tell me who's who, what makes 'em tick, all that."

I went more or less in chronological order—Abby, Patty, Angel, Lester and Buddy, Malicite, Calvin, and Tyler. "There's some other lobstermen I haven't talked to as well."

"I think I got the picture," he said. "Now what makes you think you know who wanted Buddy dead?"

"It's about revenge. When I was super angry with Seymour, Angelo told me an Italian saying about revenge that made sense."

"Huh. What was it?"

"Wait for the time and place to take your revenge, for it is never well done in a hurry."

"I get it. Keep going."

"Last night, I made a big sketch of questions and ideas related to Buddy's death like I do when I'm stuck on a research question."

"You've explained that to me. Police do somethin' similar."

"Well, I hit on the words 'revenge' and 'ambition,' and the rest came from that."

It took the remainder of the trip for me to explain my idea, answer all of Connor's questions, look at the issue from different angles, and come up with a workable plan.

I was on deck as Connor slowly circled Macomek's harbor looking for a good place to anchor for the day. Malicite, who was piling traps near the lobster shacks, spotted us.

He cupped his hands and called out, "Mara, is that you on that fancy boat?"

"Sure is." I called back. "This is my good friend Connor. We're here for the memorial and get together. Where can we moor?"

Malicite pointed to a large white ball floating at the other edge of the harbor. "See that empty mooring way out theah? It's a good spot. Go ahead an' use it."

Connor turned in the direction Malicite was pointing. "I see the mooring, but there's no dinghy on it."

"You head theah. I'll row out."

By the time we'd tied up to the mooring ball, Malicite had slid alongside. Connor stepped in first and sat center stern. I took the bow seat. Seated in the middle, the lobsterman pulled the oars with slow, practiced strokes.

"I appreciate your getting us," I said.

"Macomek gets a bad rap sometimes," he said. "Just tryin' to set the record straight that we're good folk out heah."

As Connor and I walked over to the school he said, "Since we're headin' to a memorial for a murdered island lobsterman, I think what that Malicite fella said was pretty odd."

"He was just trying to be helpful," I answered. "Malicite's terrific." I told Connor about all the time the lobsterman had spent with me.

"Really? Sorry, but that's suspicious too. Lobstermen are super busy people. Why's he trying so hard to be nice to you?"

Connor had much more experience dealing with shifty people than I did, but it was hard to imagine that Malicite had ulterior motives. He was such a good guy, wasn't he?

Since Macomek had no chapel, Buddy's event took place in the school's auditorium. Besides that good-sized open room, there wasn't much else to the tiny white clapboard building except two small classrooms and a library that looked like a large closet. But the school's setting on a hill with its expansive view of the sea was perfect for a memorial honoring a man devoted to the ocean. The day was fine for September, and every one of the auditorium's windows was cranked wide open. Instead of organ music, we would listen to Macomek's enduring song—waves smashing against the island's granite underpinnings.

The mismatched wooden chairs neatly arranged in rows were already mostly taken when Connor and I walked into the room. It was quite a scene. Mothers were trying to control restless children who stood on chairs and looked around. Heads together, white-haired men and women were talking into one another's ears. Since neither Connor nor I had known Buddy, we found seats in the back row. Before settling into my chair, I scanned the ones up front. Lester was leaning toward a younger man, hand on that person's shoulder. I assume this was Lester's son, Buddy's father.

As a man wearing a suit and tie walked to the front of the gathering, the room became quiet.

"Good afternoon. I'm pastor Clyde Bickford from Saint George Episcopal Church. While I did not know Buddy Crawford, I have known his father, Todd Crawford, for a very long time. Over the years, Todd often talked about Buddy. So in that indirect way, I have come to know the younger man."

Bickford went on to say the usual things about Buddy—he was a hard-working young man who loved the sea and should be remembered for his exceptional skill as a lobsterman and generosity toward his friends and family. The only part of the eulogy that hit home was when Bickford explained that Buddy wanted to be a lobsterman like his grandfather Lester. In fact, he said, Buddy's real name was Lester. I could hear the old man's sob all the way in the back row.

Lester, I promise you, I thought, I'll find the bastard who did this to you and your namesake.

Two of Buddy's high school friends lightened the mood a bit with a few funny stories, and Malicite, speaking for the island's lobstermen, praised Buddy's skill at lobstering.

"Buddy had only been on his own a couple years, but anyone could see he'd be a highliner. Buddy was smart and incredibly hard-working. The guy was always lookin' to the future. How can I do this better, what's happening with lobstering in Maine? Dictionary's got a fancy word for folks like that—visionary. Buddy was one of those, a visionary."

Malicite's tribute was the first time I'd heard Buddy described in this way. I couldn't help but wonder if Buddy's farsighted tendencies had cost him his life.

At the end of the tribute, Buddy's father announced that everyone was invited to Abby Burgess's place for snacks and beers on the beach.

Connor and I trailed behind the group on our way over Abby's beach. "What'd you think?" I asked.

"The only thing that struck me is what the lobsterman said. What was his name?"

"That's Malicite."

"Odd name. Anyways, in a place like this with so much tradition and history, is being visionary a good thing? Visionaries can be ambitious people with highfalutin' ideas. That might not sit well with some folks out here."

"I wondered exactly that," I said. "It's funny, but Malicite's a visionary too. He works on a NOAA program called eLobster and attaches a sensor to one of his traps. The sensor sends data about temperature, salinity—that type of thing—to NOAA scientists. Malicite can see the data as soon as his pulls the trap up. The project is pretty forward looking."

"Interesting. Two forward-looking guys on one little island? Could be there was some competition between 'em."

We stopped on the road in view of Abby's house. "Connor," I said. "how would I know? It's so incredibly frustrating being in the dark about everyone out here."

"Jus' keep your eyes open, like I said. I assume you *do* know where I can take a leak in private?"

After Connor excused himself to find the bathroom, I wandered down to the beach and scanned the group. It was obvious that the get-together was not the usual rowdy, lobster-and-brew party on the beach. Islanders sat together in small groups quietly talking as they ate a mismatched assortment of chips, cookies, stuffed eggs, and the like. As much cola was drunk as beer. A half-dozen kids ran up and down the beach trailed by two mongrel dogs.

Beers in hand and apart from the others, Patty and Calvin shared a log above the high-tide line. Their behavior indicated that the two knew each other pretty well, but on a small island that wasn't surprising. They both leaned forward, gesturing with their hands and shaking their heads. It looked like an intense conversation, and I couldn't help wondering what they were talking about. Maybe Patty was angry that Tyler was still on the loose and nobody was looking for him. Maybe Calvin was pissed off because information about how Buddy died still hadn't been released.

Maybe, maybe, maybe.

Richie and three other lobstermen walked the beach chugging beers. Snatches of their conversation—"There's this babe" and "You gotta be friggin' crazy"—told me they weren't especially upset that Buddy was gone. I was about to look away when the men stopped walking and turned toward a cluster of bushes at the edge of the forest. Richie glanced to the side as the group scrambled up a sea-scoured bank and disappeared into the shadows. Squinting, I thought I saw someone tallish and thin. Interesting, but despite my curiosity about what or more likely who had gotten their attention, I wasn't about to go after them to find out. It was time to get back to the party.

Abby was holding the hand of a young woman with waist-length brown hair. I walked closer and Abby waved me over.

"Mara, this is my daughter Angel. Angel, meet Mara Tusconi who stayed with me for a couple of days last week."

Angel was a good half-foot taller than her mother. With her dark hair and height plus chestnut eyes, Angel looked nothing like Abby. She appeared drained and exhausted.

"I understand that you and Buddy were good friends," I said. "I am so sorry for your loss."

Blinking, Angel wiped tears from her eyes with both hands.

Abby reached into her pocket for a tissue. "Here you are, baby." Abby turned to me again. "Angel was in the middle of nowhere on a camping trip. She just learned what happened to Buddy yesterday."

My hand went to my mouth. "Oh my god. You poor girl. Again, I'm so sorry. Abby, I'll see you later. I'm sure you both have a lot to talk about."

"Abby's daughter Angel was Buddy's girlfriend *and* she was away on a camping trip?" Connor asked.

Connor and I had left the get-together and decided to walk up to the harbor.

"That's what Abby said. Why?"

He shrugged. "It's one of those coincidence things. Girlfriend has gone nobody-really-knows-where when the boyfriend gets knocked off by an unknown person or persons."

"Connor, I can't imagine…"

"I've seen it all, Mara. It happens."

"She was crying."

"Could be a terrific actor."

"Still. I mean, she's Abby's daughter."

His non-answer hung in the air, and I had no idea what to do with it.

"Did you notice anything else?"

"Not much. Calvin—he's that highliner I told you about—and Patty, Abby's oldest daughter, were pretty deep in conversation away from anyone else. But they could have been talking about anything. Richie, a loud and obnoxious lobster-man, was marching down the beach with his buddies acting like they were at a Fourth of July party instead of a memorial get-together."

"Wouldn't know what to think about any of that," he said.

"Wait. Those guys were walking along like I said, but something up in the bushes caught their attention. A guy, I'm pretty sure. They left the beach and climbed up there. After that, I couldn't see them."

"Now, *that's* interesting," Connor said. "Someone in the bushes must've called out to them. Could you see anything?"

I tried to recreate the scene in my mind's eye. "The bushes were in the shadow of trees above them, but somebody was up there. Someone kind of tall."

"Any idea who that might be?" Connor asked.

"The only person I can think of is Tyler. He's tall and skinny. Tyler and Richie. What a pair."

"You're pretty sure that Buddy's killer had help. Could be one of those guys."

"Or a couple of them," I said.

When we reached the harbor, I was surprised to see a long row of wooden crates bobbing in the water. Connected to one another by trap line, the crates formed a kind of floating walkway easily a hundred feet long.

I pointed at the crates. "What the heck is that?"

"Crates for the Maine Lobstah Boat Race. Between two wharfs, folks string togethah old wooden crates folks used to use for storin' lobstahs. It's called lobstah crate racin'. Somebody, kids I'd guess, mus' be trainin' for next yeah while the ocean's still warmish."

I stared at the crates. "You mean people run on top of the crates from one end to the other? My god, they must fall off all the time."

"You got that right. If the crate runnah goes too slow, the crates sink, and down he goes. If they don't get their foot in the middle of a crate, the thing tips sideways and throws 'em off."

I envisaged shrieking kids wobbling off the grates and crashing into the water. "How many make it through the whole crate gantlet?"

"Less than one in ten," I'd guess."

"Connor, in all these years I'm embarrassed to say I've never watched a lobster boat race. What does it look like? The boats I mean."

"It's jus' wild. Guys push those boats like you wouldn't believe. Boats tipped up halfway out of the watah, speeds like forty knots."

I did a quick translation. "Wow, nearly fifty miles an hour. Just regular lobster boats, right?"

"Some designs do bettah." He scanned the harbor and pointed at *Lucky Catch*. "See that one theah?"

"That boat belongs to Calvin Ives."

Connor raised an eyebrow. "Does it now? Well, lobstahman Ives has one fine racin' craft."

"Doesn't surprise me at all. Calvin is a very competitive guy."

I looked at the sky as Connor checked his watch.

"Still want to wait 'til sunset?" he asked.

"Yeah. Hope that's okay."

"Sure. I'm gonna hang out aboard *Money Pit* an' catch some shut-eye." He winked. "Some crazy girl called me at five this morning."

I picked a random dinghy on the beach, rowed Connor out to *Money Pit*, said I'd be back in two hours sharp, and returned the little boat to where I'd found it.

Abby absentmindedly ran her hand across the rock's surface. We'd walked to the far end of her beach to get away from the group for a bit. The flat slab of granite still held some of the day's warmth. "There's an odd mood here on the island," she said.

"Mood? Wouldn't you expect that with what happened to Buddy?"

"Yes, but this is different. Hard to explain."

I turned toward her. "Abby, let your mind work on that and tell me if something pops up, okay? Connor Doyle, the guy who ran me out here, is a former cop from Augusta. He's trying to help me figure out who killed Buddy, and we've got somebody in mind. You know more than anyone about the people who live on Macomek—their fears, what makes them tick, and we need your insight."

"Of course. Anything. Who…?"

"Wait. Let me go through my reasoning and see if you come to the same conclusion. There's a brilliant female oceanographer at MOI named Betty. Wise old bird. She knows what I'm up to out here and she listed several human traits I should focus on—greed, money, and love. Does this make sense?"

"'Course it does. It's human madness in one package."

So, if you consider each trait, or all three, and think about who might have a reason to kill Buddy, does anyone in particular stand out?"

Abby closed her eyes and stayed that way so long I thought she might've fallen asleep sitting up. I was about to touch her shoulder when she popped her eyes open.

"It's more complicated."

My blank stare said I wasn't with her.

"Take greed, for instance," she said. "A person might desperately want something right now, like money. Their desperation drives them to do awful things. But what if the thing they want is in the future? It would be a lot harder for someone else to figure that out."

"They want something in the future? Can you give me an example?"

"When I was a teenager, I wanted nothing more than to be a sternman, then a lobsterman. I was desperate for it but knew my father wouldn't let me. 'That's man's work,' he'd say. The real reason, and deep down I understood this, was that he was afraid of losing me. I was his only daughter and looked a lot his sister who'd died from the plague—or what they thought was plague. Of course, I loved my father and wouldn't have hurt him for the world. But that's the kind of thing I'm talking about."

I stared at the horizon. "Boy, you'd have to know a lot about a person to figure that out. I mean, who knew you wanted to be a lobsterman besides your dad?"

"Nobody. It's not anything we talked about, but I was crazy about boats, all that. Dad must've guessed. Anyways, he never let on to a soul. It was my secret, that's all."

Secret. The word hung in the air. Who on Macomek *didn't* have secrets? I knew about Abby's and Lester's because she'd told me. I also guessed Lester loved her and the feeling was mutual. But every single one of them—Patty, Angel, Malicite, Calvin, Tyler, and the rest of the lobstermen and people in their families—harbored secrets passions, fears, and hatreds I'd never know anything about. Whether such feelings came from something that happened in the past or might happen in the future, those sentiments had been the basis for murder ever since humans had minds that could reason and scheme.

"Okay," I said. "Think about people on the island who could have killed Buddy. It might have even been by mistake if they'd argued with him, for instance."

She patted my hand. "Deah, you must know I've racked my brains with that question."

"You've no idea at all?"

"Not about the who. On the why, I'd say it's got to do with family, maybe children or someone you love."

Behind us, the crackle of footfalls startled me. Lester Crawford circled the rock and stood before us.

"Lester," Abby said. That was it, just the man's name. But the undertone, a mix of sadness and yearning, was there. What I heard was, "Isn't it time?"

I stood. "Lester, that was a lovely memorial tribute to Buddy. I'm so sorry...."

He touched my arm. "I do appreciate you comin' way out heah again."

I patted his hand, then smiled at Abby. "Nice to chat with you again. I caught a ride out here with a friend who doesn't know a soul. I'd better go find him."

On my way back to Abby's house, I turned around. Shoulder to shoulder on the rock, Abby and Lester faced the sea and what lay beyond.

As I followed the path to higher ground, the words *greed*, *love*, *money*, *passion*, *ambition*, *hate*, *past*, and *future* swirled around in my brain. I'd felt so confident about the identity of Buddy's killer. Now I wasn't sure at all.

17

ONNOR WAVED BACK AND KNELT DOWN ON *Money Pit*'s bow to release her from the mooring. Hand over hand, I clambered down the wood ladder and stepped onto the gunwale as he came alongside.

We chugged to the harbor's outskirts and drifted so nobody could hear us talk.

Out on the aft deck, Connor draped his arms over the coaming and leaned back. "Positive you want to do this? It's just a hunch you've got."

"Like I said, Connor, it's more intuition than a hunch."

He looked skyward. "Lord help us."

"Isn't there an Irish saying that a hunch is creativity trying to tell you something?"

"Could be. Okay, let's go over this again. I'll pass by his stern so *Money Pit* blocks the view. You step aboard his boat. I keep goin' to jus' beyond the habah. You slip into the wheelhouse where nobody can see you. You'll try to find what you're lookin' for. That'll take somethin' like ten minutes. You'll come back out on deck an' signal me with the flashlight. That it?"

"That's it," I said with more confidence than I felt. "Pretty straightforward plan, don't you think? What can go wrong?"

Connor put his hand on my shoulder. "If things head south, I'll be back in a flash."

Connor slowed *Money Pit* and slid past the lobster boat. The open stern made stepping aboard very easy. I was already in the cabin before Connor had motored by and turned toward the outer harbor.

I waited for my eyes to adjust to the dim light—and my heart to slow down a bit—and tried to remember Malicite's exact words.

"Lots of important information you can't keep in yer head. We all have a notebook we write stuff in and hide in our cabin where nobody's gonna mess with it."

Scanning the cabin, I looked for places a lobsterman might stash his precious notebook. In this case, a notebook listing future locations for lobster traps as the Gulf of Maine warmed up. A list originally put together by Buddy Crawford. A list an ambitious lobsterman might well kill for.

There weren't too many possibilities. The space below the wheel was free of any stowage. No surprise there, since the lobsterman steering the boat might kick something at his feet.

In the whole cabin I could see only one place to store anything. Below a low counter there were two drawers wide enough to hold marine charts. Kneeling, I slowly slid the top one open. As I expected, it held NOAA charts for Macomek's waters and elsewhere along the coast. I flipped through the pages. Nothing there and nothing beneath the pile either. Frowning, I slid the drawer closed.

Whispering "now or nothing," I slid the bottom drawer open inch by inch and peered inside. Unlike the chart drawer, this one held an assortment of items—official-looking sheets of paper, tide charts, pencils and scissors, envelops of various sizes. Nothing that looked like a precious notebook. Disappointed, I flipped through the layers until I reached the bottom of the drawer where a large manila envelope with frayed edges lay sideways. I pulled it out and stood to give my knees a break.

The sun was close to setting now, and not much light made

its way into the cabin. My intuition told me the envelope was important and worth a risk. I tugged Connor's handkerchief out of my pocket, slipped it over my flashlight's lens, and flipped it on. The handkerchief didn't do much to diffuse the light's intensity, so I lowered myself onto the cabin's deck, stretched out my legs, placed the flashlight next to one knee, and put the envelope on my thighs. My body, I hoped, would block any telltale glow.

The envelope's flap had lost its glue a long time ago. I lifted it up and peered in. A photograph, black and white and maybe ten by eight inches, lay inside. Careful not to tear one of the frayed edges, I slowly slid it out, laid it on top of the envelope, and picked up the flashlight.

The light brought to life two young people, a male and female. They looked the same age, eighteen I guessed. She, a cute tomboy type with blond braids and freckles, grinned at the camera. He stared only at her and the drape of his arm over her shoulder told me his affection was not sisterly.

The guy looked a lot like Calvin. In fact, I decided, that's exactly what Calvin would have looked like about ten years ago. I turned the photograph over. Something had been written on the back, but it was in pencil and smudged. I held the flashlight directly above the word and spelled it out.

"C-O-D-Y."

The date, more easily read, was 1993.

Cody. An unusual name I'd seen recently. Had he been one of Buddy's classmates in the photograph Lester showed me? A Macomek kid in the photo on his wall?

Then I knew. *Cody Booth September 13, 1975–September 13, 1995*

"Oh my god. Cody isn't a male. She's a female," I said. "She *was* a female."

The full realization came to me in a rush. Cody Booth

had been Calvin Ives's girlfriend. Given the much-used state of the photograph, that it was hidden in the bottom drawer, and the way Calvin was looking at Cody, I guessed she had been much more than just a girlfriend. Calvin Ives must have loved Cody Booth. A lot.

The photograph in my hand had been taken in 1993. Two years later, the young lady with braids and freckles was dead. But she hadn't die in a car crash or anything like that. Cody had died in a terrible storm off Macomek Island. And she'd been Lester Crawford's sternman.

Lester, the boat's captain, had been rescued, but his sternman Cody had been taken by the sea. No wonder Lester marked the unlucky September date in her memory.

Calvin must also mark that terrible date, but in his own way.

I put the photograph down and rubbed my eyes as an idea took form in my brain. Like most people on Macomek, Calvin knew—or at the very least strongly suspected—that Lester had been drinking the day Cody died. He would hold Lester responsible for Cody's death.

"Revenge." That's what I'd added to my list. Revenge was an intensely powerful emotion that drove people to do terrible acts. All these years, I could imagine Calvin desperately wanting to retaliate for his terrible loss.

"My god," I said aloud. "Calvin could have killed Buddy to get at Lester."

I clamped my hand over my mouth as a voice from behind answered my question. "You figured that out, damn you. You nosy, snooping outsidah. I knew you were trouble the moment I laid eyes on you."

By inches, I got to my feet and turned around. Calvin Ives stood next to the wheel of his boat. Tight lipped, his eyes burning in the fading light, he looked like a cougar about to spring. If I'd had a voice, I would have screamed.

He thrust out a hand. "You have *no* right. Give that to me."

I placed the photograph on his palm.

"The envelope."

I held out the frayed envelope. He snatched it, slipped in the photograph, and secured the precious item in the inside chest pocket of his coat.

"You have exactly one minute to tell me what the *hell* you're doing in my cabin."

I cleared my throat.

"Fifty seconds."

"Okay, okay." Speaking hurriedly I said, "Buddy spent a lot of time researching where to put his traps as the Gulf of Maine waters warmed. It was a goldmine of information for the future. I thought you wanted it and maybe murdered him to get it. I guessed you had his notebook or kept notes of your own, so I decided to poke around your cabin to find out."

He narrowed his eyes. "You thought I'd *kill* Buddy to get trap ideas? My god, that's rich."

"You asked me to tell you why I'm here. That's why."

He patted his heart. "But you found this instead, didn't you? Now tell me, Dr. Scientist, what did you deduce from that?"

"That maybe you wanted to get back at Lester for what he did to Cody and did that by killing his grandson."

At the mention of Cody's name, Calvin's eyes tightened for a moment. He blinked and said, "Lester deserved to rot in hell for what he did. Drinkin' while you're runnin' a lobstahboat. He might've just as well slit Cody's throat."

I added, "Whatever happened with Buddy, I don't think you were alone."

The man studied my face. Then, like a practiced actor, his

demeanor went from angry to clinical.

"You're a smart lady, I'll give you that. You're right. Patty was with me. She's who you should be talkin' to 'bout Buddy, not me."

Incredulous, I said, "Patty? Why…"

He cut me off. "Buddy had a big, bad secret, but Patty figured it out. He was sellin' drugs—bad stuff like heroin—to kids on the mainland."

"Kids?"

"That's what I said. Teenagers—fifteen, sixteen, like that. Too bad Buddy didn't recognize those kids grown up. Before they left the island to work or whatevah, Patty taught 'em when they were little in the school out heah. That's the school where Buddy had his memorial."

I remembered Abby's words when she described Patty's attitude toward the children she taught. "Patty, she's like a female lion protecting her cubs."

"My god," I said.

"Ayuh. Buddy picked the wrong kids."

"But what happened? To Buddy, I mean."

Again, the calculator in Calvin's brain seemed to weigh his options.

"It was an accident. Happened right on the habah when nobody was around. Patty tol' Buddy she knew what he was doin'. Buddy got high an' mighty like he always did. I jumped in with my two cents. He backed up. Next thing I knew he'd fallen off the pier an' hit his head on a rock down below. Tide was low. Buddy was dead when we got down to 'im."

I pictured the horrific scene. At low tide, the drop from the harbor's pier was about thirty feet. If Buddy hit his head on a rock when' he landed, he probably died instantly.

"But if it was an accident, why didn't you just report what happened to Marine Patrol?"

He snickered. "That shows how much you know 'bout Macomek an' cops from the mainland. Somethin' like that happens out heah 'n right off they figure those crazy island guys're killin' each othah again."

I opened my mouth to argue, but he cut me off.

"There's somethin' else. Patty's DUI three times. You think Marine Patrol'll believe Patty?" He mimicked a girl's voice. "Oh officer, it was jus' an accident." His raucous laugh bounced off the walls of the tiny cabin. "Somethin' like this 'n Patty, she's off to jail."

"Well, *I* believe you," I said.

"Sorry, but that's not worth much." He ran a hand threw his crew cut. "Now I got the problem o' what the hell to do with you."

"How about just letting me go home to Spruce Harbor?"

The laugh resounded through the cabin once more. I wondered if the man whose boat I'd visited uninvited was a little mad.

"Right. I'll jus' wait out heah 'til the cops come, 'cause you ran ovah and told 'em how it went with Buddy."

There was no point in my arguing with Calvin because he was right. I'd have to report his story to Marine Patrol, and naturally they'd go right after him.

A boat motor gurgled at the edge of the harbor. Calvin whipped his head toward the sound, back at me "Who the hell is that?"

"Connor, the guy who brought me out here."

"Guy's a cop. I could smell it a mile away."

Money Pit's motor growled. I bit my lip to suppress the grin.

"Christ," Calvin barked. "Your goddamn cop's comin' back

for you." He flung an arm at the cabin's empty corner. "Back theah, on the deck. Now!" Calvin twisted *Lucky Catch's* key and the vessel roared to life.

As Calvin scrambled to the bow to release his craft from its mooring, I considered leaping up and jumping overboard. But the man was back in an instant. He yanked the wheel to starboard, a maneuver that threw me against the open cabinet in the cabin. A piece of metal inside the drawer sliced my arm. A thin trickle of blood ran down my hand as I crawled back to my corner.

With increasing speed, Calvin wove through the moored boats like he was the lead kayak in a whitewater slalom course.

Clueless what to do, I yelled a useless warning. "Connor's boat's called *Money Pit's*. It's pretty fast,"

"*Nobody* beats *Lucky Catch*." Calvin stared ahead with the same demonic intensity I'd witnessed in the bar. "I've won lob-stah boat races ten years in a row." The man licked his lips and snickered at a joke he didn't share with me.

Once more, he jerked the wheel to starboard. I braced a foot against the cabin's doorframe and stayed upright. The view through the window told me we'd left the moored boats behind. I strained to hear *Money Pit's* engine but didn't.

Calvin's motor must be too loud, I told myself. On my knees, I squinted to see past *Lucky Catch's* stern. Boats on Macomek's outermost moorings lay quietly at anchor. Connor's borrowed vessel drifted soundlessly with them.

Calvin jerked a thumb over his shoulder. "Looks like your cop's wallowing in the watah with a dead engine."

Crawling back to my corner, I didn't give my captor the satisfaction of a response. I needed to think. Sure, I said to my-self. Think about what? I was in a fast-moving boat captained by a crazy man who could navigate these waters blindfolded.

If I tried to run past him, he'd probably throw me right back onto the cabin's deck. Even if he didn't, what would I do? If I jumped overboard, I'd be in fifty-degree water and unconscious from hypothermia in minutes.

Of course, Calvin would be happy if I'd offed myself so he wouldn't have to do it on his own. That was how this was going to end. Besides Patty, I was the only one who knew Calvin's awful secret. Year after year, Calvin's sick mind had festered with the knowledge that Lester Crawford had killed Cody. Now, after all this time, Calvin had gotten his revenge. He'd killed once—or at the very least covered up a death he claimed was accidental. There was no question in my mind that Calvin Ives wanted me dead.

Throwing me overboard miles off Macomek on the edge of the continental shelf would be a very effective way to make sure that happened. Who would know?

I looked toward the island. Connor was still back there somewhere. I could just see and hear him. He'd be swearing like an Irish sailor at a recalcitrant motor that wouldn't start. I blinked back tears.

Calvin slammed a hand against the wheel. "Christ, god-damn it!"

Had he run across a submerged string of lobster traps and snarled the motor? I got to my feet to look. Connor's drug-running craft was quickly gaining on us. Maybe the king of lobster boat races was going to see his match.

Calvin slammed the motor into a higher gear. Bow tipped up out of the water, stern buried, *Lucky Catch* jumped ahead like a filly given her head. Calvin whooped as *Money Pit* dropped behind.

Like soldiers in a trench, I got religious. "A little help for a wayward Catholic girl?," I whispered.

"Sayin' yer prayers?" Calvin sneered. "Good idea, considerin'...."

On my feet, I looked past him. Maybe a quarter mile behind, Connor was coming up fast once more.

Calvin grabbed my shoulder and shoved me toward the cabin opening.

"What're you doing?" I screamed.

"If that cop sees you in the ocean, he's gonna stop an' go aftah you an' not me."

I was about to protest when *Lucky Catch* hit a swell. The boat leapt into the air and threw me face first against the steel snatch block hanging over the side. Screaming, I pressed my hand against the gash on my forehead and flipped over the gunwale into the water.

On my back, I slammed into a wave that tossed me down into the icy brine. As frozen barbs poked into my naked skull and salt scoured the weeping gouge, I opened my mouth to scream. A primal sense forced me to clamp it shut. To scream underwater would be to die.

My dulled, frozen brain knew death was closing in. With collapsed lungs and no life jacket, I drifted downward, a soggy ragdoll at the mercy of currents and gravity. Ignoring knives of pain in my neck, I looked up and opened my eyes for an instant. I'd sunk so far from the realm of blessed air I could hardly see any light at all. Tears of anguish flooded sightless eyes as I fell into oblivion.

My screaming lungs demanded air. Bitter cold water stabbed my eardrums with unbearable force. Engulfed in silence, an image of Mom and Dad in a water-filled sub drifted through my brain.

Finally, I *had* to give up. In one desperate gasp, I sucked in water. My chest on fire, I knew what drowning was.

Right before death, I dreamed of salvation. The hand of God grabbed me, arrested my downward spiral, and dragged me up to the world of the living.

18

BLINKING, I ROLLED MY HEAD TO THE SIDE. WHY WAS I cold and drenching wet and lying on a hard surface that was moving? And why did my head feel like I'd smashed it into a door?

A man with angelic curls and blue eyes leaned his face closer to mine.

"Are you an archangel?" I asked. "Am I in heaven?"

The man spoke with an Irish brogue. "Jus' your buddy Connor, Mara. You're on a boat off Macomek Island."

"Oh," I said.

There was a noise to my left. I started to turn my head in that direction but stopped. "Ouch."

"Take it easy," Connor said. "You've got a nasty cut on your forehead."

"Cut?"

"Yes. You hit your head against a hydraulic trap hauler."

"Oh," I repeated. "They're heavy."

Suddenly, the memory flooded in. I had been on a fast-moving lobster boat that belonged to Calvin Ives. The boat had hit a wave. I'd smashed my head on something hard, something I now knew was the trap hauler. I'd gone overboard into the water.

My memory stopped there.

"It's awfully uncomfortable lying here. I'd like to sit up," I said.

"All right, lass," Connor said. "Go real slow. I'll give you a hand."

A half hour later, I was comfortably seated on a padded bench inside the wheelhouse of Connor's boat. He handed me a mug of hot water to sip. He'd already draped blankets over my shoulders and legs.

I held the mug to my chest. "Thanks."

"Feeling better?" Connor asked.

"Much. Hope I stop shivering soon. How long was I in the water?"

Calvin stood in the cabin's entryway. "Not long," he said. "Couple minutes."

I looked at him, at Connor by my side, back at Calvin. "But who got me out of the water?"

"Calvin did," Connor said.

The lobsterman looked down at his feet and said nothing.

"But Calvin," I asked. "Weren't you trying to get away?"

He ran a hand through his wet crew-cut and blew out a long breath. "Ayuh, I was. But lobstermen can't jus' take off an' leave someone to drown."

A shiver traveled down my spine. "Are you saying you turned your boat around and came back for me?"

He shrugged.

Suddenly the room began to spin. I turned to Connor. "I feel like I'm going to throw up."

Following Connor's orders I put my head down between my knees. The nausea diminished in a few minutes.

"You must've swallowed some water," Connor said.

I knew my dizziness had nothing to do with being in the water. Wanting to change the subject I asked, "So Connor, tell me what happened?"

"Here's how I saw it. Calvin's boat was in front of me. I was trying to catch up. You flipped over the gunwale into the water. Calvin turned around and went right back for you. He jumped into the water and dove down. By the time I idled up, he had you. He swam to *Money Pit*'s stern. I lifted you aboard and got you settled while he changed into dry clothes."

"That's incredible," I said. "Calvin, you could have let me drown and what you told me about Buddy would've died with me."

He shook his head. "No. It was wrong, terr'ble, that Buddy died. Shouldn't have happened. No way was I gonna let an innocent woman drown when I could save 'er."

"Even if I was a nosy, snooping outsider?"

"Ayuh," he said with the shadow of a grin. "Even then."

Even in my addled state, I sensed a shift in Calvin's demeanor. He'd never joked before, but the change was much more fundamental than that. After finally acting on an obsession he'd held for so many years, it was as if a burden had been lifted. I'd heard that soldiers who dreaded killing their enemy counterpart became calmer after they actually did the deed. Calvin's transformation was like that.

Angelo strode down Spruce Harbor's town dock as Connor slid *Money Pit* up to one of the bumpers, flipped off the running lights, and killed the motor. Connor and I walked to the stern. After an appreciative whistle Angelo said, "Connor, isn't that boat a little above your pay grade?"

"Fastest boat I ever ran an' boy did I need it." Connor patted the aft gunwale. "I'm gonna miss her. Well, here's Mara safe an' sound like I said. Striper fishing in a couple days?"

"Let's see how they're running," Angelo said.

Angelo reached toward me. I took his hand and stepped onto the dock. "Thanks."

Connor asked, "Mara, you all set?"

"Good as gold. No way in the world I can thank you."

"'Twas a great adventure that turned out okay." With a quick wave he headed back to the wheelhouse

Angelo put a hand on my shoulder as we walked toward shore. "I got the abbreviated version of events from what Connor could say on the VHF. It sounded pretty bad, and there's still a lot I don't know. I'm sure you're exhausted, but how about stopping at the house for some dinner so you can tell me what happened?"

The concern in his tone was palpable. Angelo worried about my "escapades," as he called them, and said I took too many chances. He had good reason. Since the spring, I'd gotten myself kidnapped on a British Columbian island and chased by a crazy man driving a motor boat when I kayaking. And those were just the episodes he knew about.

I took his hand. Like always, it felt warm, rough in a nice way, safe. "I'm really sorry to worry you. If you want to feed me, I'm more than happy to oblige. But next time I'm cooking, and it's at my house."

When we got to Angelo's home, I ran upstairs and changed into some clothes I'd left behind earlier. His chicken Parmesan was history when I leaned back against the kitchen chair. "Perfect. That hit the spot," I said.

He carried our plates to the sink and asked over his shoulder, "Will coffee keep you awake?"

"Tonight I'll be asleep two seconds after I turn off my light."

We'd kept dinner conversation light, but I knew questions would come out with the espresso. Elbows on the table, Angelo leaned toward me. Atypically, his curly white hair needed a trim. "Connor filled me in a little but didn't have time to say much. You're not too tired to talk about this now?"

In truth, I *was* too tired. But I knew that worry and being in the dark had taken its toll on my godfather.

"I'm okay. Go ahead."

He nodded. "All right. Mostly I'm wondering why you suspected this Calvin Ives and what's going to happen to him."

There was some coffee left at the bottom of my cup. Twirling it, I sorted through the critical parts of my story. I described the evolution of my thinking and why I'd settled on Calvin.

"So you decided that ambition was Calvin's motivation."

"Yes. Laurie Culligan, a scientist who knew Calvin, told me he was obsessed about warming, where the lobsters would migrate to, that type of thing. He really pestered her about it."

"She used that word—'obsessed'?"

I nodded. "The issue, of course, is that I couldn't prove anything. Another lobsterman told me he hid a notebook in his cabin with really valuable information about trap location, dates, numbers of lobsters caught, that type of thing. So I thought Calvin might have Buddy's notebook in his cabin. If he did, that would be solid evidence I could give to Marine Patrol."

"But you didn't find a notebook."

"No. Instead, I found a photograph of a woman Calvin planned to marry. She was Lester Crawford's sternman, and she died in a storm in 1995. Lester was saved, but he'd been drinking. Naturally, Calvin blamed Lester for her death. He's been bitter ever since."

Angelo frowned. "You mean Calvin killed Buddy to avenge a woman who died that long ago?"

I shrugged. "It's not that simple." I went on to explain who Patty was, why she hated Buddy, and why she hadn't reported him to the police herself. "In the Macomek way, Patty and Calvin took care of island business and went after Buddy together. As Calvin explains it, they confronted him at the harbor and Buddy stepped backwards.

He fell thirty feet and bashed his head on a rock. So it was an accident."

"And what do you think?"

I stared at the stone cold coffee in my cup. "Calvin's got his faults for sure. But he did jump in the water and save my life. That says a lot about him."

I looked up. Angelo rubbed his eye like it was irritated. But I knew he was wiping away a tear.

Side by side, we washed the few dishes we'd used. I dried my hands on a dishtowel and leaned back against the slate sink. "Of course, what Calvin did for me brings up some terrible guilt."

He stacked a dinner plate on the drying rack and turned toward me. Angelo was taller by a good half foot, and I felt small. "I was wondering when you'd mention that."

I looked to the side. "I don't think about it much now. But sometimes I wake up from a dream where I'm reaching for her and there's nothing there."

"Mara, that was over twenty years ago. You were only eight. The canoe you both were in hit a boulder, and she went overboard. There were adults in your canoe and in the one behind it. Two people jumped in the river to save her but couldn't swim against the current. There was absolutely nothing you could have done."

I met my godfather's gaze. His warm gray eyes had a way of calming me, and they did. "I know, but it's good for you to remind me."

Angelo walked me to the door. "So what's going to happen to Calvin?"

"Connor contacted Marine Patrol. By now, they've gone out to Macomek. I'm not sure what they're going to do, but at the very least they'll charge Calvin and Patty with withholding information related to a murder investigation. Patty's got a couple of DUIs on her record, so that might influence their treatment of her. I really don't know."

"And you'll tell them about Calvin saving your life."

"Connor already gave Officer LeClair a heads up. Of course, I went overboard after Calvin took off with me in his boat. Marine Patrol will have to untangle all of this. I'll call them first thing in the morning."

I reached LeClair at eight. The sergeant peppered me with questions, and I promised to drive up to Marine Patrol headquarters and make an official statement. When I asked what'd happened to Calvin and Patty, his response told me nothing.

"We're talking to them."

I'd just hung up when Alise walked into my office. She handed me a cup and said, "From the Neap Tide."

I pulled off the lid and peered in. "Fantastic. Sally's making lattes again."

She grinned. "Gotta keep my mentor happy. Here's the final draft of the grant proposal with Harvey. I think it's in pretty good shape."

"Thanks. I need to read it through one last time. Come back in twenty minutes, and we can give it to Seymour together. Good?"

She saluted and closed the door on her way out.

Sipping the coffee, once more I read through the NOAA Sea Grant proposal titled "Impacts of Acidification on Mussel Aquaculture in the Gulf of Maine." If funded, Alise would work with Harvey to monitor pH concentrations in the Gulf of Maine and with mussel aquaculturalists on impacts of acidic waters on mussel growth. Not a thing needed to be changed.

A half hour later, Alise and I marched down to Seymour's office. She knocked on his door. He answered with "Come!," which we did. Seymour was the only US scientist I'd met who used this typically British way to grant entry into an office. He probably thought it sounded erudite. To me, it was ludicrous.

Alise slid the proposal across his desk. "Here you go Dr. Hull. The second Sea Grant proposal, right on time. As I'm sure you know, I left the other one with your secretary yesterday."

He frowned at the tattoo on her arm, snatched the proposal, slid his glasses up his long nose, and flipped the pages. "Well, looks like everything's here"

Taking that as our signal to leave, we did. On the way up the stairs, Alise said in a low voice, "He hardly looked at it at all."

"Nope." I agreed. "He'll give it to his secretary, and she'll make sure everything—references, budget, vitas, all that—really is there. Hey, you did an absolutely stellar job. I'm sorry I wasn't around to help out more."

We'd reached the chemistry floor. "I'll tell Harvey the proposal's on Seymour's desk," she said.

I stood in the stairwell for a moment and watched the door close behind Alise. Smart, hard-working, and a great colleague, she was going to be a successful oceanographer. The woman was politically savvy too, not one of my strengths to say the least. She'd called Seymour "Dr. Hull" when other grad students did not. Harvey was, of course "Harvey" and not "Dr. Allison." If she called me "Mr. Tusconi," I'd laugh. Yes, that girl was going to do just fine.

That evening, Gordy was in my kitchen feeling pretty low.

"I'm sure it feels lousy to realize Patty was using you," I said.

Back against the wall, arms crossed, Gordy looked down at his feet. "I do feel like a total dope. She played me like a fiddle."

I'd invited Harvey, Connor, and Gordy for dinner. Gordy had arrived early. Circling the room to get out plates, silverware, napkins, and the like, I offered my cousin whatever solace I could. Unlucky in love, as they say, I was in no position to give advice.

Connor's truck came to a stop behind Gordy's as I stepped out onto the deck. "Hey, you two."

Harvey practically ran up the four steps. Holding me tight, she said, "Damn, girl, we could've lost you."

I stepped back when she let me go. "It already seems like it happened to someone else." I changed the subject. "Gordy's in the living room."

Connor dropped something wrapped in brown paper on the kitchen counter. It smelled decidedly like fish.

I patted the package. "This looks big enough to be a tuna."

He beamed. "Biggest striper I've caught. Got it right off Juniper Ledge outside the habah. Too bad Angelo missed it."

"He's down in Portland with a sick friend."

Connor pulled back the brown paper. I leaned in to admire a fillet as long as my arm. "Jeez. I've never seen one so big."

With his hand, he divided the fillet into sections. "I'll cut a piece big enough for now an' leave some for your next dinnah. I'll even grill it tonight if you want."

"I'd love that. You know where the grill is."

My Maine cottage is just that—a cottage. The combined living-dining room was the only place a group of people could comfortably sit and chat.

Feet on the coffee table, beer in hand, Gordy greeted Connor and Harvey with, "Hey, how are you guys?."

I slid cheese and crackers onto the end of the table Gordy hadn't appropriated. "If you all want to talk about what happened on Macomek, please go ahead. I'll be in the kitchen getting things ready for dinner. After that, I'd like a moratorium on the subject. There's plenty of other things we can talk about."

Gordy saluted, Harvey nodded, and Connor said "Okay." I was pretty sure they understood why I was tired of talking and thinking about the whole Macomek venture. Even if they didn't, my dearest friends would give me some slack.

As I sliced tomatoes and cucumbers for salad and red peppers and zucchini for grilling, I caught snatches of conversation. "So it really was an accident?" "What did Marine Patrol say?" After filling my biggest wooden bowl with fresh salad greens, I scattered cherry tomatoes and cukes across the top and looked around. Everything was ready for my favorite fall Maine dinner—grilled vegetables and fish, lots of salad, and fresh bread from Spruce Harbor's bakery. I leaned against the doorframe between the living room and kitchen.

The conversation had turned to a Caribbean-wide calamity.

Harvey said, "I just can't believe what's happening out there. Three category four or five hurricanes in as many weeks? Even those weather guys who broadcast when they can hardly stand up in pelting wind and rain are running out of superlatives."

Connor patted her hand. "It's called The Weather Channel."

Harvey—who, of course, only watched PBS—said, "Right. The Weather Channel."

"Okay," Connor said. "I got two eggheads to ask. I keep hearin' the weather guys say things like 'record-breaking.' I look at the storm track, and it's a huge mothah hurricane. Winds like one-hundred-fifty miles an hour. Lobstahmen get off the watah when it's, what, forty or fifty? And then there's the president sayin' it's all jus' a regular storm."

Talked out, Gordy looked expectantly at Harvey and me.

"It's complicated and it's not," I began.

Gordy rolled his eyes. I ignored him.

"Take Hurricane Harvey in Texas." I winked at Harvey. "Sorry, girl. As Harvey roared over that state, sea surface temperatures off the Texas coast were somewhere between three and six degrees Fahrenheit above average. That was one of the highest above-average measurements in the world."

Gordy nodded. "I'm with you so far."

"Good. Hurricanes happen when weather disturbances like thunderstorms interact with warm water. Heat is energy, right? So in Hurricane Harvey's case, all that ocean heat made that storm more intense, longer-lasting, and with super-high rainfall."

Scientist Harvey jumped in. "The way meteorologists explain it, hurricanes begin when water that evaporates from warm seawater gets dragged up by high-altitude winds."

"Since I got all that," Gordy said, "what you jus' said must be the easier bit ta understand."

I nodded. "Right. Now we get to predicting storm track and intensity. It's always difficult, but Harvey behaved like no hurricane meteorologists know about in that region."

Gordy's eyebrows raised.

I kept going. "Harvey got stronger and stronger and was category four when it reached land. There's no record of a hurricane doing that there."

"So why did it?" Gordy asked.

"Hurricanes churn up ocean water from hundreds of feet down. That water's usually colder than what's at the surface, and that cold water weakens the storm."

Gordy finished the lesson. "But the deep watah off Texas wasn't cold."

"That's right," I said. "People naturally want accurate predictions about where storms are going and how intense they'll be. Like I said, that's always been hard. Now it's even harder. Weather prediction computer models are based on previous storms, but the game has changed. Those models probably won't work as well as they used to because climate change has altered so many critical pieces."

"We're all gettin' the rug pulled out from undah us with this climate business," Gordy said. "That's for sure true with fishermen."

Connor stood. "Gordy, didn't you tell me that the lobster biologists found something strange they don't understand?"

"Ayuh. It's the tiny lobsters. They can't find 'em where they've been countin' 'em for yeahs an' don't know why."

Hands folded in his lap, Gordy looked as somber as I'd ever seen him. I wanted to say something hopeful but couldn't think of what that might be.

We'd just finished my apple crisp with ice-cream dessert when Gordy handed me a present loosely wrapped in tissue paper. "For the scientist snoop," he said.

The oval-shaped mystery item felt hard. I anticipated something like a "If You Piss Off the Writer She'll Put You In A Book and Kill You" mug. Instead, I held up a vintage lobster buoy.

The wood buoy was faded yellow with a reddish stripe across the middle. "This is great," I said.

Gordy reached over and ran a finger across the middle stripe. "It's a pretty special. A Maloy buoy my granddad used."

I carefully laid the buoy on the table next to my empty desert plate. "But Gordy, it's a family heirloom. You should keep it for yourself."

He shook his head. "Nah. You did one helluva a job on Macomek. And, Mara, you *are* family."

It's awkward for me to show sentiment, even with those closest to me. Blinking, I managed "Damn" and left it at that.

19

I PADDED ACROSS THE DECK AND LEANED BACK AGAINST THE railing to look up at the stars. My home had been filled with happy chatter and good conversation, but now I was ready to relish the quiet. When my spine demanded an upright posture, I sat on the top step, stared into the dark, and smiled at the thought of Gordy's generous gift. While the buoy itself was a treasure, Gordy's words were even more special.

"You *are* family," he'd said. Funny. Even though my lack of family was a stubborn ache, I never really considered my mother's sister, Gordy's mom, a kindred soul. Like many people I'd met who lived in northernmost Maine, Gordy's parents had been very conservative, extremely independent, and suspicious of outsiders. They'd viewed me as an elitist who studied books but really didn't know much about the natural world they hunted in, fished on, and cut lumber from day after day. But Gordy was different. Bright and ambitious, he'd moved to Spruce Harbor, became a leader in the fishing community, and was willing to learn about marine science, albeit reluctantly at times.

That he truly thought of me as *family* meant more than he could ever know. Next time I saw him....

My musing was interrupted by a boat motor's low rumble drifting up from the beach. It was a sound I rarely heard at the house because passing boats avoided the rocky, shallow waters off my beach, especially at night. Holding my breath, I turned my auditory synapses to high alert.

Nothing.

Convinced I hadn't imaged the hum, I followed the familiar path and walked out onto the beach. The lobster boat was only thirty feet from shore. Someone, I couldn't make out who, was pushing their way through knee-high water toward me.

She didn't seem the least surprised that I was there to greet her.

"Patty, what are you doing here?" I demanded.

"Is that any way ta welcome your Macomek neighbah?"

I repeated my question.

"Heard ya the firs' time," she slurred. She opened her mouth to say more but was interrupted by a deep hacking cough. Leaning over, she spit phlegm on the sand in front of her feet, straightened, and wiped her mouth. "You got me in a whole lotta trouble, bitch, an' I'm gonna do somethin' about it."

In different circumstances, I would have dismissed the pronouncement as irrational rambling of a sad and very drunk young woman. But a typical drunk wouldn't travel miles by boat at night, anchor off my beach, and wade through the water in search of my house. Angry and unpredictable, Patty Burgess could do me a lot of harm.

Bile bubbled up from my stomach and fouled the insides of my mouth. I swallowed to push it back down. "I only told Marine Patrol what happened. That it was an accident."

Her cackle ended in another rasping cough. Straightening up again she said, "But what, smart bitch, if it wasn't?"

She smelled horribly of alcohol, stale cigarettes, and ripe sweat. Taking a step back I said, "I don't understand."

Pointing a finger, she lunged toward me. "Tha's 'xactly right. You undahstand nothin', zero, nada."

The woman was drunk, stoned, and maybe crazy. If I kept her talking, I could buy time and think. "So tell me what I don't know."

She patted her chest. "*I'm* in charge heah. What happenin' now is we're goin' for a boat ride."

I answered with more bravado than I felt. "I'm not going anywhere with you. You're drunk, for one thing."

She reached into the breast pocket of a ratty green and black checked jacket. Something flashed in the bit of moonlight.

"Patty, what…?"

She waved the gun. "Shut up. Out ta the boat. Like I said, we're goin' fer a ride."

Extremely aware that a drunkard was pointing a gun at my back, I slogged through the water toward the lobster boat. My knowledge of guns was thin, so I had no idea what kind it was. I did know, however, that an inebriated, unstable woman had her finger near the trigger.

I climbed up onto the stern deck. Right behind, Patty gave me a shove. "Ovah by the wheel."

Glued to the deck, my legs felt like they belonged to someone else.

The jab in the small of my back sent a jolt of electricity up my spine. I shuffled forward and stopped at the cabin opening. Patty turned the key and the boat came to life.

"Go pull up the anchor," she barked. "Jump in the watah, and it'll be like shootin' fish in a barrel.

Believing her, I picked my way up to the bow and mechanically yanked and secured the anchor.

"Get right back heah," she yelled.

Again, I followed her directions.

My captor revved the engine and slammed it into gear. The boat leapt forward.

Hands on the wheel, she endured another coughing jag, spit the result into the air, stuffed a cigarette into her mouth, and lit it with a lighter.

Cigarette wagging between her lips she said, "Into the wheelhouse, bitch, where I can see ya."

Inside the cabin, I leaned back against the wall and finally snapped to. In what I could only imagine was deranged copycat behavior, Patty had decided to abduct me in a lobster boat. We were speeding away from shore through the dark in waters this witch didn't know, drunk or not, and I fully expected her to smash the boat into a rock ledge. That or some other calamity had to be in the offing. I needed a plan and fast.

Looking around, I suddenly realized I'd been in the same cabin just days ago. Patty had borrowed or—given her drunken state—more likely taken, Calvin Ives' *Lucky Catch*.

I wasn't sure why, but knowing this made me feel a little better. Probably because everything is so neat and orderly, I thought. Clean and ready for him to step into, Calvin's orange bib overalls hung on a hook. At my feet was Calvin's cabinet with all his charts and manuals. Above the cabinet, his red waterproof box labeled "Marine Emergency Kit" was secured to the wall. Hah, I thought. Streaking thought the night in a boat captained by a drunk crazy lady was an emergency for sure.

I slid down onto my butt. Legs outstretched and feeling totally helpless, I tried to come up with an escape plan. Tackling Patty was a lousy idea. The woman looked like she lifted weights. She also had a gun and was drunk. I could dash out onto the stern and jump off, but then I'd be in cold water with no life jacket and no way to contact anyone. Besides that, Patty could easily turn around and run me over.

I looked around the cabin in the hope that something would spark an idea and landed on the emergency kit. The flash in my brain was as bright as the contents of that red box. Marine emergency kits held flares mariners shoot into the sky to signal that they're in trouble. Anyone seeing the flare would report the sighting to authorities such as local police, the Coast Guard, or Marine Patrol. A key responsibility for Maine's Marine Patrol officers was following up on such sightings along the coast.

From the wheel, Patty couldn't see much in the dimly lit cabin. I slowly slid my butt across the deck to a position where I'd block any view she might have of the emergency kit. In slow motion, I reached for the box, opened it, slid out three flares, and pressed the kit closed. The lid shut with a resounding snap.

I froze. Surely Patty must have heard what sounded to me like a gunshot. But she stayed put. The boat's engine had masked the sound.

Flares behind my back, I slid back to my corner and faced Patty again. She lit another cigarette. In profile, the flame tinted orange a spiky-haired freak that Maine thriller writer Stephen King would have loved.

Patty threw the lighter on a shelf in front of her. Isolated in her own crazed world, it seemed like she was hardly aware I was on the boat.

My next move—shooting the flares off the stern into the night sky—was problematic, to say the least. I'd have to get up, walk out onto the aft deck, and discharge the flares. All without her stopping me.

Patty solved the problem for me. Once more, she doubled over with that dreadful rasping cough. But this time she gagged on her own vomit.

Between groans and "oh my gods," the woman upchucked onto the deck beside the wheel. She slammed the boat into neutral, clamped a hand over her mouth, threw her torso over the gunwale, and emptied her guts out.

It was now or never.

I sprang to my feet, grabbed the flares, and sprinted into the pitch black of the stern. Standing still, I was rewarded by another of Patty's groans. The woman was in no state to wonder where I was. Even if she recovered quickly, the unlit stern offered me cover.

There was downside to that blackness. Boating regulations specified bright white lights fore and aft for a reason. Patty had been running dark—a foolish, dangerous thing to do.

I shivered, a mixture of fear and cold. At night, the open deck of a boat off Maine's coast was uncomfortably cold even in the fall. Without a jacket and still wet from the knees down, I had to ignore the bitter wind and focus on my task.

After securing two of the flares between my feet, I cradled the third one. It had been a couple of years since I'd done a marine safety course. Now I had to remember how to set the damn thing off.

"Come on," I whispered. "What's the first thing?"

From somewhere in the computer that was my brain, "Firmly hold the ribbed handle" came to me. In the cabin, I'd fingered both the bumpy handle and the cap below it.

I wrapped my right hand around the handle, stretched out my arm, and froze. I couldn't remember what to do next.

"Picture the flare right before it's lit." I whispered. "What does it look like?"

I slowed my breathing like we did in yoga class and waited for the image to come to me. It did. There was a short cord with little ball at the end that dangled from the bottom of the flare. To set the flare off, you pulled the ball.

But where in hell was that cord?

My outstretched arm was cramping. I dropped it and fingered the device with my left hand. On the bottom was a cap.

"Duh. The cord's under the cap."

I unscrewed the cap and released the firing cord and its little ball. Really ready to go this time, I stretched my arm out and up in the direction the wind was blowing. With one quick snap of my wrist, I pulled the cord.

There was a sharp recoil as the flare hissed. Then the projectile took off, well, like a rocket. A single bright red star, it climbed higher and higher into the black sky. Mesmerized, I watched it rise to an astounding height, arc, and drop gracefully down into the ocean.

I pumped a fist in the air. One down, two to go. Reaching down, I grabbed the second flare and repeated the maneuver exactly. Pulling the cord, I looked up to watch the show. But nothing happened.

I hissed, "Goddamn piece of crap."

I took the third, final flare from between my feet and held it out. "Come on baby, come on." Slower this time, I unscrewed the cap, aimed the flare as before, and pulled the cord.

The rocket took off and leapt into the black sky. I watched until the glow blinked out. Done, I closed my eyes for a moment and also sent aloft a quiet thank you.

I suddenly wanted to run, jump, do anything but stand still on the boat deck. Adrenaline, I knew, was racing through my body. But all I could do was bounce on my heels. Anything more vigorous would attract Patty's attention.

Patty. I froze and listened. No gagging or groans. Fixed on the flares, I had no idea when she'd stopped.

My abductor flicked on a flashlight, waved the beam around the stern, and found my face. I covered my eyes.

"What the hell are you doing?"

"I, ah, had to take a leak."

She mimicked what I'd said in a little girl's voice. "She had to take a leak."

Fussing with my pants like they needed to be fastened, I walked past her and returned to the wheelhouse.

Patty took her position again and started the motor. We resumed speed, but slower than before.

Back in my corner, I waited and worried. There'd been no VHF distress call before or after the flares. Such calls weren't required since someone needing help might not have a radio, but it troubled me anyway. Were two flares enough? That depended on whether Marine Patrol or a savvy citizen was watching the night sky. Might they wonder if somebody playing Fourth of July sent up the flares? Such behavior was illegal and a definite no-no among mariners. Those who played by the rules, anyway.

Minutes went by—how many I didn't know because my watch was sitting on my bedroom bureau. As more minutes passed, worry set in. Where the hell was the Marine Patrol? If Patty was steering for Macomek, we couldn't be *that* far from the mainland. Someone should have seen the distress signals. Even if we were farther than I imagined, other boats were bound to be out. They'd see the flares and notify someone, wouldn't they?

I wasn't sure when I first noticed, but soon it became obvious that we were losing speed. Patty also wasn't consumed by that dreadful hacking cough. Legs spread and hands tight on the wheel, she stared straight ahead like a manikin.

The ill-lit lobster boat motored on, thick gloom the only witness to its journey.

20

I STOOD IN THE CABIN RUBBING MY ARMS TO WARM UP WHEN something bright in the distance flickered. Blinking, I tried to focus. Nothing. I stared, moved over a bit, stared some more. Tears filled my eyes.

No way was Patty going to see me cry.

Looking down, I wiped my eyes with the sleeve of my turtleneck and raised my head with a sniff. That's when I really did see them. Distant flashing blue lights.

Suddenly, they were on us. Lights still going, the Marine Patrol's vessel circled *Lucky Catch*. Patty didn't even try to give chase. The whole thing took minutes, and I'd barely processed what was happening when it was all over.

Sergeant LeClair escorted Patty to his patrol boat while Officer Bernadette DelBarco attended to me. After I'd finally convinced Bernie that I was cold but otherwise fine, she leaned over the gunwale and asked someone on the patrol boat for a jacket.

Inside Calvin's cabin, snug in the singular green jacket, I gave Bernie the Cliffs Notes version of what happened. When LeClair came back, I would answer his questions in more detail.

"Where are we?" I asked Bernie.

"About two miles northeast of Spruce Harbor, less than a mile off shore," she said.

"You're kidding. We hardly went anywhere."

Shaking her head, Bernie said, "Good thing. Wherever

she took you in the dark, she was only running with light from the cabin." She pointed at the starboard side of the boat. "Your beach, from where you describe it, is right there."

I'd let go of all the tension, fear, and worry. Now, exhaustion overtook me. "How 'bout a ride home?" I asked.

She grinned. "Maybe we can manage that. 'Course we'll wait for what Sergeant LeClair has to say."

I didn't have to wait long. After LeClair told Bernie that the Marine Patrol medic was taking care of Patty, he turned to me, clasped my hand, and said he was sorry to see me again under such circumstances. The man repeated many of Bernie's questions about my wellbeing and asked me to describe what had happened from beginning to end. He was especially interested in Patty's behavior and what she'd said.

"Besides being drunk, the woman must be high on something," I said.

LeClair didn't disagree or provide any details. I assumed they'd take her to a psychiatric hospital.

"She's angry because you reported what happened with Buddy Crawford," LeClair said. "I get that. But why take someone else's lobster boat, motor to the mainland, force you onto the boat, and ride around in circles?"

"Who knows," I said. "She heard what happened after Calvin found me on his boat, so in her screwed-up mind she wanted to finish the job?"

He closed his notebook. "Dr. Tusconi, it seems like this Macomek business is holding you in its web. I've certainly never had a case where someone was taken captive on a lobster boat twice in one week."

"Have to say, it's nothing I want to experience again."

His cobalt-blue eyes tightened as if my pain had stung him. "You'll need to drive up to the Rockland office again.

We'll probably have more questions, and you can go over your statement."

Since the Marine Patrol vessel would transport Patty to wherever they were taking her, LeClair decided that Bernie and a fourth officer could give me a ride home in *Lucky Catch*. They would secure Calvin's boat in Spruce Harbor, and my beach was right on the way. Bernie insisted on walking me up to my house and waiting until I gave her the okay. From the deck, I watched her flashlight dance along the path before she dropped down onto the beach.

* * *

Preoccupied with a spreadsheet, I kept my eyes on the numbers and said, "Come on in, Alise" to the knock.

Ted's said, "Sorry, not Alise."

I looked up to see him standing in front of my half-open office door. Surprise and angst had turned me into a babbling idiot. "Oh. I thought, I mean. What time is it?"

"Around nine. In the morning."

"Oh. Alise is due at ten. Sorry."

"Okay if I come in?"

I flipped down the computer screen. "Yeah. That'd be great."

He rolled back the chair next to mine and sat down. I told my heart to slow down and tried to look nonchalant.

"I've heard bits and pieces of what happened out on Macomek Island but would like to get the story from you," he said.

Months earlier, Ted had complained that trouble followed me around. His desire to learn about my most recent escapade was a sea change.

Warily at first, I laid out "the Macomek story," emphasizing for Ted's sake my duty to Gordy and reason for searching

Calvin's cabin. I didn't mention the previous night's boat trip. There was more than enough to say without adding that bit of mischief.

Between shakes of the head and "exclamations of "unbelievable!" Ted asked lots of questions. "So Calvin hid his anger toward Lester for how long?"

"Since 1995."

"Wow. Long, long time. You said Calvin was a highliner. Why would a smart guy like that sympathize with someone like Patty?"

I nodded. "Good question. I'm guessing he didn't know how unstable she was. When I first met her, I never would have thought Patty was hooked on alcohol and drugs. It's possible nobody, not even her mother, knew. Gordy sure didn't. So Calvin must've seen her as a teacher worried about her former students and outraged that Buddy could be so uncaring and greedy. People view Calvin as a leader in the community. Patty probably told him what Buddy was up to and asked for his help."

Ted digested that for a moment and added, "Maybe Patty was obsessed to protect those kids because she knew more than most what drug addiction does to someone."

"Could be," I said. "I also think Buddy's death pushed her off the deep end."

Ted circled back to Calvin's motivation. "So exposing Buddy would be a way for Calvin to get at Lester?"

"Sure. Lester was so proud of his grandson. Seeing Buddy in jail because he sold drugs to minors? You can imagine how that would hurt."

"You have to wonder why Calvin didn't just go to the police."

"Yeah, another good question. Macomek's a small island. The three of them may have ended up at the harbor together and it just happened. Apparently, Buddy could be a cocky jerk.

Maybe he said something and that set Calvin and Patty off." I leaned back in my chair and rubbed my eyes.

"One last question?"

"Hmm?"

"Do you think Buddy fell off the pier? That it was an accident?"

I shrugged. "A week ago, I couldn't imagine Calvin or Patty harming one of their own. Now?"

"It's amazing that Calvin circled back and dove into the water after you. Shows his real character."

Unsure exactly what Ted meant, I asked him to explain.

"True character comes out when someone faces a dilemma. The greater the pressure, the stronger a person's character when they make the unselfish choice."

We stood in unison. Narrowed hipped and toned in jeans and a white T-shirt, Ted looked damned good. My desire to feel and smell his body was so fierce I hugged myself to keep my arms still. I got lost in the deep blue of his eyes before looking away.

Silence filled the room. Finally he said, "You're okay and that's what really matters."

"Thanks for that and for stopping by."

"By the way, there's a party at my house tomorrow afternoon. Burgers, corn, potato salad, beer. It'd be terrific if you came."

"Celebration of fall's arrival?"

"That and Penny's heading back to Wood Hole."

"Ah. I should've asked about the submersible research."

"Really exciting stuff. You'd love it. See you at the party?"

"Um…I'll try."

I closed the door behind Ted and fell into my chair. I was such a goddamned fool. He'd stopped by as a friend concerned about what happened to another friend. There was no romance between us and never would be. Ted and Penny were a unit. He was giving her a party for god's sake. Again, I pictured the two of them in the close quarters of a submersible as they marveled at wonders they'd only seen in photographs or as pickled specimens. A marine biologist's dream.

Embarrassed and angry with myself, I couldn't share my misery with anyone, including Harvey. After all, Ted was her half-brother. Still, I really needed to vent and trudged down the stairs to the basement.

When the big open room was clean and put back in order, Homer had been transferred to his usual tank. On my way to it, I stopped at a large circular tank that held squid jet-propelling around. The otherworldly creatures led with their bulbous heads and trailed eight sucker-bearing arms behind. As a result of global warming, *Loligo pealei* could now be found all the way up to northern Maine, which spawned lots of local interest. Tackle shops sold squid jigs to anglers trying their luck with prey that looked nothing at all like fish.

Homer glided up to the glass as I looked in.

"Hey, buddy."

Like a dog looking for his treat, Homer backed up and waved his antennae upward. I returned with some mussels, cracked them, and dropped bits of meat into the aquarium. He snatched each one before it landed on the bottom and shredded it. Bits of food moved toward his mouth like they were on a conveyer belt. Watching Homer do his lobster thing helped me remember the joy of simply observing animals with no expectation of what they might do.

Expectation takes you away from what's really happening.

Finished with his food, Homer settled down on the bottom of his domain.

"I haven't seen you since we went for that ride together

during the flood. A lot's happened, but mostly I need to talk about Ted."

At the mention of Ted's name, one of Homer's antennae twitched. I believed, but didn't know of course, that Homer especially liked Ted McNight.

"So after he said he wanted to get married some day, and I freaked out, we split up. Actually, he did the splitting because of the marriage thing and my reluctance to, you know, give myself to him."

Homer kind of rolled his eyes.

"No, no. Nothing to do with sex. Actually, that part was incredible. I froze when he tried to hold me, that type of thing."

Homer kind of tipped his head. To a lobster, I guessed, the concept of "hold" was only associated with fighting and eating one another. I didn't try to explain.

"He invited me to a party at his house tomorrow. That's nice, but he's giving it for his girlfriend Penny. It'll kill me to see them together."

Homer jumped back like I'd hit the glass plate. He'd never done that before, and I didn't know what to make of it. Finally, I gave up and left.

Ongoing work throughout the day—talking with Alise, a pesky water sampler that needed repair, a department meeting, and a newspaper reporter asking about eel biology—kept me from dwelling on Ted's party.

Wing Point, a spit of land across the harbor from Seal Point where Angelo lives, has a little-used running path. During my sprint down to its end, I obsessed about Ted's party. A worthy friend, he had been genuinely concerned about events on Macomek. How could I blow him off and not show up at a get-together he seemed eager for me to attend?

At the end of the trail, I stretched my legs on top of a

boulder and watched waves smashing into rocks below. Ted's reference to Calvin's noble act haunted me. "True character comes out when someone faces a dilemma. The greater the pressure, the stronger a person's character when they make the unselfish choice."

Unlike Calvin, I didn't have to choose between someone dying and my facing the police. I'd pushed away a smart, kind, sexy-as-hell lover who wanted to marry me—then was surprised when he wanted to be "just friends." My behavior had been motivated by fear of abandonment, the aching loss of my parents, and stubborn individualism. Honest enough to acknowledge all that, I now had to choose between keeping my distance from Ted or becoming the noble friend who was happy he'd found another mate.

My psyche fought with itself. The generous part of me argued that I was quite capable of attending the party, enjoying the company of MOI scientists, and looking the other way when Ted pulled Penny close. My less charitable side said "No way," and painted a picture of me leaving the party in tears, or worse, doing something obvious like staring helplessly at the happy couple. Back and forth I went. At home, showered and sated with dinner, I'd still made no decision.

Midnight found me half asleep in bed with a book. Too distracted to read, I flipped on the light and prowled the dark house in search of an answer.

21

THE NEXT MORNING, I OVERSLEPT AND NEARLY MISSED A
prospective job applicant's talk. Seymour would surely
have whined about my absence, especially since the
speaker was a female chemical oceanographer, something rare
in the field.

I walked Harvey back to her office.

"It's not like you to be late for an important talk," she said.

I stood behind her as she unlocked her door. "I'm recovered
from the Macomek business, if that's what you mean."

She pushed the door open. "Come on in. Sorry the place
is a mess."

Harvey's version of "mess" was a desk where books and
papers were neatly piled side by side. "I meant that Seymour uses
every opportunity to go after you. The guy's so petty and small."

Driving home that afternoon, I couldn't put Harvey's
description of Seymour out of my mind. "The guy's so petty and
small." Could I allow myself to be on the same low moral plane
as a man I despised?

I ran through every excuse I could think of for not going
to the party. It was a twenty-odd mile drive and my gas tank
was low. I didn't feel like talking to anyone. I'd already turned
down my road when I came up with clothes as a pretext. Pulling
over, I checked out what I was wearing—jeans (just washed),
red turtleneck (ditto), and a flannel shirt that served as a jacket.
Pretty much what I wore every day. I adjusted the mirror to

check out my appearance. For a change, my hair was pulled back into a neat ponytail. I examined my teeth. No green bits marred my smile.

I turned around and took the nearest road west.

The party was well underway when I parked behind Betty Buttz's truck. Looking for a way to delay, I peered through her passenger window. Like Harvey, she kept her shotgun on a gun rack in her truck, but Betty's was overhead instead of behind her seat. Smart, I thought. Thieves wouldn't easily see it up there. Since there was nothing else of interest in the truck, I slowly climbed the steep driveway. The aroma of grilled hamburgers wafting by made my mouth water.

Waving, Ted spotted me before I reached the lawn. He turned back to the volleyball game about to begin. I watched as he tossed the ball in the air and delivered a killer jump serve his opponents failed to return. Damn. Could he look a little less like a Greek dude from the first Olympics?

For the next hour I talked to every person I liked—and someone I really didn't. Circling the classic New England house, I pretended to appreciate its architecture and examined the vegetable garden in the back. Beyond the garden, I watched turkey vultures circle overhead. Soon I ran out of things to occupy my time.

I was digging a beer out of the cooler when Betty walked up. We clinked beer cans.

"How're you doing, Betty?"

"Better than you are, Mara, I'd guess."

I swear the woman could read my mind. That had helped a lot when I was obsessing about Seymour's treatment of me, and she'd correctly diagnosed his lack of confidence. Today it was just embarrassing.

"Um, what do you mean?"

"I've been watching you, and it's almost funny. Every time that man comes near you, you're off to find someone else to talk to or someplace to go."

I took a slug. "You must be imagining things. Why would I do that?"

It was impressive eye roll. "You think I don't know what's going down with you? For Christ's sake, go talk to the man. It's his party, after all."

I gave up the pretense. "Fish or cut bait?"

She reached over and gave my arm a squeeze. "You're a lot stronger than you think."

Even less touchy-feely than I was, that much contact for Betty was a big deal. At MOI's founding, my father had lobbied for Betty's hire, and she'd turned out to be a leader in the early days of physical oceanography after World War II. With his and my mother's passing, Betty had stepped in as mother–father–mentor rolled into one. And every bit of advice she'd given me had been right on the money. But this was the first time she'd counseled me about Ted.

A slow smile brightened Ted's face. "Hey. I thought you'd left."

"I, ah, realized I hadn't thanked you for the party."

"Oh."

I looked over his shoulder. "Where's Penny?"

"Did you want to speak with her?"

"Um, well, I never talked to her about the submersible."

"You'll have to email her. She's already left for Woods Hole. Then she's off to Antarctica for a couple of months."

My hand flew to my mouth, and I faked a cough. "Excuse me."

Ted turned to see a couple of people who looked like they were on their way over to speak to us.

He gave them a quick wave and steered me in the other direction.

"I wanted to ask you something."

"About today's seminar?"

"I thought she did a good job," he said. "But no, that's not it."

Nervous, I wet my lips and waited. Whatever Ted wanted to ask, it seemed like it was important.

"I'm taking a test dive in a new NOAA submersible off Schoodic Ridge to see the deep-sea corals. Would you like to go with me?"

"The coral hanging gardens?"

"Yeah."

"In a NOAA submersible."

"Yes."

"With you."

"That's what I said, Mara."

Tears flooded my eyes, and there was absolutely nothing I could do about it.

He put both hands on my shoulders. "Are you all right?"

"I'm good. Real good. Do you have any Kleenex?"

22

I DROPPED ONTO THE BENCH AT THE END OF MOI's PIER where RV—Research Vessel—*Thalassa* was tied up. A couple of crewmates wandered around her aft deck, but it didn't look like the ship would pull away anytime soon. My dive watch told me only ten minutes had passed since I'd last checked the time. The boat that would transport Ted and me out to Schoodic Ridge, twenty-five nautical miles off Bar Harbor, would stay where it was for at least another half hour.

"Shove ovah."

I slid my butt six inches to the left as Betty fell onto the bench.

""So you're goin' down in a little sub to see the coral gardens," she said.

"That's right."

"I'd imagine you didn't sleep too well last night and not just because you're excited."

A gull hovering directly above released a mussel from its mouth. We watched as the bivalve smashed onto the pier's cement edge. The bird's snack cracked opened on impact.

"You're right. Not much sleep." I tried to think of something to divert the conversation, but Betty was too quick for me.

"You don't have to do this, you know. They've got good video feed, so you can watch everything from the ship."

"Might as well stay here if I do that."

"Mara, cut it out," she said.

"Nobody who's gone down in *Benthic Pioneer* lost their parents in a submarine accident."

I fixed on a distant buoy off the harbor. "I've run through the dive a dozen times in my mind—from when we climb in, slipping under the water, sinking down into the dark. All of it. I'll be okay."

"Sounds like you're prepared as you can be. Just don't try to be Superlady."

"Super*woman*. No, I won't." I changed the subject. "Hey, weren't you in Woods Hole when the sub *Alvin* found those deep sea vents? What was it like seeing the first images of the greatest biological find of the century?"

The diversion worked. "I was a post-doc at the Woods Hole Oceanographic Institute. What was it like? Imagine finding animals—big, colorful, never-seen-before animals—on Mars. That's what."

Things were a little more lively on RV *Thalassa*, but not much. I leaned forward, arms on my thighs. "Why don't you start at the beginning?"

As I'd assumed, Betty relished talking about the astounding discovery. "It was winter of nineteen-seventy-seven. Oceanographers were on WHOI's RV *Knorr* off Ecuador studying deep-sea spreading zones. The top-notch team of geologists couldn't have imagined they'd need biologists on the cruise. The bottom images they'd seen were from a camera towed behind the ship on a steel cable. The sled—that's what they called the towed steel cage—had powerful strobe lights, the camera, and a very sensitive temperature sensor to detect thermal vents in the spreading zone."

"So how deep was this towed camera?" I asked.

"Eight thousand feet below the ship. An incredible engineering feat."

I tried to envisage a heavy—maybe a couple of tons—steel cage towed at that depth, close enough to the sea bottom to take photos and measure temperature but not so close as to smash into the lava-covered seafloor. "Wow. Keep going, Betty."

"Well, around midnight, the sensor measured a spike in temperature. People got excited because it seemed like they'd found what they were looking for—a deep-sea hydrothermal vent. Direct evidence of seafloor spreading and continental drift."

"The idea that continents move. You forget how recently that was discovered," I said.

She shook her head. "I remember when scientists who pointed out how neatly South America fit into Africa were ridiculed. So where was I?"

"Um, the temperature spike."

"Right. Photographs taken right before and after that temperature spike showed what you'd expect—barren, fresh-looking lava. But in the dozen or so frames that coincided with the temperature increase scientists saw something they simply couldn't believe."

As if I were there, I held my breath.

"Clams," she said. "Hundreds and hundreds of big white clams."

"Clams," I repeated. "Over a mile below the sea surface where it's completely dark and near freezing. A deep-sea desert. Then what happened?"

"Within hours WHOI's RV *Lulu* arrived with the submersible *Alvin* on board.

"I know *Alvin* is named after Allyn Vine, the engineer who designed it. But *Lulu*?"

"The catamaran that carried *Alvin* around was named after Vine's mother. The brilliant guy could do whatever he damned well wanted to."

"Hey," I said. "It was just a question."

She waved me off. "Two geologists and *Alvin*'s pilot went down in the sub. On the bottom when *Alvin*'s sensor measured water about ten degrees Centigrade, they knew they'd found the vent site."

I did a quick calculation. "About fifty degrees Fahrenheit. In the deep sea. Astounding."

"Yeah. Looking out his viewport, one of the scientists talked to his grad student aboard *Lulu* by acoustic phone."

"What'd he say?"

"Something like, 'Isn't the ocean's bottom suppose to be like a desert?' When she answered 'Yes,' he told her there were big clusters of foot-long clams at the vent site."

"That's the site they named 'Clambake 1.'"

"Correct. More dives gave them 'Clambake 2' and a site they called 'Dandelion Patch.'"

"What about the foot-plus-long tube worms?"

"They called that one 'Garden of Eden.' Long white-stalked tubeworms with bright red tops. Never been seen before. Swaying in the water, they looked like a field of ted tulips. That was the warmest site, nearly room temperature."

"What was the reaction aboard *Lulu* and *Knorr* as all this was going on?"

"People were dancing on the ceiling. This was an enormous Columbus-scale discovery with so many unanswered questions. The biggest one, of course, was 'What the heck are all these creatures eating?'"

"Too bad the media didn't know scientists would discover a deep sea wonderland fueled by chemical energy from hot vents instead of sunlight. A whole ecosystem we never even knew existed. It could've been watched by millions like the *Apollo* moonwalk."

"Hello, ladies."

Betty and I turned in unison as Ted strolled up and dropped his backpack on the pier next to mine.

"Betty was at WHOI when *Alvin* discovered the Galapagos Rift ecosystem," I said. "First time I've heard the story from beginning to end."

"Betty, I'd love to listen to that," he said. "Over beers at the Lee Side sometime?"

I'd long suspected Betty had a bit of a crush on Ted. Her weathered skin didn't hide the crusty oceanographer's blush.

With a quick nod she said, "Yeah, sure," wished us good luck, and lumbered down the pier toward shore.

Ted took Betty's spot on the bench as several crewmembers boarded *Thallassa*.

"Ready to go?" Ted asked.

I looked down at my hands. "Before we got into deep sea vents, Betty brought up something you and I should talk about."

"Good for her. I've been thinking about this but figured I'd follow your lead."

I bit my lip. "Betty reminded me I don't have to go down. If, you know, I get a panic attack."

As Ted put his hand on my knee, his navy eyes signaled compassion and understanding "Of course, you don't. *Benthic Pioneer* has a terrific camera system. You'd see everything from the ship, and we can talk the whole time I'm on the bottom if you want."

We were discussing my very private struggle in a very public setting, and I felt exposed. I slid away from him a bit

Reaching down for my backpack, I lifted it onto my shoulder. "Really appreciate you saying that. It takes the pressure off. Naturally, I'd love to see deep-sea corals up close, but it's good to know there's a backup plan."

"If you decide to go for it, let me know if you need a little more time before you get into the sub, that type of thing. Believe me, you won't be the first scientist who got the heebie-jeebies as they dropped into a submersible."

We boarded the ship talking about the origin of "heebie-jeebies."

"I think it was coined in the nineteen twenties when nonsense rhyming pairs got popular," Ted said.

"Like the bees knees," I added.

Anyone listening to us could not have imagined that we'd just discussed how I, daughter of two oceanographers who'd died in a submersible, might react to my first dive in one.

Thalassa's captain was in the bridge. Ted, who'd met him before, introduced us. Completely bald, the man made up for his lack of hair with a neatly trimmed white beard and mustache.

He gave my hand one quick shake. "Delighted to have you on board Dr. Tusconi."

"Please call me Mara. For a marine biologist, seeing the Gulf of Maine's hanging coral gardens up close is an opportunity of a lifetime. Um, when will we reach our station, do you think?"

"Late morning, maybe noon."

"And *Benthic Pioneer's* tender is already there."

He glanced at the electronic array in front of him. "Yes. They've gone down twice already. Your dive will be the last one before *Ocean Voyager* heads south to Woods Hole.

I wanted to ask how the dives had gone but man was clearly busy and would probably think it was an odd question anyway. I thanked him, and we left. Ted and I were out on the aft deck when *Thalassa's* engines came to life. We watched as the crew cast off all lines except one on the bow. Only when the stern had swung a good distance out from the pier did the crew release the bow line.

The captain slowly backed away, shifted to forward, and carefully maneuvered the ship out of Spruce Harbor.

How long is *Thalassa*," I asked. "Seventy-five feet?"

"That sounds about right," Ted said. "A lot of ship in a harbor with lobster and pleasure boats."

After *Thalassa* passed through Spruce Harbor's headlands, we clambered down a ladder down to the mess. Ted carried a mug of coffee to a booth. I went for mint tea, and he didn't need to ask why.

Swirling my tea I asked, "This is the first submersible to go down to the hanging gardens?"

"Yup. Researchers studying Maine's deep water reefs have used real-time color video and digital photography, that type of thing."

"I assume subs are too expensive?"

"It's too bad, but they are. As you heard, *Benthic Pioneer* is headed back to Cape Cod. Schoodic Ridge isn't much out of the way, so they decided to do a couple of dives there."

"Since you can find deep-sea corals in canyons closer to the Cape, why dive on Schoodic Ridge?"

It took a moment for him to answer. "Um, well, the highest coral densities are on steep, vertical rock faces. *Benthic Pioneer*'s pilot wanted to see how the submersible operated in that type of setting."

My stomach flipped. "Operated?"

"How close he could get to the rock face so we could see the corals up close."

I let out a long, slow breath. "Oh. I guess that makes sense."

We sat there for a long while as Ted sipped his coffee and I my tea.

23

OCEAN VOYAGER IS NOT YOUR USUAL SHIP. WITH HER oversized A-frame designed to lift a submersible in and out of the water, as we approached she looked like a huge floating mousetrap attached to a boat at the front end.

I thanked one of *Thalassa's* crewmember before we boarded *Ocean Voyager* and added, "What'll you guys do while we're busy with the submersible?"

He answered with a wink. "When you're done we'll bring you home."

"Wow. I'm not used to such service."

"MOI's publicity people told us to take good care of you. Hey, get some cool photos so we can see them on the way back. What you folks are doing is exciting stuff."

Ocean Voyager's aft deck was pretty much taken up by *Benthic Pioneer.* The twenty-odd-foot submersible looked bigger than I'd expected. Given all its tanks, thrusters, tubing, lights, and viewports, the yellow-and-white sub was clearly an impressive piece of ocean engineering.

When Ted announced he'd go up to the bridge and talk to the ship's captain, I opted to stay on deck and "take in the fresh air." He nodded, said he'd be right back, patted my shoulder, and left.

Sucking on a piece of ginger candy, I spread my feet to better manage the rocking ship, leaned back on *Ocean Voyager's* gunwale, and regarded the submersible. The cheerily colored oblong machine didn't appear too menacing.

"In fact," I said aloud. "Given all your tubes, lights, tanks and what-not, you look like a fish out of water."

With his horn-rimmed glasses, crew cut, white T-shirt, jeans, and high-topped sneakers, I couldn't tell if the guy who emerged from the opposite side of the sub was a scientist or a crewmember.

He patted the submersible. "I talk to her all the time. I'm Dylan Dyer, *Benthic Pioneer*'s pilot."

"Hi," I said. "Um, it's pretty impressive."

"Ever been down in a submersible before?"

Looking to the side I said, "No. First time."

I waited for him to come back with "You're going to love it" or something along that line. Instead he said, "Then why don't I explain what's what on *Benthic Pioneer*."

Grateful Dylan was experienced with more than piloting submersibles, I nodded. "That would be terrific."

He pointed to a large black cylinder secured on its side. "I can control the sub's buoyancy by regulating air volume in that ballast tank."

"It looks like a huge scuba tank," I said.

"Yeah, but it functions like a scuba buoyancy compensator device."

I shook my head. "BCs are a total pain to operate."

"Yup. Reason number twenty-five why submersibles have it over scuba." He gestured toward dome-shaped windows on the sub's side and front end. "There are three viewing windows—those two smaller ones and a big one up front—the pilot and scientists can look through. They're dome-shaped so what you're looking at is bigger than it appears."

"Got it. What powers *Benthic Pioneer*?"

"Six thrusters, three on each side, let us move her

horizontally and vertically in the water. Let's see. You'll be especially interested in how we collect specimens."

We walked over to the sub's fore end. "See those turquoise tubes? That's how scientists get organisms they're especially interested in."

"Damn," I said. "All that tubing operated by robotic arms. I can't imagine how difficult it is to coordinate."

He grinned. "You got that right. I've heard lots of swear words I never knew existed."

"How do you communicate with the surface?"

"When you're inside, you'll see the video screen and speaker."

It took a moment before "when" sank it. Then I asked the big question. "What happens if, ah, the sub gets stuck?"

"We have life support for three days—air tanks and carbon dioxide scrubbers. Water and food too."

I swayed as my legs nearly buckled.

Dylan grabbed my arm, "Let's get you sitting down."

He led me to large plastic storage box in front of the sub, waited as I lowered myself onto it, and sat down next to me. "We can talk about it if you want."

The whole thing came out in a tumble—who my parents were, what they were doing in a submersible, why they didn't come up alive.

"Lord almighty," he said. "I knew about *Johnson Sea Link* but not what happened to your parents."

"The *Johnson Sea Link* disaster was especially gruesome because Link lost his son in the dive."

Dylan leaned over, elbows on his knees. "I get why you're here, of course. For a marine biologist from Maine, seeing these deep corals up close is a dream come true. But I've been doing this for a while now and nobody, far as I know, has had to deal with what happened to your mom and dad.

Frankly, I think it's amazing you're here at all."

I swallowed and waited until I could get the words out. "That's…um. I mean, what a great thing to say. Sometimes I feel, you know, like I should just suck it up."

"No way." He glanced at his dive watch. "Look, I'm going to follow your lead. You can skip the dive or try to go for it and back down. Whatever you want."

We stood together. "Any suggestions how I might distract myself."

He shrugged. "How about imagining you're going into a space capsule? You know, for a trip to the space station or something."

Dylan turned and very nearly walked into a short, skinny crewmember who'd just rounded the submersible. Rotating in my direction, Dylan said, "Mara, this is Bart. He'll be helping with the deployment."

Watching Dylan and Bart walk off together, I wondered why the pilot had bothered with the introduction.

When Ted came back, Dylan went over everything from the dive schedule and routine entry and exit procedures to emergency protocol. We'd already read a manual with the same information, but it was good to hear it verbally.

"We'll review some of this when we're inside the capsule," he said. With a quick glance at me he added, "Including emergency procedures."

Dylan's idea that I imagine this was on a mission to the International Space Station actually worked. Thinking about going up instead of down helped me step away from the experience, as if I were watching someone else. In this spacey state of mind, I marched down the deck toward the submersible like a veteran.

It was only after I'd climbed up and watched Bart lift the sub's hatch that the extraterrestrial ruse failed. I, daughter of Bridget and Carlos Tusconi, was about to enter a capsule and sink under the water.

With a quick glace in my direction, Ted slipped down into the submersible. I was next.

Dylan reached extended his hand and said, "Mara, I can help you."

Standing there atop *Benthic Explorer*, I froze and time slowed. *Ocean Voyager* lazily rocked to one side, the other, and back again. A light breeze lifted locks of hair off my forehead. Dylan spoke, but the words were drawn out and incoherent. I tried to ask what he said, but my mouth wouldn't open.

Seconds passed. A minute. More seconds.

The biting voice from behind came through loud and clear. "*Any* time now."

Like someone had smacked me hard, I whirled around. Bart's smirk screamed disdain. "Are you talking to me?" I hissed.

It wasn't his slouch, crossed arms, or practiced expression of boredom that almost made me feel sorry for the young crewmember. It was that his face—pale, scarred with acne, blemished with small muddy eyes—lacked anything of interest or appeal. Bart was someone you'd forget the moment you turned away from him.

His mouth hanging open, the crewmate stared at me.

"Bart," I said, "There are jackasses everywhere, and I have the same contempt for them all."

24

After Dylan's review and quick tour of the submersible's interior, Ted and I settled into half-sitting, half-lying-down positions in front of our respective viewports. A whirring noise echoed inside the capsule.

"That's the A-frame being lowered," Dylan called out. "You'll feel a bump when the crew connects us to it. Then we'll rise up into the air, swing out over the stern, descend, and stop. At that point you'll see the sea surface outside the viewports."

Seconds later, we were soaring through the air as sky rushed past the windows. High up, the sub stopped moving. Then we inched down and stopped again, the ocean just feet below the viewports.

The whole experience deserved the moniker "awesome." I was too amazed to be frightened.

As Dylan communicated with his counterparts outside, I closed my eyes, slowly breathed, and mentally talked to myself. "You've slipped under the water dozens of times on scuba. This'll be just like that. Then you'll slowly descend. You've done that too."

Of course, dropping down into the ocean in a submersible wasn't really like scuba diving at all. I'd not gone much more than a hundred feet with a scuba tank on my back. The hanging coral gardens were hundreds of feet deeper. More importantly, on scuba I was in charge and could ascend any time I wanted to. In *Benthic Pioneer*, I was a trapped passenger.

"Not trapped," I whispered. "Visiting."

Ted craned his neck in my direction and mouthed "Okay?"

I gave him the thumb-to-middle-finger scuba okay signal. He grinned.

"Here we go, folks," Dylan announced. "They tell me it's choppy out there. Either of you need a barf bag for the first part of the decent?"

Ted declined. I nodded, and Dylan handed me a bright blue plastic bag with "For Sickness Cleanup" written on the side.

Feeling like an idiot, I sat cross-legged in front of my viewport with the bag within reach. Distracted by fear, I'd forgotten to bring the patches I place behind my ear to prevent being seasick.

The submersible was motionless for a moment. Then it dropped, made contact with the water, and rocked to and fro. A lot.

"If you need to hold on, there are handles on either side and below the viewports." Dylan said.

Great, I thought.

Eyes closed, I told myself the rocking would soon stop. As we slipped a few feet below the surface, I stared at the waterline that had appeared at the bottom of my window. Bile crept up into my mouth. Swallowing, I searched for something distant to focus on like I did riding in a car. But there was nothing like that in the churning blue-green sea.

The sub descended a little further. Surely, this dreadful swaying would stop now, I thought.

It didn't.

More bile crept up into my mouth. I grabbed the bag and spit it out. Ted turned from his window and tipped his head. I shrugged, and he turned back.

Vomiting, also known as emesis and throwing up, is described as "involuntary, forceful expulsion of the contents of one's stomach through the mouth."

In other words, the victim can't stop the disgusting, smelly, totally embarrassing emptying of vomit from her gut into her mouth.

On my knees, I grabbed the barf bag, quite audibly filled it, and panting, held the top closed.

Like nothing in the world had happened, Dylan handed me a water bottle. "Trade you this for the bag."

"Really, you don't...." I began.

He grinned. "Part of my job. This happens a lot."

What a great guy. He'd made no sarcastic comment about an oceanographer who got seasick.

Sipping the water, I glanced out the window. We were well below the surface and the water's fading blue-green hue told me the depth was probably thirty-odd feet. Best of all, *Benthic Pioneer* was slipping gracefully through the water like a gliding bird.

"How's everybody doing?" Dylan asked a few minutes later.

By "everybody," he meant me, of course.

Staring through my viewport I said, "Good. There's still some light out there and the amount of marine snow is amazing. How far down are we?"

"Over a hundred feet. Yeah, I'm always surprised how much amorphous stuff floats around in seawater. Where does it come from?"

I rolled over, faced him, and sat up. "It's kind of like leaves and decaying matter falling from trees onto the forest floor. Fluffy bits of marine snow are food from the surface that drifts down into the dark waters below."

"Rachel Carson wrote about marine snow in *The Sea Around Us*," Ted added.

Surprised I'd missed this gem of information about the famous marine author, I said as much.

"Um, let's see if I remember how she described it," he said. "Something like 'Flake after flake, the most stupendous snowfall Earth has ever witnessed.'"

"That's perfect. Lord, she was a talented writer," I said.

I returned to my viewport. In the water, now deep purple blue, Carson's snowfall was still visible. As Dylan activated *Benthic Pioneer*'s lights, long, thin wandering ghosts appeared in the murk. These were salps, barrel-shaped gelatinous animals that look like slimy slinkies. I enjoyed the shimmering necklaces until I had to sit up and stretch.

"Dylan, how long before we reach the bottom?"

"Better get back to the viewport, Mara. We're very nearly there."

On my belly, nose to the window, I gasped as the hanging coral garden emerged from a murky fog. The forest of amber three-foot tall *Primnoa* corals—aptly called sea fans—blanketed the vertical rock wall of Schoodic Ridge.

Delicate orange-pink coral branches reached out toward us. Inches from this newly discovered marvel of the deep, I touched a finger to the window.

Behind me, Ted exclaimed, "Unbelievable. Just incredible."

"Mara, Ted, you're good luck," Dylan said. "I've never seen coral clusters as dense as this. It's astounding. Let's see if I can get a little closer."

The effort was delicate. By inches, the pilot maneuvered the submersible nearer to the corals and stopped.

Squinting, I stared at the coral display. On the surface of each sea fan branch, thousands of round, tiny polyps waved gently in the current. They looked like clusters of miniature fleshy blossoms in coral, pink, and orange.

Excited as a schoolboy, Dylan talked to folks on the ship above us watching the video feed. They sounded as ecstatic as we were.

I returned to my viewport as Dylan maneuvered *Benthic Pioneer* along the wall. Silver schools of fish—cod and herring—wove around the coral branches. Like a bed of squat flowers, clusters of lovely light pink anemones waved finger-long tentacles in the current. A spiny do fish chased a stout redfish that easily got away.

Dylan backed away from the wall so that we could explore the flat silty bottom. More clusters of fist-sized anemones—coral cousins—in pink, rose, orange, and white lay scattered across the soft terrain. Large orange starfish humped over unlucky prey. A squad of squid that jetted around stout sea pen corals annoyed a lobster that reached its claws up toward them. I glimpsed a large lumbering octopus before Dylan turned back to the handing garden wall. Once more, I was stunned by the abundance of life, color, and activity on the cold, dark, rocky ridge.

Too soon, Dylan said, "Folks, we have to leave."

From my viewport, I watched as the hanging coral gardens became dimmer and finally disappeared. I stared into the dark stunned, a little sad, but mostly grateful. I was one of the lucky few who had witnessed in person one of the coral forests that blanketed New England's submarine canyons and walls. Eyes closed for a moment, I winged thanks to my parents for their pioneering legacy as marine biologists in the Gulf of Maine.

Dylan asked, "Both of you, I'm curious to hear your reactions."

Facing the pilot, Ted and I knelt on our pads. Ted spoke first.

"It's incredible that such large coral communities are down here, but we know so little about them."

Dylan checked his electronic array before answering. "That's right. We don't know how many coral forests exist or are exactly where they are. They have to be mapped."

"I'm wondering about their ecological role in the Gulf of Maine," I added. "We saw herring and cod. Are these coral habitats important for fish like these so critical to Maine's economy?"

"Dylan, any idea about the age of the hanging gardens?" Ted asked

"Maybe thousands of years old. Sorry, but now I need to monitor our ascent."

Ted and I stared at each other for a moment. "Your place or mine?" he asked.

I scooched over closer to him.

"What'd you think?" he asked.

I shook my head. "It's…I don't know, so much to take in. At the moment, mostly I'm grateful for it all."

His eyes were full of things unsaid.

"Ted, I'm also so very grateful for our friendship."

Neither of us needed to say more.

THE END

ACKNOWLEDGMENTS

Ongoing thanks go to Connie Berry, Lynn Denley-Bussard, and Judy Copek, who have been with me right from the beginning. Maine lobsterman Richard Nelson helped with information about lobstering and reactions of fishermen to climate change. Cathy Billings and Bob Bayer from the University of Maine's Lobster Institute also answered questions about lobsters and warming. NOAA marine ecologist Dave Packer advised me about hanging coral research in the Gulf of Maine. Sarah Blair reviewed the book cover. I am so grateful for the enthusiasm and support of the Briggs family.

What I call eLobster is modeled on NOAA's eMOLT program. The Center for American Progress's 2014 survey of New England commercial fishermen is the basis for the study referred to in the story. I refer readers to my website for recommended books about Maine lobsters and lobstering, lobster research references, and information about climate change. Francis Collin Literary gave permission to use the quote from *The Sea Around Us*. The good folks at Maine Authors Publishing and their editors, including Jennifer Caven, continue to be immensely helpful.

Finally, none of this would be possible without the wit, patience, and ongoing goodwill of my husband John Briggs.

Stay tuned for the next
Mara Tusconi Mystery *expected June 2019*

GLASS EELS, SHATTERED SEA

MY HEADLAMP SPILLED A CIRCLE OF LIGHT ONTO THE dirt path, a bright lodestar in a still, black night. Head down, I followed the bobbing orb in front of my feet—which is why I bumped right into Gordy Maloy, a Maine lobsterman and my cousin.

"Damn. Sorry, Gordy. I can't see a thing out here."

"Shh," he said.

I flicked off the headlamp, stuffed my hands in my parka pockets, and listened.

To my left, the Gulf of Maine faintly announced its presence. One after the other, rolling waves upended pebbles on a beach a good half mile away. To my right, the rustle of dead leaves drifted across dense shrubs.

Straddling a split in the path, Gordy said, "We go right ta the rivah."

I tried not to sound impatient. "How far is the river?"

"It's only down the trail a piece. An' like I promised, Mara, there'll be millions of itsy eels an' Nelson Ives ta greet us."

He turned down the path and picked up the pace. After a quick look up at the spray of stars that was the Milky Way, I flipped the headlamp on again and followed with a bounce in my step. For the first time, I was about to witness one of coastal Maine's springtime miracles.

For once, Gordy's "only down the path a piece" was accurate. Within minutes, we emerged from the thicket as the path dropped down to a fast-moving river. Walking gingerly alongside the river on flood-scoured boulders, I caught up with Gordy, who stood in the dark waiting for me.

"Turn off yer light," he said quietly. "That's Nelson, right up theah."

Upstream a few hundred feet was an otherworldly sight. Bathed in glowing emerald green, a human figure leaned over the river and ran a long-handled net back and forth through the water.

"What's he doing, and why the green light?" I whispered.

"He's dip netting fer eels. White light spooks 'em." Gordy raised his voice and announced our presence. "Ahoy, Nelson Ives. Gordy Maloy heah."

The green apparition stepped back from the river. His voice shaky with age, Nelson called out, "That you, Gordy?"

"Ayuh. Me an' my cousin, Mara."

Nelson said, "Gimme a minute." As he turned away from us, his green headlamp illuminated someone leaning against a boulder behind him.

I touched Gordy's arm and whispered, "Why can't we just walk up to him?"

"You'll see," he murmured.

"Come on ovah," Nelson called out.

Curious about more than eels, I put my hand on the back of Gordy's shoulder and followed as he picked his way over the rocks to his old friend.

A bright white lantern at his feet, Nelson Ives enclosed Gordy's outstretched hand in both of his. "Gordy Maloy. By Godfrey, it's been a long, long time." Ives stepped back and put both hands on hips encased in waterproof orange bib pants.

"An' who is this lovely young lady?"

"Nelson Ives, meet my cousin, Mara Tusconi."

Ives stroked a white chin beard that neatly circled his lower face from ear to ear. Matching hair poked out from a tattered tan fishing hat pulled down to eyebrow level. "Well now. You look nothin' like Gordy, which is good." He winked.

"Mara's a marine biologist in Spruce Habah. She's dyin' ta see the eels," Gordy said.

The old man rubbed his beard again. "You at the oceanographic place?"

"Yes, sir," I said. "The Maine Oceanographic Institution."

"It's jus' Nelson, deah. I got lots ta show ya. Come on."

He turned around and placed the lantern on a large flat rock he was using as a kind of shelf for his dip net, a yellow slicker, a pair of waders, and other gear. He slid a large orange bowl closer to the lantern.

"Here ya go, Mara. Glass eels."

I leaned in for a better look. At the bottom of the bowl wriggled hundreds of thin translucent eels about the length of my pinky finger.

"Huh, they kind of look like clear spaghetti with tiny black eyes," I said.

"It's amazin' these little guys came all the way from the Sargasso Sea up ta where we are."

"The Sargasso Sea is in the middle of the ocean off the Carolinas," I said. "That's a thousand miles from here."

"Ayuh. Nobody's seen it, far as I know, but adult eels spawn in the Sargasso Sea. After that, the baby eels float in the Gulf Stream before they peel off an' go up rivahs all along the east coast."

I cradled the bowl in both hands. "Nelson, how much can you get for this many glass eels?"

He stroked his beard for a moment and said, "Last I knew, they were payin' fifteen hundred dollars."

I blinked and stared into the bowl once more. "Are you telling me you could get fifteen hundred dollars for this many eels?"

"Right theah, that's at least two pounds, an' it's fifteen hundred *per pound*."

Very, very carefully, I placed the bowl back onto the rock. "My god. The eels in that bowl might go for more than three thousand."

Behind me, Gordy said, "Now you understand what Nelson's son Jake is doing here."

"Jake?" I asked.

"Son," Nelson called out. "Flip on yer headlamp."

A ghostly apparition suddenly appeared not thirty feet up on higher ground. Focused on the rifle, I didn't pay much attention to guy's face or the rest of him.

"Oh," I said dumbly. "He's armed."

Without a word, Jake turned off the light.

I leaned back against the rock, looked at Gordy, and crossed my arms. "So tell me the deal here."

"Las' spring Maine fishermen caught somethin' like ten million dollars' worth of eels," he said. "That's in a couple months. On a good night, Nelson can make five thousand. Some guy could jus' come along with a bucket, hit Nelson over the head with a rock, an' end up with five grand at the end of the night."

I turned back to the old fisherman who was slowly pouring water into the bowl and talking to his eels. "There ya go, little guys."

Would anyone really harm this kindly old man over a handful of eels?

"Nelson, has anyone tried to steal your catch?" I asked.

"Ayuh. Couple yeahs ago, this punk come right down that

path theah." He pointed in the opposite direction we'd come from. "Big fella. He shoved me so hard, I nearly fell right in the rivah. Guy grabbed my eel bucket and marched back up the path. Heard 'im drive away couple some minutes latah."

The image of the old man falling backwards into that cold, rushing river was appalling. "Nelson, that's dreadful. How could they?"

"Easy money, an' lots of it. Who cares 'bout a worn-out fisherman?"

To change the subject in a happier direction, I quizzed Nelson about glass eels.

"When does the eel fishing season start?"

"March."

"What happens to eels you sell?"

"They're shipped ta aquaculture farms in places like Japan."

"For sushi?"

"Ayuh, but I never ate it."

"Why are eels worth so much now when they weren't before?"

"There used ta be eels by the zillions, but now they're gettin' fished out."

The old fisherman returned to the American eel's life history. In colorful language he described the animal's transformation from bottom-dwelling freshwater glass eels to large sexually mature adults that travel the open ocean.

"Nelson, you're a natural teacher," I said.

"Teachers ask me ta tell school kids all 'bout the eels." He gestured toward the river. "Every spring this amazin' thing happens right in our backyard. Folks hardly noticed till there was so much money in it."

"Speaking of that, I'm sure you want to get back to your work," I said.

He lifted his hat, scratched the top of his head, and settled the hat back down to eyebrow level. "Well, I guess prob'ly. It's sure been good talking with ya, Mara. I live in Friendship. Gordy knows wheah. Why don't you come ovah fer a visit?"

Affection for the old Mainer I'd only just met flowed through me. "I'd love to visit you, Nelson. Thanks for everything."

Gordy patted his longtime friend on the back, thanked him for his time, and promised to see him soon.

Walking back down the trail, the river that carried eels upstream on our right, I quizzed Gordy about Nelson's safety and the astounding amount of money eel fishermen could make in a single night.

"It's great money fer folks who work hard at their jobs and don't make much. But it comes with big, big problems."

"Like the need for protection," I said.

"Ayuh. Jack's got the rifle you saw plus a Glock."

"What other problems?"

"Trafficking."

"I've read a little about that in the paper."

"The eel fishery is regulated," he said. "Guys like Nelson have an annual quota, need a license, all that. Maine's one of the few states that has any eel fishing at all. That means glass eels are at a premium. Las' month a Portland seafood dealer got caught trafficking a million glass eels he illegally sold in Asia. That guy is goin' ta jail fer a long time."

We followed the trail up the bank and into the thicket. What I guessed were bayberry, beach plum, and highbush blueberry shrubs brushed against my parka as I matched Gordy's pace and thought about eel trafficking. I knew that in the world of illegal trade, animal trafficking ranked fourth after drugs, humans, and arms. I'd learned that every year countless birds (parrots like scarlet macaws), reptiles (turtles, snakes), monkeys, and many other animals were taken from the wild and sold live as pets or dismembered for ivory (elephants), horn (rhinos), fur (leopards, tigers), food (sharks), and bogus medicines (animal penises to improve male libido).

But, for some reason, the illegal selling of eels right in my home state of Maine hadn't registered as anything like the lucrative trafficking business it was.

The crack of the gunshot ricocheted off the low shrubs. Together, Gordy and I spun around and faced the river.

"Nelson, oh my god," Gordy cried. "Mara, we gotta run back ta him!"

Gordy jumped in front of me and sprinted toward the river with me on his tail. We bounded out of the shrubs, slid down the bank, and leapt over rocks until we reached Nelson. The lantern, still upright on the flat rock, illuminated the grisly scene. Sprawled across the trail, the old fisherman lay on his back, arms outstretched. In the middle of his chest, crimson oozed from a deep ugly crater and ran down his orange bib.